Also by Denise Swanson
in Large Print:

Murder of a Small-Town Honey
Murder of a Sweet Old Lady

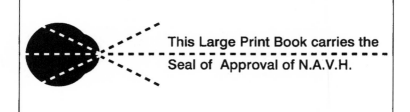

This Large Print Book carries the
Seal of Approval of N.A.V.H.

Murder of a Sleeping Beauty

Murder of a Sleeping Beauty

A Scumble River Mystery

Denise Swanson

Thorndike Press • Waterville, Maine

Published in 2002 by arrangement with NAL Signet, a member of Penguin Putnam Inc.

Thorndike Press Large Print Mystery Series.

The tree indicium is a trademark of Thorndike Press.

The text of this Large Print edition is unabridged. Other aspects of the book may vary from the original edition.

Cover design by Thorndike Press Staff.

Set in 16 pt. Plantin by Myrna S. Raven.

Printed in the United States on permanent paper.

Library of Congress Cataloging-in-Publication Data

Swanson, Denise.
    Murder of a sleeping beauty : a Scumble River mystery / Denise Swanson.
      p. cm.
    ISBN 0-7862-4402-X (lg. print : hc : alk. paper)
    1. Denison, Skye (Fictitious character) — Fiction.
2. School psychologists — Fiction. 3. Women psychologists — Fiction. 4. Large type books. I. Title.
PS3619.W36 M86 2002
  813′.6—dc21
                                    2002068706

To my dad,
Ernest W. Swanson (1927–2000),
whose quiet goodness was
taken away from us much too soon.

Acknowledgments

My sincere thanks to:

My aunt and uncle, Wilma and Al Votta, my cousins Darla and Ron Hutton, and the rest of my relatives and friends, who sustained my mother through her time of grief and helped ease her into widowhood.

My Windy City Chapter of RWA, a great group of writers.

My fellow Deadly Divas, especially Susan McBride, for all the companionship and advice. I could never have written this book while promoting my first one without you.

My Buds, for their unending support.

Luci Zahray, for her help with the pharmaceutical information.

My mother, Marie Swanson, who helped me continue despite our mutual grief.

And with love to my husband, Dave Stybr, whose devotion protects me from the slings and arrows.

Chapter 1

From Bad to Hearse

As a school psychologist Skye Denison had dealt with many recalcitrant teens, but Justin Boward would be the death of her yet. He refused to talk. She was beginning to think his entire vocabulary consisted of yes, no, and the occasional grunt. Although she knew that adolescents tended to be like cats — neither react when you talk to them — his lack of response to her attempts to draw him out was starting to make her feel like a failure. A feeling she was way too familiar with already.

Two years ago, Skye had been forced to crawl back to Scumble River, Illinois, after finding herself fired, jilted, and broke. It had been hard enough to return to the rural Midwestern town she had escaped as a teenager, but the citizens' long memories had made it worse. Hardly a week went by without someone reminding Skye of what she had declared twelve years ago in her valedictorian speech. Back then, the moment the words had left her mouth, she'd regretted saying that Scumble River was full of small-minded people with even smaller intellects. She had regretted it even more since she'd moved back home.

She snuck a peek at her watch as she pushed a stray chestnut curl under her headband. Twenty-five minutes before the Scumble River High School dismissal bell would ring. Once again, she attempted to make eye contact with the teen seated kitty-corner from her at the small table. He ducked his head and studied his chewed fingernails. Justin had not spoken three words in the previous fifteen minutes. Skye searched for some pithy comment.

Before she could come up with one, a student she vaguely recognized flung the door open and stumbled inside. The girl bent over, trying to catch her breath, and spoke between gasps. "Sleeping Beauty is dead."

"What?" Was this teen-speak for: Run, the cops are here? Was Skye supposed to answer: The gray wolf howls at midnight?

Skye's gaze raked the adolescent, who was still hunched over, hands on her knees, standing just past the office threshold. She was dressed in low-riding wide-legged denims and a hooded belly top. Her bleached two-tone hair fell to the middle of her back, and her navel was pierced.

After a quick appraisal, Skye decided that the girl probably hung with either the Rebels or the Skanks. Of Scumble River High's five or six cliques, these were the two roughest. And unlike the teacher-pleasing Cheerleaders, Jocks, and Nerds, they did not volunteer information to adults. What was this girl up to?

The adolescent finally straightened and grabbed Skye by the wrist. "Something abhorrent has happened. You have to come right now." She tugged at Skye's arm. "Hurry!"

Skye found herself half-running, half-dragged down the long hall. Orange lockers went by in a blur, and the smell of that day's lunch caught in her throat.

The teen skidded to a halt before the closed gym doors and pointed. "In there."

"Who are you, and what are you talking about?"

"This is just FYI. I'm out of here." The girl tried to push past Skye and head back down the corridor.

Skye grabbed the hood of her top. "Oh no, you don't. Explain."

"Hey, Cujo, back in your cage." The teen twisted violently, trying to free her-

11

self, then turned an anger-filled stare on Skye, who met her gaze without blinking. Finally, the girl shrugged. "So, okay, I cut my eighth-period study hall, and I was hanging around here and there, waiting until my buds got out of school. I wanted a cigarette, and knew there was no PE last hour, so I went in the gym. It was dark, but I thought I saw someone on the stage, so I went closer. That's when I saw her. The cheerleader playing Sleeping Beauty. She was laying there, dead."

The teen tried again to free herself. Skye refused to let go. "Oh no, you don't, you're staying with me. Let's check this out. Sleeping Beauty was probably just re-hearsing, or taking a nap." Under her breath she muttered, "Or maybe she was afraid of you."

Side by side they entered the unlit gym. As her eyes adjusted, Skye could just make out the stage at the opposite end of the room, cluttered with partially completed sets for the spring musical *Sleeping Beauty*. She moved forward, a firm grip on her prisoner's hood. Half walls and skeletal trees loomed in the darkness. While they climbed the steps to the stage, Skye wondered if she were doing the right thing. She didn't think the faculty handbook covered this situation.

To their right, a mock castle bedroom had been set up. Lying on the twin bed was one of the most beautiful young women Skye had ever seen. Her straight blond hair brushed the floor, and her face was a flawless oval. She had passed from the awkwardness of adolescence, and was yet to be touched by the hand of time. She was perfect.

Skye took a closer look. Her skin had a waxy appearance and was almost blue-gray in color. Her lips and nails were pale. Skye rushed to the bed and checked for a pulse. She could feel nothing over the thud of her own heartbeat. She put her ear to the girl's chest. Again nothing. Finally, she placed the back of her hand to the teen's mouth. She wasn't breathing.

Skye forced herself to remain calm and remember what she had learned in her first-aid course. Nothing applied here. Sleeping Beauty was dead.

"Run to the office and call 911." Skye looked up to find the other girl gone. "Shit, I shouldn't have let go of her."

"You shouldn't say 'shit' either."

Skye's heart thudded, and her head jerked up. She caught her breath when she recognized Justin, standing near the stairs.

It was so rare to hear him speak that she hadn't recognized his voice. She hadn't noticed, but he must have followed when the girl dragged her away.

He was the type that blended into the background. Medium height, medium build, and medium brown hair that hung straight from a center part to the middle of his ears.

"Justin, am I glad to see you. Run to the office and call 911. We need an ambulance."

"Looks more like you need a hearse." His words were cocky, but his face was pale and sweaty.

"Justin, please, just call 911. Tell them no lights or siren, and no radio." Skye wondered if there were anything else she should do. "And get the principal. Oh, and tell him to shut off the dismissal bell."

He shrugged. "He's not going to listen to me."

She searched the pocket of her gray wool skirt and found a pad of passes. "Give me a pen."

The boy handed her the Bic from his shirt pocket.

She scribbled a note and signed it, then handed it to Justin. "Hurry!"

When the boy left, Skye pulled down the

sleeves of her pink cardigan and shivered. It was the beginning of April, and it was still cold in Illinois. Of course, it didn't help that the school board turned off the furnace on March 31, no matter what the weather.

Skye felt a deep sadness settle over her. Why was this young woman dead? She had barely begun to live. This was one Sleeping Beauty who would never awake to her prince's kiss. Skye's gaze was drawn back to the girl. What had caused her death? There was no visible wound, no blood, no mark of any kind.

She glanced around. The scene looked ready for a rehearsal. Except — what was that, not quite under the bed? She got down on her hands and knees, and peered at the object. The label had been peeled off, but the bottle's odd shape teased Skye's memory.

She sat back on her heels and gnawed at her thumb. *I wonder where it came from? The school doesn't sell anything in bottles.*

Suddenly doors flew open and lights snapped on. "Miss Denison, what's the meaning of all this?" Homer Knapik, the high-school principal, scurried across the gym floor.

As he approached her, a detached part of

Skye's mind noted that between his squat build and the hair emanating from nearly every orifice and covering every limb, the principal looked like a sheepdog — one ready to bite the next lamb that veered from the flock.

Justin followed at a prudent distance, his face still chalky but his brown eyes alight with interest.

Skye met Homer at the bottom of the stairs. "Did you call 911? Did you shut off the dismissal bell?"

"Yes, and you'd better have a damn good reason for your note." He peered peevishly up at her through the fuzz hanging over his eyes.

"I do." She pointed to the body on the bed. "Maybe you'd better have the teachers escort the kids out the front door. We don't want any of them wandering back here."

Homer took a step closer and squinted upward. "Oh, my God! That's Lorelei Ingels. She isn't . . . dead?" When Skye nodded, he scribbled a note on the pad from his pocket. "Boy, take this to the front office immediately and give it to Mrs. Hill."

"Justin, after you do that, wait for the ambulance crew, and show them the side

16

entrance." Skye lowered her voice and kept an eye on the teen, who was walking away ever so slowly. "We'd better call the police, too."

"What?" Homer jumped from foot to foot, as if he were about to pee his pants. "Do you have any idea who Lorelei Ingels is? Her family is one of the wealthiest and most influential in town. She's won nearly every beauty pageant in the state. We've got to be extremely careful." He stopped hopping around, and his shoulders slumped. "What am I saying? No matter how we handle this or how she died, we're screwed."

"A young woman is dead, and that's your first reaction?" Skye shook her head. She hoped that thirty years in the school system wouldn't turn her into a bureaucratic zombie like they had poor Homer.

The PA blared into life, making them both flinch. "All teachers are to personally escort their eighth-period students out the front door. Teachers without eighth-period students are to report to the locker area and help supervise. No students are allowed anywhere in the school unescorted."

When the announcement ended, Homer tried to climb the steps, but Skye stepped in front of him. "What are you doing? Get out of my way," he demanded.

Skye didn't budge. "I think we'd better leave things on the stage alone. We don't want to disturb any evidence."

Homer gave her a withering look. "Are you saying the girl was murdered? All we need is for a rumor like that to get started."

"The police will want to know why an apparently healthy eighteen-year-old suddenly dropped dead."

As if in response to her words, they heard the sound of running feet. Moments later, paramedics rushed through the door. Skye pointed to the bed. They pushed past her and went up the stairs.

Homer grabbed her arm. "I'd better call the superintendent. I'll be right back."

Skye watched the principal scurry out of the gym and Justin step just inside the doorway, turning back to the stage only when the EMTs began to fire questions at her. "How long has she been like this?"

"I don't know."

"When did you find her?"

"About fifteen minutes ago."

"Was she conscious?"

"No, just like she is now. No pulse, no heartbeat, no breathing."

One of the paramedics turned to his partner. "Better call the police."

The chief of police, Walter Boyd, was the first to arrive. He was tall and powerful-looking, with a muscular chest. Skye watched him swiftly assess the situation, then radio for backup from the county sheriff's department and the state police. He also called in all four of the off-duty Scumble River cops.

Wally's expressive brown eyes became shuttered when he spotted Skye. "I should have known you'd be involved."

She bit her lip. It wasn't fair. She had never even dated the guy, and still her relationship with him had always been complicated: from her first crush on him when she was fifteen and he twenty-three, to their latest fight over what he considered to be a betrayal of his trust. "I'm sorry you're still mad at me," she said.

"Mad? I'm not mad at you. I just don't trust you anymore," Wally said without inflection. "I specifically told you not to go off investigating on your own."

"I explained why I had to go alone to talk to those survivalists when my grandmother died last summer." Skye moved closer. "They never would've said anything if you'd been with me."

He stepped back from her and ran a hand through his curly black hair, pain etched in the lines bracketing his mouth. "Yeah, Darleen explained why she had to leave me for another man, too. Let's stick to business." He flipped open his pad and clicked his pen. "Tell me what happened, from the beginning."

Skye noted the weariness in Wally's face, and realized once again just how much she had hurt him. She wanted to repeat her apology but knew it would never be enough, so instead she replayed the last hour for him, step by step.

"Where's the girl who originally found the body?" Wally asked.

"I haven't seen her since she got away from me, and I don't know her name."

Wally walked over to where Justin stood a few feet away from the adults. "Do you know who the girl is?"

He shrugged. "Could be Elvira Doozier."

Skye looked heavenward. She should have guessed. Anytime there was a problem, a Doozier was usually involved somehow. She had first encountered the family when she initially returned to Scumble River. In fact, Junior Doozier had helped her when her car was totaled. Then the boy's uncle had tried to kill her, and Junior had again come to her aid. She wondered where Elvira fit into that twisted family tree.

The chief sent Justin to wait on the bleachers and ordered Skye, "Tell me about the boy."

"Who, Justin?"

Wally nodded impatiently.

Skye quickly sorted out what she had gathered from their counseling sessions, and thus considered confidential, from what was a matter of record. "I've been seeing him for nearly two years, ever since I started working for the Scumble River school district. He's a freshman. We haven't made much progress. He barely speaks to me. At the end of last year, he almost came around, but thanks to Aunt Mona and her committee, he was denied an essay award he had legitimately won. Now he's reverted to his previous hostile self."

"How did she stop him from getting a school award?"

"She didn't like his essay topic — pro-choice vs. pro-life."

"Is he dangerous?"

"Hard to say. Justin's a loner, due to his deep distrust of both adults and peers.

He's a bright boy, with an IQ in the superior range, but he squeaks by with Cs and Ds, so he doesn't hang out with the Nerds. He's not athletic, so he doesn't fit with the Jocks either. He's both angry and uncommunicative, which is a dangerous combination. I'm worried about the type of group he might eventually find."

"But what about now? Is there anyone he hangs with?"

Skye shook her head. "Why are you asking all these questions about Justin? Surely you don't suspect him of being involved with this death. He was with me this period."

"We don't even know what happened, let alone when. But since this boy was around, I just want to get a picture of him. Have you talked to his parents? What are they like?"

"I've tried to warn his parents of the seriousness of his emotional state, but his mother's coping with her own depression, and his father's in poor health. They're both pretty absorbed in their own needs."

Wally made a note, and his voice turned formal. "Thanks. Please sit on the bleachers with the boy until you're dismissed."

Skye chafed at his brusque tone but did as she was told.

Simon Reid, the coroner, arrived next. As tall as the chief, he had a more sophisticated demeanor. His dark auburn hair and golden hazel eyes reminded her of Gary Cooper. As usual, he was dressed impeccably in a perfectly pressed designer suit.

He rushed past Skye, nodding coolly. He was another of her interpersonal disasters. They had dated for nearly a year after Skye had first returned to Scumble River, but had broken up last summer when he had pushed for a level of intimacy she wasn't ready for.

Skye sat on the bottom row of the bleachers. Shouts echoed through the cavernous gym. Ceiling lights in their safety cages cast ominous shadows. Justin sat beside her, sneaking worried glances at her face. She knew she should say something to reassure him, but she felt drained and unable to move, let alone make a decision.

Occasionally, she heard the voices of people trying to push past the police officers and enter the gym. Eventually, someone calling her name penetrated her fog. She rose unsteadily from the bench and made her way to the door.

Kent Walker, Scumble River High's new English teacher, the director of *Sleeping Beauty*, and the man Skye was halfheartedly dating, was arguing that they should let him into the gym. He was tall and lithe, with a casual grace that spoke of money and privilege. He had caused many heads to turn and hearts to throb when he moved to town last September. Skye had never understood why he chose to date her, especially since there was so little sexual chemistry between them. She had come to the conclusion it was because she shared his wry view about rural life.

He turned away from the officer and demanded, "Skye, tell these buffoons who I am."

She dutifully said, "This is Kent Walker. He's the director of this year's musical."

"So?" Deputy McCabe took off his hat and scratched his head. "The chief says nobody comes in or goes out. No exceptions."

She shrugged at Kent. "Sorry."

His handsome face reddened. "I need to come in." He dropped his voice. "Is it really Lorelei Ingels?"

Skye hesitated. "I can't say. The police aren't releasing the name until the next of kin can be notified."

Kent's tone turned frosty. "Why are you treating me like a stranger? I thought we had something between us."

She raised an eyebrow. Something between them? She didn't think so. True, they had gone out half a dozen times, but they weren't dating each other exclusively, and they had never progressed beyond a quick kiss good night.

Skye stared at Kent, who was frowning and tapping his foot. She hadn't noticed before, but his jaw was slightly receding, and when he tensed it, as he was doing now, it looked as if he had no chin at all. She gazed in fascination as he changed from good-looking to downright ugly. *Why am I thinking about Kent's appearance at a time like this?*

Finally, she forced her attention back to the situation at hand. "Sorry, what did you say, Kent?"

"I asked why you're acting so strangely." His blue eyes were icy.

"Well, it is quite a shock to find a body in the course of a Wednesday afternoon." Skye was beginning to feel more like her usual assertive self. Since coming out from under the spell of her ex-fiancé, she had allowed no man to take that belligerent tone with her.

"You're right, of course. I'm being a beast." A lock of white-blond hair fell over one eye as he tilted his head. "But could you please talk to that police chief of yours, and see if he'll let me through?"

She answered automatically, "He's not *my* police chief." *At least not anymore.* "But if you really want me to, I'll see what I can do. Why do you need to come in here?"

"I'd rather not explain it twice, just get the chief, okay?"

Skye had opened her mouth to say no, it wasn't okay, when she caught a glimpse of Wally standing alone. This was her chance.

She hurried over to one side of the stage just as he squatted down. "Wally, could I speak to you for a moment?"

He straightened and glared at her. "Didn't I tell you to sit on the bleachers and not move?"

He had, and she'd forgotten. "Sorry, I haven't touched anything."

"That's something." He crouched again. "So, what's so urgent?"

"Um, well, Kent Walker, the director of the musical, would like to come into the gym, and Deputy McCabe won't let him."

"As per my orders," Wally answered distractedly, his nose almost touching the floor. "Why does he need to be here?"

Skye tried to see what Wally was staring at. It looked like a small piece of tinsel. "He wanted to talk to *you* about that."

"And you didn't insist on knowing?" Wally got to his feet. "Then it's true. You two *are* an item."

"What?" Her eyebrows came together.

"Never mind. Let's go talk to Mr. Kent Walker."

Chapter 2

Waste of Death

Skye trailed after Wally as he approached the gym doors. Deputy McCabe stood talking to the crowd that had continued to gather. There was no sign of Kent.

The chief stopped at the entrance and turned to her. "Where's Walker?"

She shrugged. "Maybe he went to the bathroom."

Wally spoke to Deputy McCabe. "Where did Kent Walker go?"

"Who?" The deputy wrinkled his brow.

Skye pushed past the chief. "The guy you wouldn't let into the gym."

"Lots of those. I think nearabouts every parent in Scumble River is trying to get in here."

Skye blew a curl out of her eyes. "The one yelling my name."

"Oh, the fella with the funny way of talking. Is he English or something?"

"No, he's from Boston."

"Oh, well. He said something about

having to go, and walked off."

"That's all he said?"

"Yeah." McCabe twisted his face in thought. "No. Said to tell you he'd see you later."

Skye felt her face burn. Wally probably thought she had used this whole incident with Kent just to get his attention.

The chief narrowed his eyes, and Skye waited for the explosion. Instead he said sarcastically, "If there's nothing else you or your friends require, I'll get back to work now." He turned on his heel and started away from the door, then stopped and told Skye, "Go sit on the bleachers."

"Wally?"

"Yes?"

"I really need to make some phone calls. Couldn't I just go to the office? I won't leave the building."

"No."

"Why not?" Skye searched his face, but it was blank of emotion. "Could I at least call Justin Boward's family? They'll be wondering where he is."

"I'll have an officer call. Do you have his number?"

Skye shook her head. "But we can ask Justin." She turned toward the bleachers. "Where'd he go?"

29

The chief gave her a disgusted look. "You sit down. I'll go find him."

"But . . ." Skye trailed off. Wally was already striding away.

She examined her surroundings. There was nowhere to hide in the gym. It was just a large room with wooden floors and high ceilings. The sidewalls were made up of bleachers folded flat, except for the one extended bench on which she and Justin had been seated, and two locked doors marked GIRLS and BOYS that led to the locker rooms. On the back wall were two sets of double doors. Those to the right were chained shut, and Deputy McCabe guarded the others.

In front and up a short flight of stairs was the stage. It was brightly lit and crawling with police officers examining the scene, sketching, videotaping, and snapping pictures. Others were dusting for fingerprints and collecting evidence.

A door on either side at gym level led to the backstage area. Skye bet that was where Justin had disappeared to. She scanned the area. Wally was talking to a deputy. No one seemed to be looking for the boy. She edged closer to the door on the left. She could hear the officers on the stage talking. One mentioned a pool of vomit near the curtain that he had almost stepped in. Yech! She was glad she hadn't noticed that bit of evidence.

A quick glance assured her that no one was paying attention to her. Maybe she could take a fast look and be back before the chief noticed. Justin was her responsibility, and she needed to make sure he was okay.

Skye entered the darkened concrete stairwell. There were five steps leading upward. The light from the gym provided the only illumination, and she was surprised to feel a little afraid. Which was silly — the place was crawling with police; nothing could happen to her.

At the top, she paused. Was that voices she heard? To her left was a room used for makeup and dressing, but the sounds were coming from the opposite direction. She carefully eased through the small passage formed from the space between the wall and the stage's back curtain.

As she approached the room on the other side, the voices stopped. The door stood ajar, and she peered inside. This area was used to store sets and costumes. A space in the back had been cleared and a desk set up for the director.

Standing in the shadows was a male

figure. He moved slightly, and Skye saw who it was. "Justin Boward, what are you doing back here?"

The boy shrugged, his face sullen. "Looking around. Nothing to get bent about."

"Is there someone else back here with you?"

"Nah."

Skye decided to pursue that later. She scanned the area. There was no sign of disturbance. "We'd better get out front before the chief comes looking for us."

"Too late," came Wally's voice from behind them. He aimed his flashlight at Justin. "Stay where you are, son."

Skye saw the teen's Adam's apple bob nervously.

The chief barely glanced at Skye. "You, go sit on the bleachers, like I told you before."

"No." She stepped nearer to Justin. "This boy is my responsibility until his parents get here, and I'm staying with him."

Wally's features hardened with anger. He started to say something, seemed to change his mind, then spoke through clenched teeth. "Fine. You." He pointed at Skye. "Keep your mouth shut, or I swear

I'll arrest you for obstruction of justice. You." He pointed to Justin. "Tell me what you're doing back here, and why I shouldn't arrest you for tampering with evidence."

The boy stared at the chief, then looked beseechingly at Skye. She raised an eyebrow at Wally. They all stood silently.

The chief sighed and spoke to Skye. "Tell him to answer my questions."

"You told me to keep my mouth shut." Wally groaned.

"Right, a foolish consistency is the hobgoblin of little minds. I forgot," she said, and hastily continued, "Justin, tell the chief what you were doing back here."

"He'll be mad." The boy shuffled his feet and refused to make eye contact.

"Too late again." Wally shot Justin an angry look.

"Smart, Wally. That's the way to get someone to talk to you." Skye turned her back on the chief. "Justin, unless you had something to do with Lorelei's death, I'm sure the chief won't care what you were doing."

"Sure, I'm just concerned about this incident, nothing else," Wally confirmed. Skye could tell he was trying the "good cop" routine.

"Promise?" Justin asked.

Both adults nodded.

"Okay, I was trying to get out of here. The cop at the door wouldn't let me go, and then I thought about something I heard in PE class one time." Justin took a breath. "Someone told me there was a secret door backstage that would lead you out of the gym."

Wally's expression sharpened. "Did you find it?"

"Yeah. It's right here." Justin pushed aside a curtain and a half door was revealed.

Skye reached for the knob, but Wally grabbed her hand. "Don't touch anything. I need to get this whole area fingerprinted."

Justin's face reddened. "Ah, I already opened it."

"Son of a bitch! There goes any evidence."

Skye couldn't remember ever having heard the chief swear before. She closed her eyes, remembering once when Wally had spoken about investigating a young person's death a few years ago, and how much it had disturbed him. He must be experiencing similar feelings now, and that was why he was coming across as such an insensitive and authoritative jerk. Convinced Skye had betrayed him several months ago, and now having to deal with a senseless death, the chief was raising all sorts of emotional defenses.

She tried to save the situation by asking, "Where does the door lead, Justin?"

"The band room."

"It must be so they can hand their instruments through, without carrying them in the corridors," she guessed.

Wally focused on Skye. "Why do you say that?"

"With all the additions put on this school, there are some rooms that are right next to each other, but you have to detour through miles of hallway to get from one to the other. That must be the case here. I know the hall dead-ends at the gym." Skye paused and considered. "Hey, maybe not all is lost. You can have your techs dust the band room. Justin didn't go in there, right?"

"No."

"Good." Skye smiled.

The chief crossed his arms. "One other question, Justin. Why did you want to leave so badly?"

The boy reddened and glanced at Skye before answering. "I need to go to the bathroom."

★ ★ ★

It was nearly six by the time the police finished their work in the gym. The stage and the backstage areas remained taped off with bright yellow ribbon, a glaring contrast to the gray gymnasium. Justin had been released to his parents, and most of the crowd had dissipated. Suppers had to be cooked, farm animals had to be fed, and families had to be tended, no matter who died.

Skye, Wally, and Homer were left trying to locate Lorelei Ingels's parents. Wally had called their residence and spoken to their housekeeper, who'd told him that Allen Ingels, Lorelei's father, was out of town that day on business and his wife, Lorna, had accompanied him in order to shop and have her hair done. Lorelei's younger sister was at a neighbor's playing. They were all expected home by seven.

After a brief discussion, it was decided that Skye, Homer, and Wally would wait for the Ingels at their home. Skye hadn't been surprised when Homer insisted that she go along. The Ingels were an extremely prominent family — Mr. Ingels was the bank president — and Homer liked to surround himself with other people to deflect any possible blame that might be cast on him. Wally led the way in the squad car, and Homer and Skye followed in the principal's Taurus.

Ten minutes later, the three of them stood on the Ingelses' doorstep. The housekeeper answered their ring, and after a brief explanation from the chief, showed them into a stark white living room.

They seated themselves, and the housekeeper brought them coffee. Skye winced as Homer put his cup down on the glass table. She hoped it wouldn't leave a ring.

Skye wiggled, trying to find a comfortable position in the Jacobsen chair she occupied. Except for a family portrait done in oils above the fireplace, and several mirrors hung in strategic locations, the walls reminded her of the inside of a refrigerator.

Homer's shaggy appearance looked out of place against the streamlined leather couch on which he was perched.

Wally, on the other hand, seemed at ease in a Bauhaus chair as he made notes on a pocket-size pad. He finally looked up. "Homer, you and Skye really don't have to be here."

Homer slowly put down the magazine he had been pretending to read. "How would it look to the Ingels and the rest of the community if we let the police take over with no school representation?"

Before Wally could respond the sound of car doors slamming and the front door opening drew their attention. A tall woman dressed in a lime-colored Nipon suit entered. Her champagne-blond hair was perfectly coifed in a shoulder-length flip, and she held a Shizué purse.

The man following her had been handsome in his youth, but time had clawed its signature across his features. His Armani suit, although flawlessly tailored, couldn't hide his thickening middle. His florid complexion spoke of three-martini lunches, wine-drenched dinners, and bedtime brandies.

The chief stood and took a couple of steps toward them. Skye and Homer kept a few feet back.

Allen Ingels spoke. "What's going on? What are you doing in my house?"

Wally answered, "I'm sorry, folks, but I have some bad news for you."

Lorna Ingels paled and clutched her husband's arm. He half turned, almost as if he were ready to make a run for it.

"Bad news? What could you possibly have to say that would concern us?" Allen Ingels brushed off an imaginary speck of lint, his eyes suddenly unable to meet the chief's.

To Skye, it was almost as if he already felt guilty about something.

"Today at approximately three o'clock your daughter Lorelei was found in the high school gym, dead from unknown causes."

"My baby?" Mrs. Ingels shrieked and sagged against her husband. "What happened to my baby?"

Before Wally could speak, Mr. Ingels roared, "Nonsense! There must be some mistake. What gross incompetence. She's never been sick a day in her life. I'll sue all of you for scaring us like this."

Skye watched a veil of denial descend on both the Ingelses' faces.

Wally eased the couple down on the sofa. "There's no mistake. During the last half of eighth period, Ms. Denison here" — he indicated Skye — "was summoned by a student to the gym. Once there, she found your daughter lying on a bed that was part of the stage set for the school play. Lorelei was not breathing, nor was her heart beating. An ambulance was immediately sent for, and arrived within five minutes. The EMTs declared her dead, and called for me and the coroner. We won't know the cause of death until after the autopsy."

Mrs. Ingels screamed and buried her head in her arms. "My baby, my baby! She was so beautiful! You can't cut her up. I won't let you. I want to see my baby."

Skye moved forward to comfort Mrs. Ingels, but Wally held her back. She shot him a surprised look, and he gave a slight shake of his head. What was he up to?

Mr. Ingels sat stone-faced. "What are you talking about? How could a perfectly healthy eighteen-year-old go to school and just die?"

"I'm sorry. We don't know. There's no physical evidence."

Skye looked at Wally again. What did he mean? What about the mysterious bottle? What about the piece of tinsel, and the pool of vomit the officers had been talking about?

Allen Ingels turned to Homer, who had been hovering to the banker's left. "How could you let something like this happen in your school?"

Beads of sweat popped out on Homer's brow.

Skye stepped forward to rescue the principal. "Mr. and Mrs. Ingels, you have our utmost sympathy for your loss, but there was nothing we could do." Was their reaction a natural expression of grief? The Ingels weren't acting like any parents she had dealt with before.

"And you." Allen Ingels pivoted in Skye's direction. "Did you do anything to help? Did you try CPR or mouth-to-mouth? Or did you just let her die?"

Skye felt as if she'd been sucker-punched. *Could I have done something more?*

Wally spoke before she could find an answer. "Your daughter was dead when Ms. Denison found her. She followed the correct procedure."

Both parents glared at Wally. Lorna Ingels, tears running down her cheeks, said, "Well, we'll never know now, will we?"

"The autopsy will answer many of your questions," the chief answered. "And since we have to treat this like a suspicious death, we'll need to search Lorelei's room."

Allen Ingels drew up straighter and glowered. "Over my dead body. No search and no autopsy." He started to leave the room. "I'm calling our attorney. I want you all out of my house now."

"That's not being very cooperative, Al," a deep voice boomed.

All eyes turned to the huge man who

filled the doorway. He wore a white shirt and gray twill pants held up by bright red suspenders. An unlit cigar was clamped between his teeth.

Skye let out an inaudible sigh. For better or worse, Uncle Charlie had arrived. Charlie Patukas was really Skye's godfather, not her uncle, but more importantly he was president of the school board and had his finger in a lot of Scumble River pies.

Charlie Patukas and Allen Ingels were the two most influential men in the area, and as such, were often at odds. Charlie's first concern was the welfare of the town, whereas Allen's interest seemed to lie more in self-advancement.

Homer opened his mouth, then closed it. Clearly, he couldn't decide if he was happy or upset with Charlie's arrival. He whispered to Wally, "The superintendent is out of town at a conference, so I had to notify Charlie."

Wally folded his arms, his face expressionless.

"This is none of your business, Charlie," Allen Ingels said, his bloodshot blue eyes locked with Charlie's clear ones.

"Most everything in Scumble River is my business, Al. 'Specially when it happens on school property." Charlie leaned against the doorframe, which creaked in protest, and crossed his arms. His voice turned deadly serious. "So," he said, "why don't you want to cooperate with the police?"

Chapter 3

Lend a Tear

Skye sat next to Charlie as he piloted his white Cadillac Seville through the darkness, toward the cottage she rented down by the river. She tried to concentrate, to figure out what she should do next, but her thoughts kept turning to Lorelei Ingels, the Sleeping Beauty who would never wake again. It was difficult to face mortality at any age, but the death of a young woman on the verge of independence just wasn't right. No words could comfort the family or soothe Skye's own sense of waste. *It was her time. At least she didn't suffer,* certainly didn't work. And the old standby, *Now she's with God,* didn't cut it when the corpse was an eighteen-year-old.

Charlie interrupted Skye's thoughts. "She was a beautiful girl."

"Yes, she was."

"What do you think happened?" He concentrated on steering the huge car into Skye's narrow driveway.

44

"It could be just about anything." She didn't want to have this conversation, but she knew she had better get used to it, as everyone in town would be asking the same question. "It could be suicide, heart attack, an overdose. We may never know, if Mr. Ingels squelches the autopsy."

"Bob Ginardi is both the school and city attorney, and he says Al can't do that. But he's not sure if Al can stop the search of Lorelei's room."

"So what'll they do?"

Charlie bit down on his unlit cigar. "Tomorrow they'll go before a judge and try to get a search warrant, but our lawyer doesn't think we'll have a good case until we nail down the cause of death. It's real touchy, the Ingels being who they are."

"What do you mean? The rich get different treatment than the poor?"

"Sure. And you know it." Charlie reached over and pinched her cheek. "Normally, Wally would post a guard at that bedroom door while he tried for a warrant, but he can't do that with the Ingels."

"So, we're all responsible for what we do — unless, of course, we're rich?"

"That about sums it up. The more money, the better the lawyer and the more rights you have."

Skye closed her eyes and took a deep breath. Charlie had a point, but no matter what happened now, no matter what any of them did, an eighteen-year-old was dead. Were they all about to fight over her corpse like children over a Barbie doll? Once again Skye felt caught in the middle, and there was nothing she could do to make things better.

She slid over and kissed Charlie's rough cheek. "Thanks for the ride." She tried to keep the resignation from her voice.

"You should let me buy you a car," Charlie said.

"I'm supposed to get money from the insurance company by the end of this week, so I'll finally be able to buy my own car," Skye countered.

Ever since Charlie had inherited a fortune, he'd been trying to spend it on Skye, her brother, Vince, and her parents. He claimed they were his only family, and he wanted them to be happy. Skye tried to resist the temptation of his gifts — at least most of the time.

"Can you believe they stopped payment on the check for the Chevy," Skye said, "just because the Buick was totaled a few months later? Good thing the insurance agent is my cousin. Can you imagine how strangers are treated?"

She'd had bad luck with cars since she'd moved back to Scumble River — two years, two cars, two wrecks ago. Her insurance company was not at all sure they wanted to pay up for either vehicle, and with her bad credit rating and nonexistent savings account, she couldn't afford to purchase one without that check for a down payment. This meant she'd been borrowing cars and hitching rides for the last eight months.

"You should have let me talk to Kevin," Charlie said. "Sometimes cousins need to be reminded of their family duties."

"I can handle him. Time to hit the sack. Tomorrow's going to be a rough day."

She slid across to the passenger door, then got out and waved as Charlie pulled out of the driveway. Bingo greeted her at the cottage door. He was a beautiful, nearly solid black cat, and had previously belonged to Skye's recently deceased grandmother. He twined around Skye's ankles, meowing and purring simultaneously. She dropped her tote bag and coat on the hall bench and scooped him up, burying her face in his velvetlike fur. He purred louder and kneaded her shoulder with his front paws.

After a moment she carried him to the kitchen and prepared his supper with one hand. As soon as she popped open the can, he began to squirm, insisting on being put down. She placed him on the floor with his bowl of food, sorry to lose the feeling of something alive in her arms. Bingo sniffed delicately.

"Come on, don't be silly. You've been eating the same stuff for over nine months now."

He looked up at her out of slitted eyes.

"I don't care if Grandma prepared hand-cooked meals for you. You're lucky that on my budget I buy you the name-brand cat food and not the generic."

He took a tentative lick.

"That's better."

Skye glanced at the clock in the microwave. Nine-thirty. She should eat something. Her tuna sandwich at lunch had been a long time ago. But she wasn't hungry. Suddenly she was bone-tired. She dragged herself to the bedroom, undressing as she went. Her flannel nightgown hung from a hook on the back of the bathroom door, and she wearily inched her way into it, then climbed into bed, too exhausted to bother with her usual nightly ritual of facial cleanser and moisturizing cream. She didn't think missing one night would cause her to wake up looking like a shar-pei.

Skye dreamed she was in college and had forgotten to go to class all semester. Now it was time to take the final exam. A blank blue book stared up at her from the desktop. She couldn't breathe. She struggled up through layers of unconsciousness. She still couldn't inhale. Her mouth felt dry and fuzzy. Her eyes flew open. Everything was black. Bingo had settled on the pillow next to her, his rump covering the lower half of her face.

She pushed him away and flung back the covers. She was sweating, and it felt as if she had run the Chicago Marathon. To calm her racing heart she tried one of the deep breathing exercises she taught to kids who suffered from anxiety.

Suddenly Skye bolted upright. *Shit, shit, shit!* She would bet her next paycheck that the high school had no crisis-intervention strategy. She had read recently that only seventy-eight percent of all schools had such a plan, and since neither a psychologist nor social worker had ever remained in Scumble River for more than a year, it was highly unlikely an emergency procedure had ever been written. And without a plan spelling out who would do what in case of a disaster or a tragedy, nothing would be in place to handle the students' grief.

She'd bet another week's salary that Homer would see no need for such an intervention. But whether the principal agreed or not, many of the students would suffer severe emotional trauma once they heard about Lorelei's death. For the majority of those kids, it would be their first taste of mortality. Most would act as if Lorelei's death didn't bother them, but if the situation wasn't handled properly, they'd be vulnerable to suicide attempts, substance abuse, and other risk-taking behaviors.

Skye pulled the covers over her head. How could she deal with such a crisis alone? She needed help from other mental-health professionals, but there were none in Scumble River.

After a few moments, she forced herself out of bed and into the shower. By five-thirty, she was sitting at her kitchen table with a cup of Earl Grey tea, the phone book, and a legal pad.

One bright spot. The superintendent was out of town. Dr. Wraige and Skye had a mutual-avoidance policy going, and she was happy not to have to deal with him. That left the principal as her first call. She hoped he was an early riser.

"Hi. Homer? Skye Denison here. Time? Yes, I know the time. It's five-thirty-five. I'm sorry I woke you, but we have a problem, one connected with Lorelei's death." Skye held the phone away from her ear and let him rant for a few moments. "I'm really sorry, but do we have some sort of policy on how to deal with this type of situation with the other kids?"

Homer's end went silent. Then he said, "No. Well, we do have something from the special ed co-op, but we never filled in the blanks with names or anything."

The Scumble River School District belonged to the Stanley County Special Education Cooperative, an entity that, in theory, furnished them with programs and personnel on an intermittent basis, as needed. The cooperative had started out by providing school psychologists, social workers, occupational therapists, physical therapists, speech pathologists, and teachers for such low-incidence handicaps as vision and hearing impairments. Now that most of those professions were needed full-time by school districts, the co-op had become more or less a watchdog to deal

51

with the bureaucratic red tape of special-education funding.

Skye covered the mouthpiece and swore. She tapped an angry tattoo on the kitchen table with her pen, then finally spoke into the phone. "Who do we have available who's qualified to help deal with the kids who are upset?"

"Besides you?"

"Yes, besides me." She was glad Homer couldn't see her expression. Forcing her tone into a pleasant range, she asked, "Who can I have today? Who will have had some training?"

A longer silence fell this time. "Ah, no one I can think of. Maybe we should call off school today and let the parents handle it."

Skye considered Homer's suggestion. It was tempting, but it probably wouldn't be best for the majority of the kids to sit home and brood, or worse yet, get together in groups and egg each other on to do something stupid, to prove who loved Lorelei best.

If Lorelei had been an average student, Skye could have called together the girl's two or three closest friends and helped them deal with their emotions. But Lorelei was a star — head cheerleader, lead in all the school musicals, majorette in the band, and secretary of the student council — so almost everyone in the school would feel her loss. Even those who were jealous of her would experience some emotion.

"No, we'd better have school today. I'll call the co-op, and see if they have a crisis team we can borrow. And we need to have a faculty meeting before school. Quite a few teachers will be upset, too."

"The staff will be fine," Homer protested.

Skye contemplated crawling back into bed. Instead she continued to sweet-talk him until Homer agreed to hold a teachers' meeting at seven-thirty. She fed Bingo and got dressed. It was still only six o'clock. She decided to try the co-op anyway and got an answering machine. She left her message and headed out the door.

It was a long walk to the school, and what with yesterday's excitement, she had forgotten to arrange for a ride. Skye vowed she would buy a car this weekend even if she had to sell her body to get the cash. Looking down at her generous curves, she hoped the car salesman liked cuddly women.

As Skye pulled the cottage door shut, a white Oldsmobile turned into her driveway. Skye closed her eyes and prayed for strength. Her mother, May Denison, was fifty-seven but had the energy of a twenty-year-old. She kept her house immaculate, exercised four times a week, and worked part-time as a police, fire, and emergency dispatcher. Along with this already-busy schedule, May's primary cause in life was taking care of her children. This would have been noble had Skye and her brother, Vince, been under sixteen, but both were well over thirty. Skye was finding it tough to keep her independence.

May shot out of the car and yo-yoed Skye, first grabbing her in a tight hug, then pushing her away, then grabbing her again. "Why do I always have to hear about things from Minnie first?" May demanded.

"I thought you were dispatching last night, and would already know more than I did."

"No, I traded with Thea so she could go to her granddaughter's dance recital. I worked days yesterday." May crossed her arms. "Fill me in."

Skye thought she knew what her mother was referring to, but she was taking no chance in revealing a secret that May might not actually know. "What did Aunt Minnie have to say this morning?"

"Don't try to act dumb with me, Missy. Lorelei Ingels's murder, of course."

"No one has said she was murdered, have they?" Skye wondered if a cause of death had been announced while she was sleeping.

"Everyone in town knows that the police and coroner were at the school. Not that my own daughter would pick up a phone and call me." The salt-and-pepper waves on May's head appeared to bristle.

"Sorry, Mom. It was after nine-thirty by the time I got home." Skye tried to look innocent, fighting a sly grin that was trying to escape. "Besides, I thought for sure Uncle Charlie would have told you."

"Charlie knew?" A look of betrayal crossed May's face. Charlie and May had been trading secrets and gossip for nearly thirty years.

"Sure, he was there. He drove me home."

"Mmm." May paused for a few moments, then continued on a different track. "That reminds me. Your father's found a car for you."

Skye felt her heart sink. Her dad's idea of a great car was good transportation — paint and fenders were optional. After driving her father's eyesores all her life, this time she wanted something with a little more beauty than the beasts he usually chose. She knew it was shallow to care about a car's looks, but she didn't care. This time she wanted something hot. A Miata if she could swing the payments.

"Ah, well, that's really nice of him, but I did tell Dad I was going to pick out a car myself."

"Just take a look at it." May played her trump card. "You don't want to hurt your father's feelings, do you?"

"Sure, I'll look at it." Being a bridge player, Skye recognized an ace of spades when she heard it. "But I'm not buying it."

"Sure. No one said you had to." May nodded. "Want a ride to school?"

Skye weighed her options. A three-mile hike, hoping to see someone she knew who would give her a ride, or five minutes of interrogation by her mother about Lorelei's death. "Sure, thanks. Is that a new jacket?" She took a stab at trying to distract May's attention.

"No. Now tell me what happened yesterday, from the beginning."

The drive to school was short, and Skye was only up to finding the body when May steered the Olds into the empty parking

56

lot. "Keep going. No one is here yet, so you have time."

"Not really, Mom." Skye grabbed the door handle and pushed. It seemed to be stuck. "I've got to get some plans in place before everyone else arrives." And if she were lucky, she might be able to squeeze in her morning swim in the school's pool.

"Five more minutes."

"I'll call you tonight." Skye tried the door again.

"Childproof automatic locks." May smiled serenely. "Tell me the rest."

Skye sagged against the seat. Why were her relatives always kidnapping her? As she told her mom what May wanted to know, Skye realized they had all forgotten about the girl who had sounded the alarm. She would have to confirm that it was indeed Elvira Doozier and talk to her ASAP.

When Skye finished, May pressed the button to release the doors. "You know," she said, "from what you said, Allen and Lorna Ingels's attitude is really pretty strange. You ought to talk to your cousins. They know a lot about Lorelei and her mother."

"Which cousins?" Skye stood on the blacktop, straightening her navy wool pantsuit.

"The twins. They're involved with all that beauty-pageant nonsense, and so are the Ingelses." May looked at her watch and frowned.

Before Skye could question her mother further, May leaned over, shut the passenger door, and drove away. Skye gazed at the red taillights, wondering where her mother was off to before seven on a Thursday morning.

The phone was ringing as Skye unlocked the front door of the school. It stopped while she was still trying to open the door to the front office, but started up again almost immediately. Should she answer it? Probably not, but what if it were the co-op with a list of helpers?

She dropped her tote onto the counter and reached for the phone, pressing the button for an outside line. She'd call the co-op back rather than run the risk of playing telephone roulette, with a thousand-to-one odds in favor of the caller being an irate parent.

This time she reached an actual person. A secretary. Skye identified herself and asked to speak to the coordinator for their district. She had met him only a half dozen times, as he rarely attended any of Scumble River's meetings. She was told that he wouldn't be in until nine.

"Could someone else help me? We have an emergency, a student death. Does the co-op have a crisis plan?" Skye heard her voice become shaky. It was just starting to hit her that she would have to handle the situation all by herself.

"I'm sorry. That has to go through your coordinator. But I can page him if you like."

"Yes, definitely page him."

"Please hold." Music suddenly blared into Skye's ear. Appropriately enough, it was Patsy Cline singing "Lonely Street."

Twenty minutes later, Skye finally got to talk to the coordinator. "As I've explained at least a dozen times, I need help," she said. "What can the co-op do for me?"

The faculty and staff of the high school were beginning to arrive. She heard excited voices and sobs, and Skye wondered if by the time the announcement was made at the faculty meeting, the stories going around would resemble in any way what had really happened.

"We'll try to pull some social workers and psychologists who are employed by the cooperative, rather than by individual school districts," the coordinator replied. "But this could take a while, and they may not be available for the whole day."

"How about you? Couldn't you come down for at least the morning? Didn't you say you have a degree in social work?" Skye couldn't keep the desperation from her voice.

"Working directly with students is not part of my job," the coordinator's emotionless voice droned. "As I said, I'll see what help I can get you."

"Fine." Skye recognized when someone really didn't care.

Her mind raced as she hurried down the hall toward the guidance room. Coach would not be happy, but she was commandeering his office for the day. She stopped suddenly as an idea formed. If Coach were a real guidance counselor, he should be able to help with the day's crisis. She had always suspected he wasn't truly qualified. Now she'd find out.

Who else could she get to talk to kids with minimal instructions from her? Trixie and Abby. Trixie Frayne was the school librarian and cheerleader coach, a natural listener, and a lot of kids already confided in her. Plus, she was Skye's best friend and could be counted on to do her a favor. And Abby Fleming was the school nurse. Surely she would have had some training in at least rudimentary counseling.

Skye talked to Trixie and Abby, who were glad to help, although a little unsure of their ability. Next she approached the coach. As she expected, he flat-out refused. Most teachers were happy to do what they could for the school and the students, but there was a small coterie of those who had been teaching too long and had essentially retired before the actual papers were signed. Coach belonged to the latter group.

Skye went in search of Homer. She found him sequestered in his office and explained what she had already done.

Homer shook his shaggy head. "Not good. Not good. Mrs. Frayne and Ms. Fleming are not qualified to provide counseling, thus they are not covered under our liability insurance."

Skye bit back a retort and searched frantically for an answer. "Wouldn't they be covered by the Good Samaritan law?"

"I'll call our lawyer and find out."

The attorney wasn't in his office yet.

Before Homer could say no, Skye asked, "What do you suppose would be worse in the eyes of the law: do nothing or make a good-faith effort?"

After a few minutes of agonizing, Homer

grudgingly gave Skye permission to follow through on her plan. Then, without warning, he stood, and said, "Time for the faculty meeting. I'm turning it over to you to run."

He was halfway down the hall before Skye could protest. She raced after him, but as soon as she caught up with him, in the Home Ec room where the meetings were held, he turned to the teachers who were already assembled and introduced her.

Suddenly she felt her own grief and despair fighting their way to the surface. She fleetingly considered faking an appendicitis attack so she could go home sick. Instead, she pushed her distress back down, nodded to Homer, and began. "We have all had a terrible shock. As you know, Lorelei Ingels was found dead in our gymnasium yesterday afternoon. As of this morning we do not know the cause of death.

"Many of us feel a personal sense of loss, and those of you who think you cannot handle your classes, please let Mr. Knapik know immediately, so other arrangements can be made."

Skye paused, but no one came forward. She didn't expect anyone would. They would come later in private. "Here is our plan for today. We're a small school, so as soon as the bell rings to signal the beginning of classes, we will assemble all students in the cafeteria, since we still aren't allowed access to the gym. I will announce Lorelei's death, and give them what little information we have about the circumstances surrounding it. At that point, I ask that all teachers return to their first-period rooms. Any students who want to talk more about Lorelei's death will be asked to stay in the cafeteria. The rest will be dismissed to their classrooms."

Skye swallowed hard and forced her voice to remain steady. She could not afford to break down. "The students who remain in the cafeteria will be counseled by me, the school nurse, and the librarian. As the need arises, we will break into even smaller groups or see kids individually. I'm hoping that some social workers or psychologists from the co-op will arrive this afternoon. When that happens, if any of you would like to talk to someone, please feel free. Of course, if you need to see someone before then, find me, and we'll speak with you immediately."

Most of the teachers looked as numb as Skye felt. Some had tears rolling down their cheeks. Skye asked, "Any questions?"

After dealing with the usual queries about who should say what to the students' questions, Skye dismissed the faculty. There were two more things she had to do before the day officially started. She wanted to ask the secretary to get some coffee, soft drinks, donuts, and snacks for the counseling rooms. And she had to call Wally and find out if a cause of death had been established. *How* was usually the first thing teens wanted to know. Too bad that question was followed closely by *why*, something that the adults could never answer.

Chapter 4

More Than Meets
the Lie

The students filed silently into the cafeteria. There was none of the joking, laughter, or raised voices Skye had come to expect at an assembly. They found seats on the benches, without the usual fuss of who sat next to whom, and stared forward. Skye felt as if she were about to address the Stepford children.

She walked nervously to the front of the room, near the window where food trays were usually handed out. The pea-green cinder-block walls were hung with posters advertising the seven basic food groups and nutritionally balanced meals. Many had been altered with Magic Marker and teenage wit. Skye blinked; was that supposed to be a condom on that banana?

A heavy odor of Tater Tots and hot dogs hung in the airless room. Skye opened her mouth, but found she couldn't remember what she had meant to say. The eerie silence and concentrated stares were making her nervous.

This was one of the many tough parts of her job. She had to keep her own emotions in check in order to create an atmosphere in which the students would feel safe to expose their feelings. Teens only felt secure if the adults around them exhibited a calm, unruffled, it's-all-being-handled type of demeanor.

With an effort, she pulled herself together and began, "As many of you know, my name is Ms. Denison, and I'm the school psychologist." Skye smiled slightly and nodded at several students she recognized. "I'm sure you've all heard the sad news — Lorelei Ingels was found dead yesterday on the school stage. We don't know the cause of death, but we will share that information with you as soon as we do find out. There is no reason to believe that she suffered, or that there is any danger to anyone else."

Skye studied the faces in front of her. Most of the teens were staring back at her. She could hear whispers starting as she continued, "In a few minutes Mr. Knapik will ring the bell, and everyone should go to their first-hour classes. Anyone who feels too upset should stay here and we'll talk some more."

After the teens were dismissed, Skye did a quick count of how many were left. About forty kids remained seated. They ranged from clumps of eight or ten, to single students hunkered by themselves.

Forty was far too many for an effective group intervention. She'd have to divide them among the helpers she had available. Weighing the personalities involved, Skye resolved to give Abby the least upset kids. The school nurse tended to be a bit clinical, which would be appropriate for the teens who would be fine as soon as they could sort out the experience in their minds.

Trixie was a great listener. She could take the kids who were upset more with the idea of someone dying than with Lorelei's death in particular.

Skye would take Lorelei's closest friends — the cheerleaders, the drama crowd, and the student council.

"Okay, in a little bit we'll divide up into three groups. Mrs. Frayne will take some of you to the library to talk, Ms. Fleming's bunch will go to the music room, and the rest will come with me to the guidance office."

Skye scanned the crowd. How to decide who was the least upset? She shrugged.

Maybe this wasn't the correct way to approach this crisis, but it was all she could think of. She hadn't been given much training for this type of incident. "Before we break into groups, I'd like you each to tell me a little bit about how you knew Lorelei."

Three girls were clustered together at the front table. One with short blond curls met Skye's gaze and lifted an eyebrow. Skye pointed to her. "Would you go first?"

"I was her best friend. We were co-captains of the cheerleading squad."

Skye thought she heard a small voice say, "Lorelei let you be her assistant. You were never the co-captain."

It was interesting how quickly people jumped in to get their version across. Skye dipped her head to the two other girls. "Were you on the squad, too?"

They nodded and whispered.

That triad would come with Skye.

A muscular young man sitting with two other guys caught Skye's attention next, and she walked over to them. "And how did you know Lorelei?"

His voice cracked when he answered, "She was my girlfriend."

"I'm so sorry." This boy would probably be the chief mourner. She would have to watch him closely. "Are these your friends?" Skye indicated the teens flanking him.

"Yes, we're on the football team together."

My group, too. She worked her way through the rest of the kids. The last girl sat by herself in the back, staring into space and looking out of place among the ultraslim blondes who had been in Lorelei's inner circle. She had a voluptuous figure and long, wavy brown hair. It took Skye several tries to get the girl's attention.

Finally, the loner said, "I'm no one. Lorelei didn't know I was alive."

Skye looked at her quizzically.

The girl rose from her seat. Her brown eyes blazed. "I hated her. I'm glad she's dead."

It was close to ten-thirty by the time Skye left the guidance office. Several of the students had asked for individual sessions. She was heading for the faculty lounge and the staff bathroom when Opal Hill, the school secretary, came flying down the hall. Normally Opal reminded Skye of a mouse, but today, dressed all in black, she looked more like a bat.

"Oh, thank goodness I found you. Mr. Knapik is in with the coordinator from the co-op and has ordered me not to disturb them, but the police are here. What should I do?"

"Tell Homer immediately."

"No, I can't."

"Well, I can." Skye marched toward the office, trailed by the secretary.

Wally, Officer Quirk, and two other Scumble River policemen were standing in the main office. Skye walked past them, ignoring their words, and knocked on Homer's door. No answer. She knocked again and leaned her head against the wood. Not a sound. She tried the door. It opened easily, but no one was in the room.

Skye turned to Wally. "Did you see Homer leave this office?"

The chief shook his head. "No, but we don't need him. Just give us the class lists, and we'll pull the students we need to talk to."

Skye ignored Wally and tried Opal. "Was Homer in his office when the police arrived and you left to get me?"

The secretary nodded.

"How the heck did he get out?" Skye scanned the inside of Homer's office, and walked over to the closed drapes. Come to think of it, she had never seen them open. She stuck her hand underneath the fabric and fished for the cord. Nabbing it, she yanked. The curtains swished back to reveal not the window Skye was expecting, but a door designed to look like a window from the outside of the building.

Opal murmured, "I guess they went to lunch."

"At ten-thirty?"

The other woman shrugged.

Skye turned to Wally. "You'll have to wait for them to get back. Opal and I don't have the authority to let you have the list or interview students."

Wally's face was rigid. "We don't need your permission."

Skye didn't know what the law said, but she knew what parent reaction would be if they allowed Wally free rein. "Sorry, but if you insist, we'll advise students not to talk to you until we can reach their parents."

"You're out of line." Wally sighed. "I understand you want to protect your kids, but the longer we wait, the colder the trail gets."

What he had just said finally sank through to Skye. "Are you saying she was murdered?"

Skye screamed. It felt good, so she did it

71

again. One more time, she decided, and then she could face returning to the chaos inside the high school. She had borrowed Trixie's car keys and locked herself in the Mustang in order to blow off some steam and refrain from hitting someone.

The question wasn't whom to smack, but whom to smack first? The coach/guidance counselor, who hated sharing a room with Skye and kept trying to sneak into the guidance office and force Skye out? The insufferable coordinator from the co-op, who had finally dropped by but still refused to interact with any of the students, and instead had locked himself in with Homer, then had had the nerve to go out to lunch? Or Wally, who continued to try to freeze Skye with his indifference every time they were in the same room together?

Reluctantly, Skye emerged from the small car. The dark interior had been soothing, almost like being inside a mug of hot cocoa. Too bad a cup of Swiss Miss wasn't inside of her; she could use a shot of chocolate comfort right now. As she entered the school, she could hear sounds of male bonding — guffaws, chuckles, and snickers — coming from behind the principal's closed door. She looked at her watch — nearly noon. Obviously the co-op coordinator and Homer had returned from their early luncheon.

All the buttons on the telephone were lit, and as fast as Opal answered one, another line would light up. Her part of the conversations consisted of, "Sorry, we can't give out that information." Then she paused as the person on the other end yelled at her. She finished with, "I'm really sorry, but I'm not allowed to say."

The secretary's sparse mouse-colored hair stood on end, and her watery brown eyes were red-rimmed from the tears she kept dabbing away with a shredded tissue. Obviously the woman was overwhelmed by the volume and vituperativeness of the calls.

Skye stared at Homer's closed door. Opal was nearing a breakdown, and the principal needed to do something about it. A sudden wave of male laughter helped Skye make up her mind. With some principals she used reason to achieve what she wanted. With others she used diplomacy. Homer reacted only to frontal attacks.

She knocked sharply on the door and entered without waiting for permission. "Homer, the phones are ringing off the wall. Opal needs someone to help her with all the calls."

The jovial expression on the principal's face changed to one of annoyance. "What do you want me to do about it? You've confiscated all my personnel."

Skye counted to ten and reminded herself of Homer's age and position before she replied. "Two, I'm only using two of your people."

"Sure, but how about all the teachers who are too upset to teach their classes?" Homer's tone was sarcastic.

"I did suggest hiring some floating subs for today," she reminded him, keeping hold of her temper with great difficulty.

"It's not in the budget." Homer sat back in his chair and shook the hair out of his eyes. "Did you know the co-op is going to charge us for the people they sent over? You didn't have authorization to request help. We may have to take that from your salary."

Skye opened her mouth and closed it without speaking. She glanced at the silent coordinator. She could swear he had a smirk on his face. Between gritted teeth she muttered, "Fine. Now, about some help for Opal . . ."

Homer sighed. "Who did you have in mind?"

"Coach," Skye answered. "It's his guidance counselor day, and since he has refused to do any crisis counseling, and the guidance office is occupied, he's just sitting around in the teachers' lounge stirring up the faculty."

"He won't like this," Homer said.

"Really? And I'm having such a good time today myself." Skye knew she shouldn't be so sarcastic, but it had just slipped out, and she couldn't back down now.

"Okay, Coach can answer phones." Homer leaned back in his chair. "You stop and tell him on your way back to the guidance office."

"I think it would be better coming from you." Skye pushed the phone toward Homer. "For some reason, Coach thinks I'm out to get him."

As Homer dialed and spoke, Skye smiled. She loved a twofer — help for Opal and a way to keep Coach out of the guidance office.

After the principal got off the phone, Skye said, "Did you know that the police were here and tried to question the students?"

"No, that must have been when we were . . . ah . . . at that special meeting we had to attend."

"Right." *Was that the one Ronald Mc-Donald chaired?* Skye tried to keep the sarcasm out of her voice. "Anyway, what will we do when they come back?"

"I'll check with the school lawyer and see." Homer reached for the phone he had just pushed aside. He spoke for a while, and after he hung up, he said, "Nope, Bob says not to let the police question the students. The law is unclear, but we could be in trouble if the parents could prove we were negligent in protecting their child's rights. Either school personnel or a parent must be with the child when he or she is interviewed."

"Better let people know because Wally will no doubt return any minute." Skye waved and backed out of the door. Without warning, she felt icy fingers grab her arm. She yelped and spun around.

Kent Walker's pale blue eyes stared into hers.

"Oh my gosh, Kent, you scared me to death." She shook off his arm. "What's wrong?"

"Are you aware that the police chief is interrogating some of the students right here in school? I tried to sit in with the kids as he questioned them, but one of his storm troopers threw me out."

One thing she had liked about Kent was his high level of involvement with the students. So why didn't what he had just said sound right? She didn't have time to think about it now. "Show me where they are."

Kent guided her down the hall to the Home Ec room. The space was divided into two. The half nearest the door was filled with sewing machines, several teens, all of whom avoided looking at each other, and the police officers who were guarding them.

The other half of the room was set up as the cooking area, and Wally had confiscated this section for his interviews. The heavy stoves and refrigerators that formed a wall between the two areas filtered out most of the conversation.

Skye marched through the sewing area before the police could stop her. The officers were quicker where Kent was concerned, and nabbed him as he tried to follow her into the interrogation section.

As he was escorted away, he yelled, "Tell the kids they don't have to say anything."

She yelled back, "I'll take care of the students; you tell Homer to start calling their parents."

Wally was speaking as she entered the kitchen. "We're just trying to figure out what happened to your friend. There's no need to be afraid." He leaned casually against the counter.

The blonde sitting at the aqua Formica kitchen table did not look frightened. The girl's cold blue eyes sparkled with disdain as she turned them toward Skye. "You're that shrink that talked to us this morning."

Skye nodded. "I'm Ms. Denison, the school psychologist. And you're Zoë VanHorn, Lorelei's best friend."

"Right on the first try." Zoë examined her long purple nails. "I don't have to talk to the cops, correct?"

Before Skye could answer, Wally moved from the counter to her side and ordered in a low voice, "Get out."

"No." Skye wrinkled her brow. Darn, this whole business was so much harder with Wally still mad at her. Maybe he was right. Maybe she had betrayed his trust by investigating alone last summer, but she had apologized repeatedly. What more could she do to make things right between them? She had never dreamed he would be this hurt.

Wally took her arm and tried to lead her away.

She refused to budge. "Have you called Zoë's parents?"

Wally released his grip. "Get out, or I'll have you removed by force."

"A school representative must be present if a minor is to be interrogated without a parent in attendance."

"That's not the law."

"No? Well, it's in the school handbook, which I'm obligated to follow, and the school attorney has advised us to handle things this way." Good thing she had actually read the manual when she was first hired.

"Tough. Get out." Wally turned his back on her.

Zoë waved her hand. "I want her to stay."

"No." Wally's face was beginning to turn red.

The teen shrugged. "Then I want a lawyer."

Wally's face went from cherry to maroon. "Have a seat, Ms. Denison."

"Thank you, Chief Boyd." Skye settled herself in a chrome kitchen chair and studied Wally. Once his face had returned to its natural tan hue, he was a handsome man. He had recently turned forty, but except for a few gray threads in his curly black hair, and a couple of lines radiating from his brown eyes, there were few signs of his age.

Skye shook her head. She had been half in love with him since she was fifteen. When she first met him he was fresh out of the police academy. Everyone liked him, especially the teens. He was fair and honest with them. She had developed a huge crush on the young officer, and he had handled it kindly without ever embarrassing her or taking advantage of the situation.

In the ensuing years she had moved away, he had gotten married, she had moved back, and they had become friends. But last summer she had destroyed that friendship by going behind his back. That betrayal, and his wife's leaving him for another man, had changed Wally. Skye kept hoping it was a temporary situation and that he would return to his old self, given enough time.

Skye suddenly noticed that both the chief and the teen were staring at her, waiting for her to speak. "So, what were you and Zoë discussing?"

"I had asked Zoë to tell me a little about Lorelei's movements yesterday."

The girl ran her fingers through her short curls and wet her already-glossy lips. "Let's see. It was pretty much same old, same old."

Wally drew up a chair and sat opposite the females. "Start at the beginning. When was the first time you saw Lorelei yesterday?"

"I picked her up at her house around seven, and we buzzed the gut for a half hour or so."

Wally and Skye's eyes met. "Buzzing the gut" was what the teens called driving down Basin Street, Scumble River's main drag, and circling back by cutting through the McDonald's parking lot on one end and Mayor Clapp's used-car lot on the other. It was also called "shooting the loop," and it was technically illegal, although that law was not often enforced.

Skye spoke, earning a glare from Wally. "What did you girls talk about?"

"Stuff." Her bony shoulders under a tight-ribbed sweater moved up and down. "You know, whose clothes are so 'last year,' who's a trendoid wannabe, who was slipping who the tongue at the party last night."

"Did you pick up anyone else?"

"Well, no, I drive a Miata." Zoë looked at the adults, who appeared clueless. "No backseat."

"Nice wheels," Skye murmured. It was pretty pathetic that a teenager owned the car that she could only dream of buying. It was clear that Skye had taken a wrong turn somewhere on life's highway.

"Yeah, right." Wally tried to regain control of the interview. "So you arrived at school at approximately seven-thirty, but classes don't start until eight."

"We had a cheerleader meeting." Zoë bent down and adjusted the ankle strap on her black sandals.

"Who was there?" Wally asked, taking out his notebook.

Skye itched to do the same.

"Mrs. Frayne, me, Lorelei, Caresse, and Farrah. Tara was on vacation, and we're down a girl since DiDi moved away. That's what the meeting was about. Picking a new Black Widow."

"What the he—ck is a Black Widow?" Wally asked.

Zoë rolled her eyes. "The name of the cheerleading squad, of course. The baseball and football teams are the Scorpions, so we're the Black Widows. Get it?"

The chief nodded wearily. "What are the other girls' last names?"

"Farrah Miles and Caresse Wren."

"Next, you went to your first-period class, right?"

The teen nodded. "We have all our classes together."

"Lorelei wasn't out of your sight all day?" The chief frowned.

"Well, except for seventh and eighth hour."

"What happened during those periods?"

"Since there was no PE, and Lorelei and Chase had back-to-back study hall, Mr. Walker called a rehearsal for *Sleeping Beauty*." Zoë pulled a mirror out of her purse.

"You aren't in the play?" Skye's question earned her another scowl from the chief.

"Of course I am." A tiny line appeared between the teen's perfect eyebrows. "But Lorelei and Chase were the leads."

"What is Chase's last name?" Wally slid back his chair.

"Wren. He's Caresse's twin." Zoë spread another coat of scarlet gloss on her lips.

Wally looked at Skye. "Ms. Denison, is Mr. Walker the disappearing teacher you dragged me over to meet yesterday?"

"Yes." Skye thought a moment. There was someone missing. "How about Troy Yates? I thought he was her boyfriend. Wasn't she with him at all yesterday?"

Zoë shrugged. "Probably. Who knows?"

The chief nodded thoughtfully as the three sat in silence.

Finally, Zoë asked, "Is everything Crystal Light—clear now?"

Wally didn't look up from his notebook. "Clear as mud."

Chapter 5

Mind Your Ps and Clues

After Zoë left, Wally said to Skye, "She didn't seem overly grief-stricken, did she?"

"One of the first stages of grief is denial. Maybe it hasn't hit her yet. So many adolescents have no concept of mortality." Skye felt she had to support the girl, but in her heart she agreed with the chief. Zoë had not come across as sad.

"That girl's period of mourning is about as short as her skirt."

Skye didn't want to argue, so instead she changed the subject. "Have you talked to Elvira Doozier yet?"

"She's not at school today. I sent someone out to her house."

"I hope she's okay."

"The Dooziers just don't like talking to the police."

"Too bad she's not here today. I'd like to be with her when you question her."

Wally slumped in his chair. "I suppose you plan on sitting here for all the interviews?"

"Until their parents arrive."

"You called the parents? That was a mistake."

"I told you if you tried to see the kids alone, we had to contact the parents."

Wally shook his head. Before he could speak, the PA system crackled. "Ms. Denison, line one."

Now what? Skye shot out of her seat and hurried toward the office. They would never page her for a phone call if it weren't extremely urgent. Most of the time, she was lucky to get a message slip stuck in her mailbox.

She rounded the corner and grabbed the receiver. "Skye Denison, may I help you?"

"Skye, it's Caroline Greer. Thank goodness I found you. We need you right away."

"What's up?" Skye couldn't remember the last time she'd heard the elementary-school principal so shaken up. Caroline Greer was famous for her calm demeanor.

"Linette Ingels."

Shit! Skye had forgotten that Lorelei had a sister. She should have had a crisis team at the elementary school, too. "She's not at school, is she?"

"No, but she was on the phone last night with her friends. They're all upset, and the hysteria is spreading through the school faster than lice." Caroline's tone showed her strain. "How soon can you get here?"

Caroline was a great principal. If she said she needed help, things must be really bad. Skye looked at the clock. It was a little past twelve-thirty. The kids must have just gotten in from lunch recess. "I'll be right over. Just let me tie up some loose ends." Skye could hear excited voices in the background.

"Hurry."

The line went dead in Skye's hand. Opal was still busy answering phones. Through the open door to the health room, Skye could see the coach with a receiver in one hand and an aggrieved expression on his face as he grunted into the mouthpiece. It made her whole day to see that man actually work.

Homer was still with the co-op coordinator when Skye entered his office. She explained the situation at the grade school and suggested that the principal sit in on the rest of the chief's interviews with their students.

As Skye talked, the coordinator stood and picked up his briefcase. "Well, Homer," he said, "looks like things here are under control. I've got to get going."

"Since you're leaving, could you drop

me at the elementary school on your way?" Skye asked.

A look of annoyance crossed the man's face. "Are you ready to leave now? I've got an important meeting at one."

"Just let me grab my purse. I'll meet you in the parking lot. What kind of car do you drive?"

"A red Corvette."

Somehow his answer didn't surprise her.

After a brief stop in the grade school's office, Skye went directly to Linette Ingels's fifth-grade classroom. The teacher and principal were each surrounded by several students. Other kids were wandering around the room. The children were talking excitedly in loud, high-pitched voices.

Skye whispered in the principal's ear, "Shall I take over?"

Caroline nodded, and eased out of the grasp of several girls. The teacher took the signal and followed suit.

Skye raised her voice. "Hi, I'm Ms. Denison, and I work at this school. One of my jobs is to help kids who are feeling bad. Anybody here feeling sort of bad or sad?" She knew she had to build some rapport with this age level before talking directly about Lorelei's death.

Two-thirds of the students raised their hands, as did their teacher, who smiled wearily.

"Okay. Let's sit on the carpet in a circle." Skye eased onto the floor. "I know many of you talked to Linette last night. A lot of times when something happens that makes us feel sad, it helps to talk to other people about it. I'll bet that's why Linette called you."

A girl with long red curls bounced up onto her knees. "Linette said her sister died, but we don't believe it."

Skye saw several nodding heads. Good. The little girl had given her the opening she needed to talk about Lorelei's death. "Why don't you believe Linette?"

"She tells stories," the redhead answered.

"I see." Skye tucked that info away for later examination. "Well, I'm sorry to say she's telling the truth this time. Lorelei did die yesterday."

A timid voice asked, "At school?"

"Yes, but that is very unusual. You don't have to worry about that happening to you, or anyone else you know." Skye said a silent prayer that she was telling the truth.

The kids fell quiet.

"How many of you knew Lorelei?" Skye asked.

More hands than she expected were raised.

"Wow. Did you meet her playing at Linette's?"

A boy in the back answered, "Nah, she came to class one day, and showed us her crown and junk when she got to be Miss Stanley County. She looked like a princess in a fairy tale."

One of the girls chimed in, "Linette is going to win that same pageant sometime. She's already won two more than Lorelei did at her age."

Skye decided to walk the mile or so back to the high school rather than waste time looking for a ride. It was a clear day, and the temperature had finally broken out of the forties. Birds twittered from telephone wires, and the slight breeze smelled of spring. She barely noticed either the buds on the trees or the cracks on the sidewalk. Her mind kept turning over everything she had heard that morning.

It bothered her that no one seemed to be very sad about Lorelei's death. People were upset, but more about the passing of an eighteen-year-old in general than Lorelei specifically. She seemed almost more of a symbol than a person.

Skye glanced at her watch; the day was getting away from her. She still had to find the girl from this morning who said she hated Lorelei. The girl needed to be turned over to the police, but Skye wanted a chance to talk to her first. She also wanted to touch base with Justin. Being present when a body was discovered couldn't be good for that boy's fragile mental health.

About a block from the school, Skye heard yelling and screaming. As she got nearer, she saw police cruisers with their lights on and civilian cars parked everywhere — even in the sacred bus lane.

Skye edged her way up the steps through a mob of people. Stanley County deputies guarded the doors.

She tried to step around them and was told, "You can't go in there, Miss."

"I work here. I'm the school psychologist."

"Do you have any ID?"

"Nothing that shows I work here."

"No faculty card?"

"I wasn't in this building the day they took the pictures." Skye was feeling desperate. "I'm assigned to all the Scumble

River schools. Just step inside and ask the principal."

"Sorry. We can't leave the door."

Skye fumbled in her purse and found her Illinois School Psychologists Association membership card, her National Association of School Psychologists membership card, and her Nationally Certified School Psychologist card. She pressed these into the officer's hand.

After studying them closely, he said, "Okay, you can go in."

She always knew that belonging to ISPA, NASP, and NCSP was important, although this wasn't what she'd had in mind when she joined.

The officer opened the door a sliver, and she squeezed inside. Homer pounced on her as she popped through. Immediately, she wished she hadn't tried so hard to get back to work.

"Good. You're finally here. Where were you? The secretary at the grade school said you left twenty minutes ago."

"I walked."

"Bad time to take an afternoon stroll." Homer dug his finger between his collar and neck. "We've got parents up the wazoo."

"How did they get in, with all the police

surrounding the place?"

"These are the ones that got here before we called the cops."

"Oh." Skye let the confusion show on her face. "And why did you have to call the police?"

"They were out of control. They wouldn't sit quietly and take turns talking. Worst of all, they refused to move their cars from the bus lane." The principal raised alarmed eyes. "The transportation director will kill me if I don't get those vehicles out of the way."

"I know this isn't the time, but I've always wondered why everything in the school revolves around the buses. Is the bus company owned by the mob or something?"

Homer paled. "The superintendent has ordered us never to discuss the transportation contract."

"Okaaay." Skye lengthened the word and narrowed her eyes. Another mystery to look into sometime. "What's your strategy?"

"Ah . . . that is . . . why don't we go with your plan this time?"

She took a deep breath and counted to ten. Homer found it easy to criticize others, but he always froze the minute he had to take action himself. "It's not even two yet, so we have more than ninety minutes before the buses arrive." Skye paused to gather her thoughts. "Use the PA to do an all-call announcement, saying that any cars that are not parked in legal spots within the next ten minutes will be towed. Then call the mayor."

At the look of apprehension on the principal's face she changed her tack.

"Come to think of it, the best thing to do is call Charlie. Have him call the mayor and ask for the city tow truck."

"That sounds good. How about the parents?"

"What are they here for?"

"You had me call them," Homer answered.

"You called all of them?" Skye asked. "I only wanted you to call the half dozen or so parents of the students being questioned by the police."

"That's who I called. The rest came to support their friends and relatives, or in a panic over their own children, or out of morbid curiosity."

"Is Chief Boyd still interviewing students?"

"Nope, he talked to four or five after you left, and a couple of faculty members, then left about an hour ago."

She chewed her bottom lip. "Also announce that Wally and his officers have left the building, and that no students are currently being questioned by police. Ask everyone to leave unless they have urgent business with school personnel. Have them get a number from Opal, and tell them you and I will see them in order."

Homer looked skeptical. "Why should they listen now? They haven't been listening to me for the last couple of hours."

"Two reasons. Their cars are about to be towed, and by using the number system, we pit them against each other. It'll be competitive — who can get the best numbers."

The principal didn't look convinced, but he moved off to follow Skye's directions.

Skye took a quick scan of the hall. No more parents. Good. She really needed to see some kids, but every time she ventured out of her office a parent grabbed her. She checked her watch. *Damn.* Only half an hour of school left. Which student should she talk to first? Who would know the identity of the girl she needed to see? Justin. For someone on the fringes, he seemed to know a lot about what the other kids were up to — if he'd talk.

She had Opal send for him and waited in the guidance office. It was beginning to feel like home. *I wonder how I could get Homer to let me have this room permanently.* She eyed the rows and rows of metal filing cabinets and the big old wooden desk. *Coach has an office in the gym. He really doesn't need two.*

Justin walked in as Skye was admiring the comfy leather chair. As usual, he didn't say anything.

Skye greeted him and asked him to sit. "Quite a day yesterday, huh?"

"Yeah."

She was encouraged. At least he had verbalized an answer. "I noticed you stuck around the cafeteria this morning after most of the kids left. Were you close to Lorelei?"

He shrugged. "Nah. Better than going to class."

"Do you know the girl who said she hated Lorelei?"

"Sure, that's Frannie Ryan."

Skye was surprised by Justin's willingness to answer. Could it be that this incident had actually been good for him? Maybe it was helping him to be less self-absorbed. "So, are you okay about yesterday?"

Justin looked at her blankly.

"I mean about finding Lorelei like that, and talking to the police and everything."

Another shrug. "No biggie."

Skye waited to see if he would add anything. After several minutes, she said, "I guess you better go back to class before the bell rings, so you can get your books."

Justin levered himself out of the chair. He put his hand on the doorknob and turned. "You know, Ms. Denison, one thing I figured out from yesterday is that even someone who seems perfect is probably more messed up than you'd think."

Wow, Justin had spent time and effort thinking about someone other than himself. That was real progress. Before Skye could formulate a response he was out the door.

In a counseling session, the last few words as the client left the room were usually the most significant. Justin must have been referring to Lorelei. But how had Sleeping Beauty been messed up?

The bell rang as Skye was noting Justin's statement in his file. She pulled her appointment book from her purse and flipped to the next day's page. She penciled in Elvira Doozier at eight, followed by Frannie Ryan at nine, then added Zoë

VanHorn, Troy Yates, Farrah Miles, and Caresse and Chase Wren. It would be a full day.

Skye stood and stretched. She needed to talk to the social workers the co-op had sent, debrief Trixie and Abby, and check to see when the body would be released. And if there was time, she also wanted to question Trixie about the cheerleader meeting Zoë had mentioned, and ask Kent about the *Sleeping Beauty* rehearsal.

She had set up the co-op social workers in the band room. She was impressed by their ingenuity. They had shoved most of the chairs and music stands into the center of the room, and arranged portable bulletin boards on either side, giving them each privacy.

"I see you guys are old hands at this." Skye gestured to their construction.

The male social worker nodded. "Too much so. Seems like we're called in to do crisis counseling more and more often."

"We really appreciate your help." Skye looked over to the woman to include her. "I'm here by myself."

"No problem." The woman picked up two sheets of yellow legal paper. "Here's a list of who we saw, our impressions, and suggestions for follow-up."

"Thanks. This is great." Skye looked over the names, about twenty in all.

"You should send this out to these kids' parents." The man handed her a sheaf of photocopied forms. "It tells them we talked to their child. You can check one of the boxes on the bottom as to what, if any, follow-up is recommended."

"I can't thank you enough." Skye was overwhelmed. It was so nice to have help, not to have to think of everything herself.

The two social workers gathered their belongings. The woman said, "There doesn't seem to be a need for us to come back, but if the situation changes, call us and we'll be right here."

Skye shook both their hands. "Thank you. Thank you so much."

As they walked toward the entrance the man turned to her. "You really do need to get a crisis-intervention plan in place. I'll put an outline in the mail to you tomorrow."

"Great." Skye waved. "Thanks again." For a moment she almost believed she saw halos around their heads. Of course, it was just the afternoon sun shining through the outer door . . . wasn't it?

Clutching the papers they had given her, Skye went in search of Trixie and Abby.

Staff were required to stay half an hour after the dismissal bell. Skye had five minutes to find them.

They were together in the IMC, formerly known as the library. Both women clutched cans of Pepsi. Abby was sprawled in one of the few upholstered seats. Her white-blond hair cascaded over the chair's back; a tanned hand was laid across her eyes. Trixie sat on the counter, her short, compact body bent at the waist as she clasped her knees.

Abby greeted Skye as she entered the room with, "I'm never doing this again. My throat hurts, and my head is pounding."

"It really was a lot harder than you said, Skye," Trixie chimed in. She ran her fingers through her short brown hair. "We don't have the training."

"Well, I really appreciate your pitching in. And I understand how hard it is. But unfortunately . . ."

Abby straightened, her aquamarine eyes narrowed. Trixie jumped down from the counter. They both said, "What . . ."

"Sorry." Skye ran a finger around her suddenly tight collar. Trixie and Abby didn't know the half of it . . . yet. "But we'll need to draw up a crisis strategy. Now that you two have some experience, it's logical for you to be included in that plan."

"How could you do that to us?" Abby advanced on Skye. "We only did this as a favor to you."

Trixie closed in from the other side. "You wouldn't do this to your best friend, would you?"

"Sorry. Trying to make me feel like this is my fault won't work. You both know my mom. May is a certified travel agent for guilt trips. In comparison to her, you two haven't even gotten your learner's permits yet."

Abby and Trixie muttered ominously under their breath and moved closer to Skye.

When she realized she was being backed into the circulation desk, Skye offered words of appeasement. "Don't worry. You won't be in this alone. Scumble River High has a lot of caring teachers who often aren't noticed because the bad ones get all the attention. I'm sure we'll get plenty of volunteers, so no one will have the entire responsibility on his or her shoulders."

"You'd better be right." Trixie was now knee to knee with Skye. "Because if I have to go through this again, I'm putting that

101

picture of you and the goat in the school paper."

Skye cringed. She knew the photo Trixie meant. When they were twelve their Girl Scout troop had visited a petting zoo, and a huge goat had developed a crush on Skye. He had followed her everywhere, finally butting her to the ground and standing guard over her so she couldn't get up.

"And I have a picture Vince gave me while we were dating. It's you and him attending your junior prom. How would you like everyone reminded that the only escort you could get to the dance was your brother?" Abby leaned in from the other side until they were nose to nose, and said, "Now, you were saying that Trixie and I had done our part, and you'd get someone else for the next crisis, right?"

"Right," Skye mumbled.

Chapter 6

Sweetness and Slight

"Ms. Denison, Ms. Denison." A high-pitched fake-sounding drawl shot through Skye's aching head.

Her hand was inches from the knob of the office door when she turned. "Yes? May I help you?"

"I'm Priscilla VanHorn, Zoë's mother. Do you have a minute?" The overblown redhead wore a dress that looked as if it were made out of leftover wallpaper that had been poorly hung.

"Sure. Let's use the health office." Skye ushered the woman through the main door and into a small room to the left.

Skye took the seat behind the desk, forcing Mrs. VanHorn to perch on the vinyl cot. "Now, what can I do for you?"

"I'm concerned about my daughter. I understand you were with her when that awful police chief interrogated her?" The woman raised her voice at the end of her statement, making it sound like a question.

"Yes, but I wouldn't say he interrogated her. He asked her a few questions — mostly trying to get a picture of Lorelei's last few hours." Skye wasn't sure where this was going.

"Well, Zoë was very upset by the whole ordeal." Mrs. VanHorn rummaged in her purse and pulled out a lace-trimmed hankie. "Zoë and Lorelei have been best friends forever. They've been together in every pageant, play, and performance. They're in the same clubs and have been cheering together since junior high."

"I had no idea they were so close." Skye thought of Zoë's demeanor during both Wally's interview and the crisis counseling. "She really covered up her feelings well."

"Lorelei was like a sister to Zoë and a daughter to me." Mrs. VanHorn touched the corner of her eye with the handkerchief. "We were closer than her own family."

"Really?"

"Yes. Her mother was only interested in Lorelei when she was winning a crown. And Linette's only use for her sister was as a tape measure — to show how much better she was at everything."

"My, how sad for Lorelei." Skye frowned, trying to remember what she had

104

heard about the young woman. "She seemed like such a golden adolescent — winning all the school prizes and honors."

Mrs. VanHorn heaved a big sigh. "So, you can see how being grilled by the police is too upsetting for Zoë?"

"Yes, we'll try not to let it happen again. And I'll talk to Zoë myself tomorrow, to make sure she's okay." The woman didn't move. "Is there anything else I can help you with?"

"I just had a thought." Mrs. VanHorn widened her eyes and fluttered her lashes. "I'm sure the school will go ahead and put on *Sleeping Beauty.* After all, the show must go on. Zoë would be the perfect replacement for Lorelei's part." She leaned forward and lowered her fake drawl a notch. "Zoë really should have had the part to begin with. She has a superior voice, and is a much better actress than Lorelei."

"I really don't have anything to do with the play."

Mrs. VanHorn ignored Skye's statement. "Zoë and I decided to let Lorelei have the part, to get her mother off her back."

"How . . . nice of you." This woman was amazing. She must subscribe to the new magazine, *Better Living Through Denial.* Skye tried again. "I don't have anything to do with casting the musical. You need to see Kent Walker." Skye forced down a snicker as she pictured Priscilla VanHorn trying to influence Kent's decision. Skye remembered his endless monologues in the teachers' lounge as he tried to decide who should get what part. The faculty had learned quickly that suggestions were not welcome.

"He's still in charge?" The woman looked confused.

"Yes, why wouldn't he be?" Mrs. VanHorn didn't answer, so Skye finally asked, "Do you know where his room is?"

"Why, yes I do." The woman hoisted herself off the cot and picked up her purse. "Now that Lorelei's gone, you just keep my Zoë in mind for those honors and awards you were talking about."

Skye waited until Mrs. VanHorn had disappeared down the hall. She looked at her watch. It was nearly four-thirty. She had forgotten to ask Trixie about that cheerleading meeting when she talked to her earlier, and the librarian would have left for home a half hour ago. She needed to speak to Kent, too, but if he weren't gone, he'd be tied up with Mrs. VanHorn.

Skye left the health room and looked toward Homer's office. To her surprise, the lights were still on and she could hear voices. This was not a good sign. The principal usually beat the kids out the door when the final bell rang.

It was time to head home before another crisis was dropped in her lap. Her purse was still in the guidance room. She had taken only one step in that direction when a booming voice asked, "Is that you, Skye, honey?"

It was Charlie standing in Homer's doorway. She turned and walked back. "Hi, Uncle Charlie. What's up?"

Homer was sitting at his desk, his head in his hands. After giving her a kiss on the cheek, Charlie guided Skye to a chair and sat opposite her. "Homer was telling me how he handled the parent situation today. That was quick thinking."

Skye skewered Homer with a look he didn't see. "Did everything work out all right with the buses?"

Without lifting his head, Homer talked to his desktop. "Yes, all the cars were moved, and most of the parents left."

"Good."

Homer stole a peek at Charlie. "Skye was a big help."

"I'm sure she was. I know she always is to me." Charlie stared at Homer. "So, what's the plan for tomorrow?"

Homer grabbed a file and flipped frantically through its contents. "Well . . . ah . . . things will probably be pretty much back to normal tomorrow. Don't you think?"

Charlie looked at Skye. "What's your guess?"

"Until we know for sure what happened to Lorelei, and the police release her body so there can be a funeral, I doubt things will be back to normal."

"Any idea what we should do?" Charlie asked.

Skye struggled to concentrate and formulate a thoughtful answer. "We need to know where the police are on this. Are they ready to say officially she was murdered? The chief won't say, but his actions sure point to it. I don't think he'll share much information with me this time."

Charlie took a small spiral notebook and a stubby pencil from the pocket of his white shirt. "I'll talk to Wally and get back to you before school starts tomorrow."

"Also, I have a list of about twenty kids who should be talked to again tomorrow, to make sure they're okay. Can we get one of the co-op social workers back?" Skye's gaze bounced between Charlie and Homer.

"No."

"Sure."

The men's voices overlapped each other.

"Charlie, we have to pay extra for them," Homer whined. "We don't have the budget."

"Take it out of the fund for administration's raises if you can't find the money anywhere else." Charlie turned back to Skye. "Anything else, sweetheart?"

She tapped the arm of the chair. "One more thing. We ought to be ready for another onslaught of parents."

"How can we prepare for that?" Homer asked.

"Well, we could call an informational meeting ourselves. Tell them what we know, answer their questions, maybe even persuade Chief Boyd to speak."

Charlie jumped up. "That's a good idea. Let's call it for first thing in the morning. I'll get the PTO to put the announcement over their phone tree."

The Parent Teacher Organization always came through, whether they were asked to raise money for a new science lab or spread the word about an early closure.

★ ★ ★

It was after five by the time Skye and Charlie left Homer's office. They had started toward the front door when Charlie suddenly pulled her into an empty classroom. "Listen, I didn't want to say this in front of old Homer, but I need your help."

Skye nodded cautiously. It was easier to agree with Charlie than argue, but his requests usually meant trouble.

"If it turns out that girl was murdered, I need you to find out who did it. Wally's a good cop, but he's not part of the school, so he's bound to miss some of the less obvious clues. Besides, a psychologist should be pretty good at getting at the truth."

"Uncle Charlie, I really don't think —"

"You solved Honey's and Antonia's murders. And that mystery at the recreational club last summer. I just thought you'd want to help out your old Uncle Charlie."

"But . . ." she trailed off.

"I remember when I called you in New Orleans to let you know you had a job in Scumble River. You were so happy. You said, 'If there's anything I can do to repay you, I'll do it.' But I guess that was a long time ago."

"I'm not sure what I could do," she said

110

lamely. It really was useless to argue with Charlie.

"I want the school absolved of all responsibility. There is no way I'm letting Al Ingels say it was our fault." Charlie crossed his arms. "Besides, there's something funny going on with Al, and I need to keep an eye on him."

The rivalry between Charlie and Al Ingels was well-known. Mr. Ingels had run against Charlie for the school board — a sin not easily forgiven.

Skye let her weight sag against the teacher's desk. "What if I do investigate, and we *are* responsible?"

"We'll deal with that later," Charlie said. "I have a gut feeling this has nothing to do with the school."

Skye's head ached, her stomach growled, and her feet hurt. She wanted to go home. And Charlie was probably right. It would take an insider to uncover all the inner workings of the high school. "Okay," she agreed. "I'll see what I can turn up. But be prepared. Lorelei deserves to have the truth about her death exposed, even if other people's secrets have to come out, too."

"Whatever you say. All I ask is that you tell me first."

They started out of the classroom. "Homer won't be too happy about me poking around," Skye said.

"You don't have to worry about Homer. The wheel's spinning, but the hamster's dead. He won't even notice what you're doing."

The principal's blue Taurus was pulling out of the lot when Charlie and Skye emerged from the building. A storm front had passed through, prematurely darkening the sky. The outdoor lights shed an eerie green gleam on the two remaining cars. Charlie and Skye headed toward the white Seville with the bumper sticker that read: AT MY AGE I'VE SEEN IT ALL, DONE IT ALL, HEARD IT ALL . . . I JUST CAN'T REMEMBER IT ALL. But before they reached the Cadillac, the other vehicle started up and headed in their direction.

It stopped a few feet in front of them and Kent Walker slid out of the driver's side. "Good evening, Mr. Patukas."

"Hey." Charlie's halfhearted greeting conveyed his opinion of Kent.

"Need a ride home?" Kent asked Skye.

"Thanks. Charlie's going to drop me."

"I thought we could get a bite to eat."

"Thanks, but I'm really tired."

"You've got to eat. We'll just go to the Feedbag."

Skye frowned. She was hungry, and as usual, her refrigerator was bare. "Okay." She turned to Charlie. "Why don't you join us?"

Both men scowled. Charlie answered, "No, I've got to get home. I've got a lot of phone calls to make."

Skye kissed Charlie good-bye and squeezed into Kent's car. The Acura NSX was slung so low that one practically had to know how to levitate to get in and out of it.

Kent shoved the gearshift into drive, and they roared out of the parking lot. "Why doesn't Charlie like me?"

"You're not from town. He'll warm up eventually."

"He likes Simon, and he's not from Scumble River." Kent turned to look at Skye, and the NSX veered sharply to the right, narrowly missing a parked car.

She bit her tongue to stop from screaming at him to keep his eyes on the road. "Simon's got roots here. That gives him an in."

"There's more to it than that." Kent screeched into a parking space directly in front of the restaurant.

"Maybe it's your accent. He just needs time to get used to you." Skye levered herself out of the low seat. "Anyway, don't worry about it. He doesn't influence my opinions."

Kent ushered her through the glass doors. "Yeah, but he does control a lot of what happens in Scumble River."

"I see." Skye wondered, not for the first time, if Kent was dating her because he liked her or because he wanted to get in good with Charlie. Their relationship had started out nicely. Kent was a great conversationalist. He could discuss literature and travel, and some of his quips about Scumble River citizens were hilarious. But lately Skye had begun to notice his flaws. He was too much like her ex-fiancé — shallow and snobbish. It was probably time to end it before they got in any deeper.

The restaurant owner showed them to a table. Mauve upholstery and walls intermixed with wooden tables and brass accents. Neither the decor nor the food had changed in the two years she'd been home. Skye didn't need to look at a menu to know what she wanted.

The waitress approached them. "What can I get you?"

"Is your fish fresh or frozen?" Kent asked, studying his menu.

Skye stiffened. They went through this

every time they ate here. She could recite the server's part from memory.

"Gee, let me check." The waitress hurried away.

"Why do you do that?" Skye asked.

"What?"

"You always ask stuff like that, and I've explained that you can't do that in Scumble River. Believe me, it's frozen. Nothing on the menu is fresh. Everything is frozen here."

A stubborn look settled on Kent's features. "I've spoken to the owner. He said he'd think about changing that."

"Never mind." Skye didn't want to argue about seafood. She knew she shouldn't have agreed to eat with him tonight. She had just about made up her mind to stop seeing Kent. The relationship wasn't working for either of them. Still, the realistic part of her had argued that she needed to talk to him about Mrs. VanHorn and about the rehearsal Lorelei was supposed to attend. It felt a little mean, but the practical part of her won out. "Did Priscilla VanHorn find you this afternoon?" she asked.

"No, why?"

"She wants Zoë to play Sleeping Beauty."

"Well, she was my second choice, but she makes a wonderful evil fairy." Kent stood up. "Where is that waitress?"

"Punishing you for asking a stupid question," Skye muttered under her breath. Aloud she said, "Speaking of Zoë, she said something that confused me."

Kent walked over to the kitchen and stuck his head through the opening. "We'd like to order now," he called.

Skye covered her face and considered bolting for the door. "Sit down," she hissed.

Kent came back to their table, followed by their waitress, who said, "Frozen."

He opened his mouth, but Skye kicked him before he could speak, and said, "We'll both have the steak sandwich, medium rare, and fries. Iced tea for me, red wine for him."

After the waitress left, Skye interrupted Kent again. "Did you have a rehearsal scheduled yesterday, during seventh and eighth periods?"

"Yes, for Sleeping Beauty and the Prince, but Chase didn't show up, so I told Lorelei she could go back to study hall."

"What did *you* do then?"

"Chief Boyd wanted to know that, too," Kent complained. "I went back to my classroom and graded some essays."

"Did Lorelei leave the gym while you were there?"

"No, she said she had a headache and didn't want to go back to a noisy study hall, so I said she could lie down for a bit." Kent looked guilty. "I know I'm not supposed to leave a student alone, but she said she'd only stay a little while."

"Was anyone else around when you left?"

"Not that I saw. I wasn't paying much attention. Why are you asking all these questions? Are you working for Wally?"

Skye laughed uncomfortably. "Nope, I'm just curious."

She changed the subject to the new rules on copy-machine use at the high school. They chatted about school issues until they finished their meal. To ease her conscience, Skye insisted on paying for her half of the check.

Once they were settled in the car and headed toward her cottage, Skye ventured one more inquiry. "Why did you need to get into the gym so badly yesterday afternoon, and why did you disappear when I went to get Wally?"

Kent reddened. "I wanted to get some personal items from backstage, but then I realized how silly I was being and left."

"What personal items?"

"That was the silly thing. Just some poetry I had been working on. I was afraid the police would make fun of it."

"Oh, did anyone say anything?"

"No, I doubt they even noticed."

"Wally's pretty good about keeping things confidential." Skye laughed. "Unless your poems were to Lorelei, he wouldn't mention them."

Kent's attention seemed focused on pulling the car into her driveway. "That's good to know." He walked her to her door and turned to go. "Well, good night."

"See you tomorrow." During all the time they'd been dating he'd never once indicated a desire to accompany her inside, which now that she thought about it was a little strange. Skye stared at his retreating back. There was something odd about Kent Walker, no doubt about it.

Chapter 7

Finger in Every Why

Two eyes glowed eerily in the dark foyer as Skye opened her front door. A small shriek escaped her as she fumbled for the light switch, hit it, and saw Bingo sitting on the top of the hall table.

She scooped up the cat, bringing him nose to nose with her. "Never do that again. If you give me a heart attack, you'll have to live with May, and you know how my mother feels about animals in the house."

Bingo yawned, revealing needle-sharp white teeth and a tongue like a pink emery board. He wiggled out of Skye's grasp and trotted into the kitchen.

She checked his bowls. Water and dry food were available, but Skye knew that the feline was waiting for the canned stuff he preferred. A few months ago, the vet had suggested giving Bingo only dry diet food. Bingo had refused to eat for a week and never lost an ounce. Skye eventually caved in and gave him what he wanted.

It occurred to her that perhaps Bingo's supposed weight problem was similar to her own. Maybe, like Skye, the cat had reached his set point, and the only way he would shed pounds would be to exist on so few calories that life wouldn't be worth living.

As she was dishing out the cat's dinner, Skye noticed the light on her answering machine blinking like a drunken firefly. How many calls were there?

Skye resisted the urge to play the messages immediately. She needed to get out of the clothes she had put on fifteen hours ago, and wash off whatever remained of her makeup.

After a quick shower, she slipped into her robe and poured a silken pearl of lotion into her palm, smoothing it over her face. It was such a luxury to be entirely comfortable. Now she was ready for round two of the day from hell.

Skye settled at the kitchen table with a glass of Caffeine-Free Diet Coke, a pad of paper, and a pen. She pressed the play button and listened to the first message.

"This is your mother." May didn't believe in answering machines and had only recently been persuaded to speak into them; she drew the line at leaving any actual information.

The next few missives were from parents who had somehow gotten Skye's unlisted number. Not a truly difficult feat in a small town, where everyone knew someone who knew the person you wanted to track down.

Skye decided to return their calls from school. They weren't emergencies, and if she started talking to parents from home, she'd end up working twenty-four seven.

The next three messages were from May again. On the last one she actually said something besides her name. "Skye, call me at the police station. I'm working three to eleven tonight."

Skye turned to the wall unit and dialed. Her mother hadn't sounded like herself on the tape. She hoped another relative wasn't under arrest, as had happened more than once before.

The phone didn't ring even once before it was answered. "Scumble River Police Department, May speaking."

"Hi, Mom. What's up?"

"Where have you been?"

"I was at school until after five, and then I grabbed a bite to eat with Kent."

"You're not really interested in that boy, are you?"

"Ma, he's nearly forty. I think he qualifies as a man." Skye wondered how they had gotten so far down this road when she didn't even remember making the turn.

"He acts about fifteen. You need to get back together with Simon." May paused. "Heck, now that Wally's divorce is almost final, I'd rather see you with him than Kent 'my shit doesn't stink' Walker."

"What in heaven's name did Kent say to you at Christmas to tick you off so badly?"

"I'm not saying. Just stop seeing him."

Skye considered telling her mother that she was about to quit dating the English teacher, but decided it was only fair to Kent to let him be the first to know. It was highly unusual for May to take such an intense dislike to an eligible bachelor. Ordinarily she was happy with any male Skye dated, as long as he was single and breathing. She just wanted to see her daughter married with children.

"Let's change the subject," Skye suggested. "Why were you trying to find me?"

"I figured you'd want to know the latest on the Ingels case."

"Why would I want to know that?" Skye hedged.

"Charlie told me he wants you to investigate, on behalf of the school. And since you've upset Wally and broken it off with Simon, I figured your list of informants is getting mighty short."

Her mom had a point. This time Wally would not sit down and tell her what was going on. And even when they were dating, Simon had never revealed much. May might be the only source she had left.

"You're right, Mom. As usual, I need your help." Skye reached down and scratched behind Bingo's ears as he twined around her ankles.

Skye could almost hear May purr over the phone as she said, "Did you know that Kent Walker was the last person to see her alive — if you believe his story? You see why I want you to dump him? He's probably the killer."

Skye took a sip of soda pop and considered how to answer that statement. Ignoring it was always a good option. "Interesting. Anything about cause of death? Time-wise there was a pretty small window of opportunity. Kent left her at the beginning of seventh period, and I found her about fifteen minutes before the end of eighth period. That leaves nearly an hour and fifteen minutes for whatever happened to take place."

"They found fragments of pills in the

bottom of a bottle that was near her body," May answered. "The pills and bottle have been sent to the lab for analysis. No clear fingerprints, except Lorelei's, and the label was peeled off."

"I saw that bottle. It looked sort of familiar — it had an unusual shape." The connection Skye was searching for wouldn't surface.

"Wally sent officers to check both grocery stores, the liquor store, and the gas stations. They didn't find anything like it."

"So, they're pretty sure it's murder?"

"Like you pointed out with your Aunt Minnie last year, how many people crush tablets and put them in a drink if they're going to commit suicide? I imagine the same is true for an accidental overdose, and Lorelei's father claimed she didn't have any trouble swallowing pills."

"Anything else?"

"Nope. Wally plans to talk to some more kids tomorrow and check out where everyone was during seventh and eighth periods."

"Are you working tomorrow?"

"No, not until Monday."

"I'll call this time Monday night, and you can update me."

"Oh, before I forget, I promised Gillian

you'd call her tonight, no matter how late I spoke to you."

"What does she want?" Since this was the cousin who had abducted Skye last summer, they weren't on casual chatting terms.

Skye could almost hear her mother's shrug. "She didn't say, just told me it was vital she talked to you. Maybe it's something about the Ingelses. They're in that beauty-pageant circuit together. Linette is in the eight-to-ten-year-old age range, same as Kristin and Ginger's daughter, Iris."

Ginger, Gillian's twin, had been in on the kidnapping scheme, too.

"Okay, let me hang up and call Gillian. Bye."

"Dad has to pick up a part tomorrow in Brooklyn, so if you can be ready by seven, he'll give you a ride to school."

"I'll be ready. Bye."

"Bye, honey."

Skye smiled. She could tell her mother was thrilled that they were on a "case" together. May hardly ever used endearments.

After listening to the rest of her messages, Skye punched in her cousin's number. It rang several times, and she was about to hang up when a little girl answered. "Hello. Who is this?"

"This is Skye. Can I talk to your mother?"

"She's in the bathroom."

"Oh. Could you tell her I — ?"

Before Skye could finish her sentence, she heard the phone thunk down and a high-pitched voice scream, "Mom, it's Aunt Skye."

The minutes ticked by, and Skye was considering hanging up when her cousin finally said, "Skye, glad you called. Ginger and I need a huge favor. Don't say no until you hear the whole deal."

"I'd be glad to help you if I can," Skye forced herself to respond. Her New Year's resolution was to be nicer to her aunts, uncles, and cousins.

"Here's the thing. Both Kristin and Iris are signed up for the Junior Miss Stanley County pageant this weekend. Ginger and I can take them Friday, but we need you for Saturday. We were supposed to be off work, but since the bank was turned over to its new owner last week, all vacation days have been canceled for the first month, and anyone who doesn't show up is fired."

"Didn't you know this was going to happen? The bank was bought out last year sometime."

"No, they didn't tell us slaves when the change was going to be made. Only the big shots knew."

"Oh." Skye thought fast. "How about their grandmas?"

"Mom's going back down to Carle Clinic to get her meds adjusted and you know our husbands' mothers don't live in town."

"I don't have a car and wouldn't have any idea what I was supposed to do at the pageant."

"You can drive our minivan. The thing is, the entry fee is nearly three hundred dollars, and we can't afford to just flush that down the toilet. Especially since the new owners at the bank cut everyone's salary last year."

"I see." Skye considered what May had told her earlier. "Is Linette Ingels in this pageant?"

"Yes, although she'll probably have to miss because of her sister. That's another reason I'd hate for Kristin and Iris to have to drop out. Without Linette, they both have a decent chance of winning, or at least finishing in the money."

"Sure, I'll take them." Skye doodled a tiara on her yellow legal pad. "Anything special I should know?"

"We'll drop the TransSport and the girls off at your place at seven on Saturday. You have to be at Laurel High School by eight, and ready to go on by nine. Kristin and Iris pretty much know what to do, but I'll jot down some instructions for you."

"Seven A.M.?" Skye squeaked. She was not a morning person.

"Sorry about that." Gillian didn't sound sorry. "Anyway, I've got to run. Thanks a million for helping out. Bye."

Friday morning Skye walked through the deserted high school. Although she had arrived nearly half an hour before anyone else was due, she wouldn't have time for a swim this morning. She headed directly to the guidance office and unlocked the door. Once inside she thumbed on the desk light, opened her appointment book, and put her purse into the right-hand drawer. Settling into the butt-softened leather chair, Skye reached for a pad of passes and started filling them out. She would give these to Opal, who would hand them out to the kids during homeroom.

The old wooden desk was big enough to spread out files and sort through forms. Skye had managed to keep her tiny office in the junior high, even though she was supposed to have had it for only one year. This year, the elementary school had given her a space to work, but she had to share it with the speech pathologist. The high school was the only holdout in providing her with a room, but she was still working on Homer.

Skye had just finished writing the passes when Charlie entered her office. "Wally's going to talk to the parents at three-thirty. He was busy this morning."

She noticed today that Charlie looked every one of his seventy-plus years. His normally fluffy white hair lay flat, and his usual vigorous gait was slow and plodding. She had to find the murderer before the stress killed her godfather.

"Should be okay if the parents were notified." Skye reached for her appointment book and made a note.

"The PTO phone tree got the message out."

Skye nodded. She knew that the PTO phone tree was a better communication device than anything in the Department of Defense. Once the president made the first call, it would take the end of the world to stop the rest of the ladies from calling their designated list of names, who would then call their lists, and so on, until every parent in Scumble River had received the message.

Charlie paused at the door. "I'll be back after school. Give me a jingle if you need me any sooner."

A few minutes later, at precisely seven-thirty-five, starting time for teachers, Coach poked his head into the guidance office and groaned. "You here again?"

"Yes. Do you need something?"

"My office back," he grumbled.

"Sorry. How about using your office in the gym?"

"Have to share it with the other PE teacher," he complained.

"I certainly know how hard it is to have to share space."

The barrel-shaped man backed out, muttering.

"Let's chat again," Skye trilled to the slammed door.

She hurriedly delivered the passes to the school secretary and grabbed a cup of coffee, sliding back behind her desk just as the first bell rang.

A few minutes later Elvira Doozier, her first appointment, erupted into the room. "Yeah, what do you want?"

The girl looked almost exactly as she had the day she ran into Skye's office and announced that Sleeping Beauty was dead. Same type of low-riding pants and belly shirt. Same pierced navel. And same long, straight, two-toned hair.

"Have a seat, Elvira. When you weren't at school yesterday, I was concerned that maybe finding Lorelei like you did might have upset you."

"Nope, just didn't want to talk to the cops." The teen glared at Skye. "I don't want to talk to anyone."

"I can understand that." Skye paused and changed her direction. "So, are you related to Earl and Junior Doozier?"

"Earl's my brother and Junior's my nephew. You know them from the time they pulled you from the river, right?"

"Right." Skye smiled. "Junior helped me out a couple of times."

"Yeah, by helping you out last year, he got my other brother, Hap, thrown in jail."

"Are you saying that was a bad thing?"

"Well, it kept him off of hitting on his boy," Elvira admitted. "Earl takes care of my nephew Cletus now."

"Sounds like maybe things turned out for the best." Skye leaned forward. "So, tell me about finding Lorelei."

"Like I told you that day, I cut class to sneak a smoke in the gym, saw her laying there, and grabbed you."

"How close did you get to Lorelei?" Skye was sure Elvira would have gone up for a close-up look.

"I never stepped much past the door."

"How could you tell she was dead?"

Elvira's smile was that of a very old woman. "I've seen dead people before. Dead people is easy to spot."

Skye didn't particularly want to know why the teen had such an intimate knowledge of corpses. "Did you see anyone in the hall when you were going in and out of the gym?"

"No one was around."

"You're sure?"

"Yeah. Just me and the dead cheerleader." Elvira fingered the ring in her navel.

"Why, out of all the adults, did you come get me?"

"Remembered seeing you here on my way to the gym." Elvira spoke to her lap. "And Junior thinks you're okay."

"Did you know any of Lorelei's friends?"

"No way, man." Elvira shook her head so hard that her long hair formed a cloak. "Those girls are brutal."

Frannie Ryan marched into the guidance

office and sat down facing Skye. "I didn't kill her."

Skye fought for a neutral expression. "Do you mean Lorelei?"

"How many dead bodies have you found around here?"

"Should we be looking for others?" The hair on the back of Skye's neck rose. She could feel this girl's anger from across her desk.

"None that I know of, but I wouldn't be unhappy to see a few more princesses added to the list." Frannie's long lashes veiled her expression.

"They've hurt you?" Skye had seen first-hand the devious, self-esteem-destroying tactics commonly used on some teenage girls by the more popular girls.

Frannie snorted. "Their brand of social fascism is so galactically brutal, you end up bleeding to death before you even feel the knife go in."

"Was Lorelei like that?" Skye asked. Talk about a motive for murder.

"She was more subtle. Most kids think she was so nice, but they didn't realize that anything her posse did, she approved beforehand." Frannie sat rigidly, waves of hostility pouring off of her.

"That sounds like a lot of power."

"Lorelei Ingels was the sun, and the student body of Scumble River High revolved around her."

"And she didn't like you?" Skye asked.

"In her world, I didn't even deserve that much respect. I've been taking dance since I was six, and I'm good. Despite my size, I'm also good at gymnastics. Obviously with these boobs, I'll never make the Olympic team, but I have talent. Mrs. Frayne noticed me at a dance recital, and asked me to try out for the cheerleading squad. I was so up."

"You thought this was your chance to fit in," Skye ventured.

Frannie nodded, color rising in her cheeks. "I've never seen my dad so proud of me. I practiced and practiced until I knew the routines cold. I was great at the tryout."

"What happened?" Skye was afraid she could guess the answer.

"The next day Mrs. Frayne took me aside and said she was sorry, I didn't make the squad." Frannie looked at Skye with tears shining in her eyes.

"That must have been painful."

"I couldn't figure what I had done wrong until the other cheerleaders surrounded me after school. Zoë was the one who talked, but they were all there. She said if I ever told anyone that they had even let me try out, she'd make my pathetic life even more miserable." Frannie bit back a sob.

Skye handed her a tissue. "What did you do?"

"I asked why." Frannie shot Skye a look. "Pretty stupid, huh?"

"It's hard to make good decisions when you're experiencing that kind of hurt."

"Zoë said it would be too humiliating for the school to have it known that a fat girl was even considered for cheerleader." Frannie sat back. "She said she didn't know what Mrs. Frayne was thinking when she asked me to try out. That it was a good thing all the cheerleaders got to vote, or Mrs. Frayne would load the squad with fat girls."

"How devastating."

"I'm just so tired of always being on the outside looking in," Frannie whispered. "Your destiny is determined by the color of your hair, the shape of your body, and the label on your clothes. Despite all the crap you endure, they always pick someone else."

There was little Skye could say to that, but she gave it a try. "I know this sounds bogus, but things usually get a lot better once you're out of high school. In college you have a much wider choice of friends and can find other kids who think like you do. A lot of times the princes and princesses of high school find the rest of life a lot different. For them the best time is their teenage years, but the rest of us are happier as adults."

The girl looked at her skeptically. "I sure hope you're right."

"Me too." After a moment, Skye gently asked, "Frannie, where were you seventh and eighth period Wednesday?"

The girl sat up. "Art and math, with about forty other kids. Hard to say if anyone would remember me or not."

"The bell is going to ring any second. If you ever want to talk again, just leave me a note, and we'll set something up."

Frannie got up from the chair and gathered her things. "They say you should never say anything about the dead unless it's good." She waited for Skye's nod. "Lorelei's dead. Good!"

Chapter 8

Sin and Bare It

Skye didn't have any time to recover from the session with Frannie before Troy Yates, Lorelei's boyfriend, arrived. The blond Adonis with a buzz haircut strode into the office as if he owned the place and was considering selling it.

He nodded at Skye and sat. "You wanted to see me, Ms. D.?"

"Yes, I wanted to check and see how you were today. Sometimes a loss doesn't hit a person right away." Skye noticed the boy sat perfectly straight in his chair.

"I can't believe she's gone."

"Had you been dating long?"

"We've gone steady since eighth grade." He dug his wallet out of his pocket. "These are pictures of us at every dance."

Skye shuffled through the small pile of photos. "They're wonderful." She handed them back to Troy. "Were you planning on attending the same college?"

A cloud crossed Troy's face. "I'm going

to Notre Dame on a football scholarship. Lorelei tried to get into their theater department, but she didn't make the cut."

"Did she have backup plans?"

He shrugged. "She didn't like to talk about it."

"No, I imagine that would be a difficult subject for someone who's used to winning."

Troy nodded and launched into a story about Lorelei and a game of Trivial Pursuit. Skye made encouraging sounds, and the teen reminisced for the rest of the period.

Skye noticed they were almost out of time, and said, "Troy, do you think you need to talk to someone a few more times about Lorelei's death?" During his talk about their past he'd seemed sad, but not devastated. Of course, with adolescents it wasn't always easy to tell how they really felt. They often put on a cool demeanor that covered up their real feelings, sometimes even from themselves.

"No, I think I'm okay."

"If you change your mind, leave a note for me with the secretary." Skye pointed toward the main office.

"Okay."

"Just a couple more things. Was Lorelei

in the habit of bringing bottled beverages from home?"

"No, we're not supposed to bring any drinks into school except milk."

"And she never tried to sneak something in?" Skye had always thought this was one of those stupid, unenforceable edicts that small schools seemed to love. She knew the truth behind this particular policy — Scumble River High got a kickback from the milk vendor.

"No, ma'am. Lorelei wasn't one to break the rules."

Skye hated being called "ma'am." It made her feel older than dirt and half as attractive. "Where were you Wednesday, during seventh and eighth period?"

"Study hall and baseball practice."

"Does Chase Wren play on your team?"

"Sure. We're in all the sports together."

"Was he there Wednesday?" Skye had a sudden inspiration to ask.

"No. And Coach was mad."

Mmm. Chase hadn't shown up for either of the activities he was scheduled for. Skye made a note to follow up on that.

As soon as Troy's session ended, Skye scooted out of her office to make sure things elsewhere were running smoothly. When she stuck her head around the corner of the band room, the co-op social worker gave her a thumbs-up.

In the library, Trixie was deep into a conversation with a student. Skye didn't want to interrupt, so she wasn't able to ask about the cheerleading meeting, as she had planned to.

Since she heard no sobbing or screaming in the building, she concluded the situation was under control and went back to her office.

Zoë strolled in nearly ten minutes after the bell rang. By rights she should have been issued a detention, but Skye was in an awkward position. Follow the school rules to the letter or establish rapport?

"I hope you're okay," Skye said, as Zoë took a seat. "I was worried when the bell rang and you weren't here."

"I had to fix my eyeliner. It had totally smudged."

"Were you upset about Lorelei?" Skye wondered if maybe the tough act was just a veneer, and Zoë really was grieving over the other girl's death.

The teen looked surprised. "No. We were cooking in Home Ec today, and that old-maid teacher made us chop onions rather than use the food processor. She has no concept that hers isn't the only class, that I have to look good for the rest of the day, too."

"Oh, your mom dropped by yesterday afternoon and said you were very upset."

"Yeah, well, things change." Zoë slouched in her seat.

"So, you don't need to talk about Lorelei's death?"

"I don't need a shrink, if that's what you mean." Zoë straightened. "Listen, between you and me, our mutual-admiration society was screeching to a halt."

"You and Lorelei were fighting?"

"No. Like they say in court, irreconcilable differences. She was starting to bring the group down. She bagged on a bunch of parties."

"Oh."

"We were going to different cheerleading camps this summer and different colleges in the fall. We were, like, drifting."

"One last question and I'll let you go." Skye studied the teen. "Did Lorelei bring any beverage in a bottle to school?"

"No. She was always trying to get rid of water weight, so she didn't drink much of anything."

"Okay. Well, if you change your mind about talking to someone, leave me a note."

Zoë paused at the door. "Can I be blunt with you?"

A voice inside her head was yelling no, but Skye's curiosity made her say, "Yes."

"FYI about your clothes. Whatever kind of look you were going for . . . you missed."

The door closed behind the teen. Skye gazed down at her navy pin-striped skirt and vest, and wondered where she had gone wrong.

After a delicious lunch of a peanut butter and jelly sandwich — she *really* had to go grocery shopping — Skye saw Farrah Miles and Caresse Wren, the other two cheerleaders.

It was hard to keep straight which was which. They both wore their cheerleading uniforms, had straight blond hair and blue eyes. They both had been in study hall Wednesday during seventh and eighth periods, and neither remembered Lorelei with a bottled drink in school. And they both managed to cry without ruining their elaborate eye makeup. Skye was impressed. At least they showed some emotions about their friend's death.

Skye's last appointment for the day was with Chase Wren. He sauntered into her office and ran his eyes up and down her body. She immediately hit the record button on the small tape player she kept in her top drawer. She usually used it so she wouldn't have to take notes, but in some cases it was good to have an exact record of what transpired.

Chase was cast from the same mold as Troy, but made of inferior materials. His hair wasn't quite as golden, his muscles were overdeveloped, and when he opened his mouth, it was obvious he had been shorted in the brains department, too.

"So, Chase, I just wanted to check and see how things were going with you today."

"Huh? Okay, I guess. Why?"

"Well, you were a friend of Lorelei's, and I wanted to see if you were upset by her death," Skye explained slowly, trying to use one-syllable words he could understand.

"Gee, that was real sad. But we got to go on. That's what Coach and Mr. Walker say."

"Speaking of Coach and Mr. Walker, on Wednesday you didn't show up for rehearsal or practice. Where were you?"

Chase screwed up his face. "Do I gotta tell you?"

"No, not if you'd rather not. I thought it might help to tell me first, so you have a little practice before Chief Boyd asks you."

The big teen was silent for a moment before saying, "Look, I ain't never said I was a genius. I know I'm no Delbert Feinstein, but I'm going to graduate this year, no matter how many semesters it takes."

"I see." Skye tried to follow the athlete's convoluted thinking.

"So, I'm not doing so good in math, so my teacher tutors me during seventh hour, and that day we ran over into eighth without noticing. But I don't want the other guys to know I need help."

"I'll make sure that doesn't get around," Skye vowed. "I have one more question. Have you ever noticed Lorelei with a bottle of water or juice or something at school?"

"Nah, that chick followed all the rules."

As the adolescent exited her office, Skye checked the time. An hour of school remained. Time to make the rounds again.

Everything seemed back to normal. The co-op social worker reported no concerns. Skye didn't see any parents in the halls, and the parking lot held the usual number of cars. Even Homer was back to his usual routine — she could hear a baseball game blaring from the radio behind his closed door. Now they just had to make it through the parent meeting.

There were two people she still wanted

to talk to. Kent had seventh and eighth period as plan times, so he was free. Her questions for Trixie about the cheerleader meeting would have to wait. Skye wanted to ask Kent about Lorelei's bottle before talking to Wally. She had forgotten to ask about it last night.

As she approached Kent's room, she heard voices and wondered if he was rehearsing. She knew the stage was still off-limits, but maybe he had decided to run lines with some of the students. He hated being interrupted or observed during rehearsals, so Skye hung back.

"Kenny, darlin', Lorna Ingels told me about you two. No need tryin' to pretend with little old me." Skye recognized Mrs. VanHorn's distinctive drawl.

"Priscilla, you know that isn't true." Kent's voice was pitched low and persuasive.

"Well, if my Zoë were to play the lead in *Sleeping Beauty*, I just might believe you."

"Of course, Zoë shall have the lead. She deserves it. It was a tight contest between her and Lorelei." Kent's tone was soothing.

"It was the hair, wasn't it?" Mrs. VanHorn demanded. "I told Zoë it was a mistake to cut her hair."

"It makes no difference now. I shall begin working with Zoë this very afternoon."

Kent and Lorna Ingels! A couple? Stunned, Skye leaned against the wall for support.

If it was true, Mrs. VanHorn's accusations filled in pieces that Skye had only suspected. She had wondered why Kent had continued to ask her out long after it was obvious there was no chemistry between them. She'd thought his reasons were the same as hers — no one else halfway interesting around — but maybe she'd been wrong.

As Skye hurried back to the guidance office, part of her felt shocked and betrayed, but her cooler, more rational side was asking if she really was all that surprised.

If he'd been having an affair with Lorna, Kent had been using Skye as a front — someone appropriate to date so no one would suspect he was sleeping with a married woman. That might explain why Skye had never heard any rumors about him. Either he had covered his tracks well, or she had never cared enough about him to notice.

The dismissal bell had sounded ten minutes ago. Normally the halls would have begun to quiet, but today Skye watched as parents drifted in, mostly in pairs, some in sizable groups. Voices were subdued, but there was a steady drone. They beelined to the cafeteria and carefully felt their way onto the picnic-style tables with the attached benches. Many a panty hose would be ruined before this meeting ended.

Little changed at Scumble River High. The pea-green cinder-block walls and matching linoleum were the same as when Skye had attended high school. Even the smell was what she remembered — pine cleaner mixed with overcooked mystery meat.

Chief Boyd entered exactly on time, and the already-quiet murmur faded completely. He was dressed in uniform, and his gold shield glinted in the drab room. A small podium had been set up in the front, near the serving windows.

Charlie emerged from the kitchen area and grabbed the mike. "I'd like to thank Chief Boyd for taking the time to speak to us. He's going to give us a brief summary of what the police know and will answer a few questions. After he leaves, we'll answer any school-related questions you have."

Wally took the mike from Charlie and said, "Wednesday afternoon, Lorelei Ingels was found dead on the gym stage here at Scumble River High. Certain pieces of evidence led us to believe this was not a death by natural causes. The coroner ordered an autopsy. Our preliminary finding is that she was poisoned. A toxicology screen takes some time, so we do not know the nature of the poison. We are acting as if this is a homicide.

"Because of the suspicious manner of death, we have had to interview many students and staff. I understand that some of you are upset because we've spoken to your child without your presence. Legally a parent doesn't have to be in attendance unless we press charges."

Wally waited a few minutes for the buzz to quiet down, then asked, "Any questions?"

"Do you got a suspect yet?" asked an old man in the back.

"There are several people we are considering."

"Any motive?"

"Several possible motives have come to our attention."

An emaciated woman waved her arm frantically.

"Yes?"

"I heard this was part of a satanic cult

ritual. That her blood had been drained, and she was holding an upside-down cross."

The audience gasped, and an immediate roar of voices was heard.

"That is absolutely not true," Wally shouted above the noise.

"I heard it was part of a serial killing," said a man in front, shooting to his feet. "They say there's already been three others, but the police are covering it up."

"Again, there is not a shred of truth in that rumor." Wally wearily ran his fingers through his crisp hair. "Sorry to cut things short, but I have another appointment. Be assured, the Scumble River Police Department is on top of the investigation. There is no need to worry about the safety of your children."

Skye wondered if he really believed that. She caught the chief's arm as he passed her, and whispered, "Do you have a second? There's something I want to share with you."

He scowled, but nodded, and they walked into an empty classroom.

"I'm pretty sure Lorelei did not bring the bottle with her from home."

"Oh, and how did you come to that conclusion?" His voice was deceptively gentle.

"I asked her friends if they had ever seen her bring something like that to school. Since it's against the rules to bring beverages other than milk into the building, I was sure they would notice."

"I see, so you've been tampering with suspects?"

"No, I was trying to help you." Skye frowned. Had she done something wrong?

"Keep out of this, Skye. Since you can't be trusted to work as a team player, just stay the heck out of it." Wally turned on his heel and marched out the door, his back rigid.

She felt her throat clench. It was so painful to see Wally act like that, and know it was at least partly her fault. He was normally such a sweet guy.

"Skye, Skye, are you okay?"

Skye opened her eyes and raised her head. After Wally left, she had slipped into a desk. A wave of hopelessness had washed over her, and she had put her head down for a second. Now she was staring up at Trixie. "What time is it?"

"Four-thirty. What are you doing sleeping in a classroom?" Trixie shook her head. "Why don't you go home if you're tired?"

"Because there's something I want to do first." Skye shoved the hair from her eyes. "Are you busy?"

"Not right now," Trixie said.

"Let's go visit the Ingelses."

"No."

"Why?"

"Because it will be awkward, and I don't want to. Why do you need to go?"

"I need to get a better impression of them and get a look around their house." Skye frowned. "I understand the police are still unable to get a search warrant, but a condolence call is altogether different."

"That seems pretty cold."

Skye sighed. "You're right, and I do feel bad, but why wouldn't parents want to do everything in their power to help find their daughter's killer?"

"It does make you wonder, doesn't it? But why do I have to come?"

"You're my best friend, and I have no car."

"You need to get a car," Trixie said flatly. "How have you been getting around the last eight months or so?"

"I used my cousin's scooter until the weather turned bad in November. Then my Grandma Denison let me use her car

151

until March — she spent the winter down in Florida with her sister. So really I've only been without transportation for a few weeks."

"Don't you think it's time to bite the bullet and buy a car?"

"I was going to tomorrow, but I got roped into helping the twins. Maybe I should just take whatever monstrosity my father has dug up. At least I know it'll run."

Trixie shuddered. "Don't do anything hasty. Your last car looked like it had finished last in a demolition derby."

"Well, then I really need a friend who doesn't mind driving me for a few more days." Skye stood and put her arm around Trixie's shoulders. "Please?"

"Okay, but if we're going to make a condolence call, shouldn't we bring a dish?"

"You're right. What can we bring?" Skye bit her lip. "I know. Mom left a chicken-and-rice casserole in my freezer last weekend. We can grab that."

"Do you know where the Ingelses live?"

"Oh, yes. I was out there Wednesday with Wally and Homer. It's on South Basin, past McDonald's, past that little subdivision, and backs up to the cemetery. It's all by itself on ten acres. Every time I drive past, I expect to see a moat. Wait till you get a load of this place."

Trixie wheeled her Mustang through the wrought-iron gates and onto the concrete driveway that curved in front of the Ingelses' redbrick manor-style home. She parked the car on a paved apron that already held a red BMW.

As she got out of the Ford, Skye noted the huge trees and perfectly trimmed bushes. The house was less than five years old, and mature landscaping like that did not come cheap. How much did a bank president make?

The women approached the double front doors. Trixie glanced uneasily at Skye before pushing the bell.

A long minute passed before the door was swung open by a middle-aged woman in an apron who spoke with a Polish accent. "Yes? May I help you?"

"Hi, I'm Ms. Denison, we met a couple of days ago, and this is Mrs. Frayne. We're from the school. We brought this for the family." She handed the casserole over. "Are the Ingelses receiving visitors?" Her time in New Orleans society was finally paying off. She knew the right words to use when calling on the rich and snobbish.

The woman ushered them into a soaring two-story foyer with a curved staircase. She indicated that they wait, and then disappeared down the hall toward the kitchen. A few minutes later she returned, minus the casserole dish, opened a pocket door to the right, and led them into the library.

Mr. and Mrs. Ingels sat in matching wing chairs flanking a massive stone fireplace. Mrs. VanHorn was perched on a sofa situated between the two chairs.

The housekeeper withdrew silently, leaving Trixie and Skye to introduce themselves. Skye observed Trixie's frozen expression and took over. "Mr. and Mrs. Ingels, Mrs. VanHorn, I'm not sure if you remember me. I'm Skye Denison, school psychologist at the high school, and this is Trixie Frayne, the librarian. We stopped by to offer our condolences, and see if there is anything we can do for you."

Allen Ingels rose from his chair, his face expressionless. "Yes, I do remember you."

Skye braced for another attack about why she hadn't saved his daughter, but the man continued. "I wanted to apologize for my rudeness the other day. We realize now there was nothing you could have done to prevent Lorelei's death."

"Thank you." Skye's heart returned to its normal beat. "We all say things we don't mean in the heat of the moment."

Mrs. Ingels spoke from her chair. "Won't you have a seat? Anna is getting coffee."

Skye and Trixie squeezed in beside Priscilla VanHorn. Today Mrs. VanHorn wore a tight black suit with crochet cutouts circling the sleeves and the hem of the short skirt. Her red hair was arranged in an array of curls that flowed past her shoulders.

Trixie was still silent, so Skye said, "Nice to see you again, Mrs. VanHorn." Even after a couple of years in the school system, it still seemed awkward to Skye to use Mr. and Mrs. instead of first names. It was one of the quaint customs that those in education seemed to cling to. Probably so the kids wouldn't take to calling their teachers Debbie and Robin.

Skye turned to Lorna Ingels. "Is there anything I can help you with in regard to school-related matters?"

Before she could answer, Allen spoke. "Right now we can't do anything. The police have managed to tie our hands at every turn. We can't clean out her locker, we can't collect her belongings, we can't even plan the services, because they won't tell us when they're releasing the body. For all we know, they're cutting open our beautiful daughter as we speak."

At his last sentence, Lorna gasped, then crumpled in a sobbing heap. Everyone froze and stared at the distraught woman. Finally, Mr. Ingels leaned over and patted his wife's hand. This seemed to release the rest of the group from their paralysis, and Skye and Priscilla leaped to their feet. Priscilla reached Mrs. Ingels first and guided her out of the room.

Trixie rose from the couch and uttered her first words since their arrival. "We'll leave you now. We're sorry for your loss."

Skye plastered a look of embarrassment on her face, which wasn't far from how she really felt, and said, "I'm sorry to be a bother, but could I use your powder room before we go?" She had come here to see Lorelei's room, and she would fulfill her mission, come hell or high water, as her grandmother used to say. She'd show Wally what she could accomplish without him.

Allen Ingels's expression grew colder, but he nodded. "The guest bath down here is being remodeled. You'll have to use the one at the top of the stairs. It's to your right."

Skye quickly backed out of the library

and ran up the steps. How could she tell which bedroom was Lorelei's? The house was so huge. Plus, she had to worry about where the two women and the housekeeper had gone.

Since Mr. Ingels had just told her the bathroom was to the right, she went left — if confronted, she would act confused. The first door she tried, she struck gold. It had to be Lorelei's room. It was full of pageant trophies, crowns, and pom-poms. Done in ice blue and silver, it was a stunning setting for Lorelei's blond, snow-princess looks.

Skye didn't dare go in, but she tried to get a sense of the teenager from the posters and memorabilia. When she eased open the next door, she caught her breath. It was a huge dance studio, complete with barre and mirrors. These people didn't kid around with their daughters' futures.

She checked her watch. She had been gone only a couple of minutes. She'd check out one more room, then flush the toilet. Skye turned and found herself facing a miniature version of Lorelei. If possible, this rendition was even more beautiful. She wore an ice-blue leotard and silver tights. Skye wondered briefly if those were the family colors.

Skye gathered her wits and said, "Hi, you must be Linette. I'm Ms. Denison. Could you show me where your bathroom is?"

The ten-year-old was silent. Her perfect face remained expressionless. She turned and walked down the hall a few feet, stopping in front of a closed door. "Here it is."

Skye wondered what was going on behind the child's exquisite exterior.

Chapter 9

It's the Shame of the Game

"Tell me again why I'm here," Trixie demanded into her coffee cup. The oversize red velour seat of Gillian's TransSport swallowed Trixie's tiny figure, and she looked like a cameo nestled in a jewelry box. A cranky cameo.

Skye, Trixie, and the twins' daughters, Iris and Kristin, were on their way to the Junior Miss Stanley County pageant in Laurel. For fourteen of the fifteen minutes they had been on the road, at least one of Skye's passengers had been complaining, yelling, or crying. She was ready to turn the minivan around and head back to Scumble River. Only the fear of her cousins' wrath kept her going in the opposite direction.

Skye glanced at the rearview mirror. The girls had finally settled down and were busy talking, not paying attention to the adults in the front seat. Still, she lowered her voice. "I told you last night, this is the

159

perfect way to find out the real scoop on the Ingelses."

"I understand that," Trixie retorted, "but why am I here?"

"Because I can't go off and leave the girls alone. One of us needs to stay with them while the other investigates."

"Great." Trixie took a big gulp of her coffee. "This is going to be like yesterday when you left me with Allen Ingels, isn't it? The man kept looking at his watch. I finally had to tell him you had irritable bowel syndrome."

"Gee, thanks." Skye grimaced, imagining that rumor flying through town. That would certainly attract eligible bachelors to her door. "Is that the high school over there on the left?"

Trixie squinted. "Yes. The sign says, 'Contestants please park by the south entrance.'"

"Which way is south?" Skye had no sense of direction.

"Around back, Aunt Skye," Iris instructed.

Skye cringed. Since her stint as a lifeguard last summer, her cousins' kids had started calling her "aunt." Even though it was kind of sweet, it made her feel old. But it would be too Grinch-like to tell them to stop. She was stuck with the title.

Skye eased the minivan into a pull-through spot. The long pointy nose on the vehicle made it difficult to park in a regular slot. The girls tumbled out, and the two women followed at a slower pace. Skye opened the back hatch and started handing out boxes, suitcases, and garment bags.

The four staggered toward the entrance, balancing enough luggage for a world cruise. Once inside, the girls led the way to the registration desk.

Skye let her burdens fall to the floor and said, "Hi, I've got Iris Allen and Kristin Tubb checking in."

The woman behind the table had big hair, big breasts, and a short, sequined gown. She looked over her rhinestone-edged glasses and frowned. "And you are?"

"My name is Skye Denison. I'm their guardian for today." Skye leaned closer to peer at the woman's name tag, half-hidden by the marabou feathers that trimmed her neckline. "Ms. Reiter."

"I'm afraid that's a problem. A parent must be present."

"Really?" Skye held on to her temper as the girls started to cry. She picked up a blank entry form and turned to the rules. She read them twice and turned back to

Ms. Reiter. "I can't seem to find that rule. Could you point it out to me?"

Ms. Reiter snatched the papers from Skye's hand, and flipped through them furiously. "It's not here. It's just understood."

"Oh, I don't think so." Skye started to pick up her things. "Which room do we report to?"

"I can't let the girls compete. It wouldn't be fair." Ms. Reiter's bosom puffed out like dough rising.

"If I put these things down again, somewhere other than our dressing room, it will be to make two phone calls." Skye paused to make sure she had the woman's attention. "The first will be to our attorney, and the second to the *Chicago Tribune*. You know how popular these kiddy pageants are ever since the JonBenet murder. I'm willing to bet the *Trib* would love to do an article on how unwholesome this contest is."

Ms. Reiter's mouth formed an outraged O.

"Where did you say our dressing room was?"

"Room 102."

"Great. You have a real nice day now." Skye led her little band away.

Trixie didn't bother to lower her voice. "Not one of the sharper crayons in the box, is she?"

From the constant chatter Kristin and Iris engaged in, Skye learned that Friday had been the Talent portion of the pageant. Kristin had performed a gymnastic routine, and Iris had demonstrated fly-fishing. This morning would be Modeling and Interview. In the afternoon there was Beauty and Crowning.

Skye's gaze swept Room 102. Monday through Friday it held Laurel High's Home Ec class. Cubicles had been made by rolling in portable blackboards. Since their group had two contestants, they had been assigned adjoining spots. Skye quickly pushed the center divider against the wall to give them more space.

Even though she knew that the pageant was being held in a high school, Skye was disappointed to see how drab everything was. If these girls were going to exhibit themselves, shouldn't there be some glamour involved? This setup reminded her more of her Scholastic Bowl team than a beauty pageant. Not that she approved of these contests.

While Skye was brooding, the girls

changed into their costumes for Modeling. They led Skye and Trixie to the backstage area, where they were supposed to wait for their cue. A dozen eight-, nine-, and ten-year-olds milled around in a space not much bigger than a spare bedroom. Each of the girls was fussed over by one or two adults. The whole scene reminded Skye of an anthill.

Skye watched as a tiny, raven-haired beauty dressed in a red-and-white-striped halter top jumpsuit, red bolero jacket with ruffles at the wrist, and white hat, stood as her mother made last-minute adjustments.

The girl finally shook her mother away, protesting, "Get off me. You're always hanging on me."

The mother took the girl by the upper arms and shook her. "This is for you, it's not for me. We went to McDonald's. I got you the whole Pretty Kitty kit. We stopped and bought you the little box with the key. So now all you got to do is walk through this itty-bitty dance."

The girl stuck out her lip and started to cry.

Skye turned to Kristin, who had been watching the same scene. "Do you feel that way?"

"No, me and Iris like to dress up and go

164

to the pageants, but lots of kids don't really want to." Kristin put her hand in Skye's. "Lots of moms are real mean if their kids don't win. But Mom and Aunt Ginger are okay. They swear a little sometimes at the judges, but they don't yell or get drunk."

"I'm glad to hear that." Skye squatted to Kristin's level. "If you ever want to quit doing this and your mom won't let you, tell me. Okay?"

"Sure." Kristin swung their joined hands. "We better get in line now. It's about to start, and I'm number two."

Skye checked that Trixie had Iris, who was number eleven, and they moved into position. Each girl had three minutes to strut her stuff in front of the judges. The music started, and the first contestant moved on stage.

This girl wore a silver leotard with a cape that had the U.S. flag done in sequins across the back, a Statue of Liberty crown, and silver shoes.

Skye watched in fascination as the ten-year-old pranced gracefully around the stage on three-inch heels. She herself could hardly wear two-inch pumps without falling on her face.

Kristin was next, dressed in a sleeveless

hot pink dress, matching hat, and muff. The outfit had marabou trim around the neckline, hem, and accessories. Kirstin moved across the stage in rhythm to the music, twirled in front of the judges, and winked.

Skye let her mind wander as the other girls performed. She was startled out of her reverie by Trixie tapping her on the shoulder. "A woman wants to know if Iris will trade numbers and go on next. One of the contestants just got here, and she needs to have the last spot so she has time to change. Is that okay?"

"If Iris is ready, go on and trade. It's no big deal."

"She's all set."

A few moments later Skye watched as Iris danced onto the stage. She swirled her blue jacket like a cape and popped her sunglasses on top of her head without missing a beat. Skye was sure Iris would win this portion of the competition.

The girls wanted to change clothes, but Skye wanted to see the rest of Modeling, so Trixie volunteered to take them back to the dressing room.

Skye found a seat in the rear of the auditorium just as a buzz spread through the audience. She craned her neck to see what was happening. The curtain parted, and Linette Ingels strutted out. The little blonde was dressed in silver Spandex tights with a white fur jacket and a white-and-silver circlet holding back her hair.

The audience gasped as she started her act. The sinuous movements reminded Skye of a striptease, and when the little girl peeled off her jacket to reveal a plunging neckline and backless top, Skye heard herself exhale.

The lady sitting next to her poked her in the ribs with an elbow. "Can you believe Lorna Ingels's gall, having one sister perform when the other's barely cold?"

"It sure is a surprise," Skye agreed. "Is that a typical costume for Linette?"

"No, in fact, that looks a little like one Lorelei wore in the last pageant — just made smaller."

It was only ten-thirty, the girls had finished with their interviews, and Beauty didn't begin until after lunch. Skye checked the dressing room and found Iris and Kristin playing Hungry, Hungry Hippo, and Trixie reading the latest Charlaine Harris mystery.

"Are you guys okay?"

167

They all murmured yes without looking up.

"I'm going to poke around. I'll be back at noon, and we can eat lunch. Okay?"

As Skye left the dressing area, she heard laughter and animated voices to her right. A couple doors down, a classroom was crowded with women and girls. Up front, a man with his back to the room was working on the hair of a nine-year-old girl.

Skye wiggled her way through the crowd. "Vince, what the heck are you doing here?"

He whirled around. "Skye, what the heck are you doing here?"

Her brother, Vince, was one of the handsomest men Skye had ever met. He was also charming and a talented hairstylist. Why he remained in Scumble River was a mystery to Skye, who had escaped for several years before being forced to come crawling back.

"I'm chaperoning the twins' daughters," she said.

"I'm doing hair. The contest organizers pay me to be available, and the moms pay for the appointment." He twirled the little girl in the barber chair. "What do you think?"

Skye bit her tongue. The only substitute

for good manners was fast reflexes. "She certainly looks . . . perfect." Skye thought that the little girl looked like a Barbie clone, only less animated. "How do you get her hair that big?"

Vince smiled thinly, obviously not fooled by Skye's words. "That's called the 'pageant pouf.' To get that effect you need extensions."

The little girl jumped off the chair, and another one took her place. At six-foot-two, Vince towered over his tiny customer. He tightened his ponytail and narrowed his green eyes. Muscles bulged as he flexed his shoulders.

Skye knew he was about to go into a creative trance. "If you get a lunch break, come eat with us. We're in Room 102."

He nodded distractedly, and Skye moved away.

As she walked the hallways, she saw several familiar faces. From what she overheard, the whole pageant was buzzing with talk of Linette Ingels's performance so soon after her sister's death.

"Skye!"

That sounded like Charlie's voice. Was everyone she knew here? Skye turned back to the door she had just passed. Sitting in what was normally the teachers' lounge were a group of men and women eating boxed lunches. Charlie held center court.

He motioned her to a chair at his side. "What are you doing here? You usually preach against exploiting little girls."

When her cousins had asked her to take their daughters to this contest, Skye had felt a momentary tug of conscience. She had been talking against the whole pageant idea for many years, but the lure of investigation had been too great, and she had stomped down that little voice.

"Well, the twins were in a bind," she told Charlie. "They had already paid the fee, but it turned out both Gillian and Ginger had to work. So I said I'd take Iris and Kristin so the girls wouldn't be disappointed."

Charlie raised an eyebrow, but didn't pursue the matter.

"What are you doing here, Uncle Charlie?"

"I'm a judge. They always ask me, the mayor, and the newspaper editor." Charlie motioned with his thumb.

Skye lowered her voice. "Who are the women?"

Charlie's voice boomed. "This here is Miss Stanley County 1978, and that lady in the corner is Miss Central Illinois 1960."

170

Skye nodded to the former beauty queens. "Come out in the hall a minute," she whispered to her godfather. "I need to ask you something in private."

Charlie lumbered to his feet, grumbling.

"Did you know that Linette Ingels competed today?" she asked.

"I heard." Charlie shrugged. "I'm not surprised. The Ingelses seem to think that because they got money and power, they don't have to play by the rules."

"What do you mean?"

"Let's just say no one in town will play poker or buy a used car from Al, and the missus isn't welcome at any bridge game."

"So how does he stay bank president?"

"That's a good question. One I'm going to find the answer to." Charlie turned and walked back into the lounge before she could ask anything more.

Skye stood stunned at what Charlie had said. Was he really implying that Allen Ingels was a crook? What did Charlie know that he wasn't telling her?

"Skye Denison!"

Who was it now? Skye looked up in time to see Abby Fleming, the school nurse, sweeping down on her. Abby was Vince's ex-girlfriend, and although the breakup had not been pleasant, she and Skye had stayed on good terms.

"Abby," Skye greeted her. "Before you ask, I've got Gillian and Ginger's girls entered, that's why I'm here."

"Me too." Abby smiled. "I've got my niece, I mean. Her mother's not interested, but since I used to do the pageant circuit, I take her."

Skye was surprised to hear Abby had been in beauty contests. Abby was a stunning woman — tall, thin, with white-blond hair and aquamarine eyes — but she was more striking than pretty and didn't seem the type the judges usually chose.

"Hey, you want to get a pop and meet some of the other pageant moms?" Abby asked.

Skye checked her watch. It was eleven-forty-five, and she had time before she had to get back to Trixie and her charges. "Okay."

Abby led Skye through the maze of corridors and into the cafeteria. After they each purchased a can of soda, Abby approached a table occupied by several women. "Hi. This is a friend of mine from work, Skye Denison. It's her first contest. Mind if we join you?"

A brunette in red leggings and an oversize T-shirt spoke for her friends. "Pull up a piece of bench. Did you see Linette Ingels's performance?"

Skye couldn't believe her luck. That was exactly the subject she wanted to discuss. She kept her mouth shut and listened, wishing she could take notes.

"No, but I certainly heard about it," Abby said.

One of the other moms chimed in, "I'm not surprised. My daughter competes in the same age range as Lorelei, and that mother would do anything to make her other daughter win."

The brunette tsked. "That's for sure. My daughter used to compete with that crowd, and Lorna Ingels deliberately stepped on the hem of her formal and ripped it, right before she was supposed to go onstage."

"Lorna Ingels is famous for that type of thing," an older woman added. "She grabbed my granddaughter and gave her a big old hug just as she walked on stage. I didn't notice until it was too late that she had smeared bright red lipstick down my grandbaby's sleeve. And it wasn't no accident. The lipstick Lorna was wearing was pink."

"I'm surprised Linette was never kicked out of the pageant," Skye said.

"Lorna's sneaky. It's hard to prove that

she deliberately sabotages the others," Abby explained.

"We almost caught her in the act last year," chirped a birdlike woman at the end of the table. "Someone stole my daughter's makeup case. Lorelei's space was right next to ours. We all went to the stage for Talent, and when we came back, the case was missing. Lorna had been the last one out of the room, and she refused to let us search her things."

Skye couldn't contain herself. "So, what happened?"

"The contest coordinator was going to throw her out, but she came up with an alibi. Priscilla VanHorn came forward and said Lorna had been with her the whole time the girls were onstage, and they had walked to and from the dressing room together."

"That's odd," Abby said. "Wouldn't Priscilla have been thrilled to eliminate Lorelei from competing against Zoë?"

The other women murmured their agreement.

Skye asked, "Did they ever find out who stole the makeup?"

"We figured it out later," the brunette said. "Maybe Lorna was with Priscilla, but Linette was in and out of that dressing room, and no one thought of checking on her."

"I was under the impression Linette wasn't too fond of her sister," Skye said, confused. "I'm surprised she'd steal for her."

The bird woman piped up, "This wasn't for Lorelei. This was against my family. My youngest daughter competes against Linette, and she had won the last contest they were in together."

"Boy, this is more cutthroat than graduate school," Skye commented.

"There's more at stake," Abby said.

"What? I understand that it's a rush to compete, and winning is really ego-building, but the level of intensity I've seen here today seems way more than what I would expect. What's the deal?"

Abby lowered her voice and leaned closer to Skye. "Money."

"Money? You mean there's big money up for grabs?"

"Yes. Not so much at these little contests, but as you go up the line we're talking cars, trips, clothes, scholarships, and thousands of dollars in cash." Abby paused to take a breath. "And that's not all. There's also a lot of money spent. You've got to have pictures, a professional coach, costumes, makeup, and hairstylists. Add to that the travel expenses and the fee to enter the contests. Then figure that many of these people enter a contest nearly every week. You can easily spend twenty thousand a year." Abby shook her head. "I know of women who have taken a second mortgage on their houses, or work another job, just to pay for these pageants."

"Makes you think, doesn't it?" Skye added money to her list of motives for Lorelei's killer. "I've heard a lot about Lorna Ingels, but no one says much about Lorelei. Any idea why?"

"Not really, but if you want to know about Lorelei, you should come to next week's contest, Miss Central Illinois. It's for the older girls, over seventeen. If Lorelei had won that one, she'd be a sure bet for Miss Illinois, which is a step away from the big one. I'm one of the judges." Abby's eyes gleamed.

"Was Lorelei a contender for Miss Central Illinois?"

"From what I've seen of the circuit, it was between Lorelei, Zoë, and another girl." Abby shrugged her tanned shoulders. "Of course, there's always a chance a wild card will show up."

"A wild card?"

"Some girl from east of nowhere who has never done a pageant but is such a natural she takes the prize," Abby explained.

"All this work and money, and someone can come out of left field and take it away." Skye glanced at the clock. "Hey, I've got to go get lunch ready for the girls. See you later."

The remainder of the pageant went without incident. Kristin won the Talent section, but Linette took Modeling, Interview, and Beauty. No one was surprised to see her win the crown.

When Linette's name was called, Skye studied her expression. After puzzling for some time, Skye could best describe it as a look of entitlement. It seemed that Linette never had any doubt that she'd win.

Chapter 10

Cut to the Chick

"The Mass is ended. Go in peace," Father Burns intoned. The congregation responded, "Thanks be to God," as they gathered their belongings and started to edge out of the pews.

Skye smoothed down her new blue linen dress. She had bought the dress to wear for Easter, but couldn't resist this warm, bright Sunday. Looking around, she noted that a lot of people had had the same idea. Most of the women were dressed in spring pastels.

A snippet of conversation about the Ingelses, coming from somewhere in front of her, snared Skye's attention. As she merged into the exiting crowd, straining to hear more, the heel of her sandal caught on the edge of the carpet running the length of the aisle. She tripped, falling into the person behind her. Warm, masculine hands gripped her arms and steadied her.

Blushing, she turned to thank her rescuer. Goldenhazel eyes gazed into hers. Simon Reid smiled at her.

Instead of releasing her, he said, "Well, I wasn't expecting to hold an angel in my arms today, even though it is Sunday, and I am at church."

Skye's blush intensified. What did he mean by that? He had broken up with her. Was he trying to make up? Did she want him to? She had to admit it felt good to be held by him again. "Sorry, new shoes."

He looked her over seductively, ending at the offending footwear. The thin blue straps emphasized her high arches and nicely shaped ankles. "Very pretty."

She wasn't sure if he meant the shoes or her. Feelings that she had suppressed for the last nine months were fighting their way to the surface, and she forced herself to move out of his arms. "Thanks. I got them at Spiegel." *What a dumb thing to say.* She mentally hit her forehead with her hand. *Like Simon cares where I buy my shoes.*

As they reached the double glass doors, Father Burns stopped them. "Skye, Simon, just the people I've been wanting to talk to. Do you have a few minutes?"

The priest had saved Skye's life last summer. Anything the man wanted, she was willing to try and do. "Certainly, Father."

Simon nodded, and Father Burns said, "Good, good. Why don't you wait for me next door?"

The housekeeper greeted them at the door to the rectory, guided them to the priest's office, and offered them seats.

Once the woman left, Skye finally broke the silence. "So, how have you been?"

"Fine. And you?"

"Okay." She tried to think of something else to say. "Play any bridge lately?"

"No, I haven't found another partner. You?"

Her heart lurched at his words. They'd had a great bridge partnership — among other things. "No. If it weren't for my little computerized handheld game, I'd forget how to play."

"I bought one of those too — Nintendo for adults. Did you get yours at K's Merchandise in Kankakee?"

"Probably. My parents got it for me for Christmas, and they shop there."

"Mine has a cord to connect to another unit. Does yours?"

"Yes. Maybe we could try it out sometime," Skye blurted out before she realized what she was saying.

Simon started to nod, then seemed to catch himself. A veil dropped over his features. After a long silence he remarked, "So, I hear you talked to Xavier's daughter."

"Who?" Skye was still going over her incredibly stupid gaffe and hadn't followed what he meant.

"Frannie Ryan is the daughter of my assistant, Xavier Ryan. Frannie comes to talk to me when she needs a shoulder to cry on. Her mom's dead, and since I haven't had a mother since I was fourteen, we have a common bond. Xavier isn't always the easiest person to confide in. Frannie liked talking to you."

"I didn't get the connection. Ryan's a fairly common last name." Skye remembered the teen's hatred of Lorelei and her clique. "Was she upset by Lorelei's death?"

"No. I'd say more half-afraid, half-thrilled. She doesn't want you to think she killed Lorelei, because you're so cool, but she was really psyched to finally tell someone how she was treated by that group of girls."

"She's welcome to talk to me anytime, about those feelings or anything else, although she will need to have her dad sign a consent slip," Skye explained. "Unless it's an emergency."

"She'll never ask her father." Simon

shrugged. "It's really too bad. He'd do anything for her, but somehow he and Frannie just butt heads when they try to communicate."

"Speaking of Lorelei, when will you have the results of the autopsy and tox screen?" As soon as the words left her mouth Skye experienced an "oh no, second" — that minuscule fraction of time in which she realized she had just blown the tiny chance she had to make up with Simon. Now he would never believe she was being nice to him for any reason except to gather information about Lorelei's murder. *Damn.* Why had he brought up the subject?

Skye was saved from trying to explain herself when Father Burns strode into the room and smiled beatifically at them. "Sorry to keep you waiting. Today the parishioners had many things to discuss."

"No problem, Father." Skye gazed fondly at the priest.

"I wanted to talk to you about helping out your church. Our youth committee is in dire need of leadership."

"Oh." Simon raised an eyebrow.

"You two would be perfect," Father Burns continued, leaning forward. "We need someone young, with an understanding of teens today. Skye, you have the training, and Simon, I've seen how well the kids react to you."

Skye was silent. Did she really want to take on another job? On the other hand, maybe it would do her good to be around "average" kids without major problems. It would give her perspective. Besides, how could she turn down Father Burns's request after all he'd done for her? She slid her gaze to Simon. What would his reaction be?

"What does the job entail?" Simon asked.

"Planning monthly youth activities mostly, and chaperoning them, of course."

"Is there a budget?" Skye asked.

"Not really. Mostly they fund-raise. For some of the activities we do charge a small fee, but that's waived if a family can't afford it."

Skye and Simon turned to each other. Both gave slight shrugs. Simon answered, "Okay, we'll give it a try."

Skye nodded in agreement. How hard could it be? "Sure, we'll formulate a plan, then get back to you." She convinced herself that the chance of seeing Simon on a regular basis had nothing to do with her acceptance.

Father Burns thanked them and escorted

them out of the rectory. They parted at the end of the sidewalk with a promise to get together in a couple of days and talk.

The church was located on the corner of Stebler and Basin. Simon headed toward the parking lot and Skye toward the street.

At the bench on the corner, Skye sat and exchanged her sandals for the Keds she had stuffed into her purse. She held her breath as Simon drove by in his Lexus. She squinted to read his bumper sticker: LOTTERY: A TAX ON PEOPLE WHO ARE BAD AT MATH. Typical of Simon's dry sense of humor.

Skye sighed. He hadn't even offered her a ride. Of course, he didn't know she was without a car. Giving herself a mental shake, she bounced to her feet. She didn't need a ride or anything else from anybody. It was less than a mile to her cottage, and a beautiful day to walk.

As Skye neared her house, she noticed several cars parked in the driveway. She recognized her parents' white Oldsmobile, her brother's Jeep, and Charlie's Caddy, but the glimpses of aqua worried her.

Her father, Jed, greeted her enthusiastically and took her right arm. "Skye, we've got a surprise for you," he exclaimed.

He was much more animated than she

could ever remember seeing him. His deeply tanned face was wrinkled with a smile, and his faded brown eyes were twinkling. Even his gray crew cut seemed to be standing at attention.

"Oh, today is full of surprises," Skye remarked dryly, and tried to edge closer to whatever her family was trying to hide from her. A tarp covered most of the object, but she was afraid she knew what it was. They had gone against her wishes and bought her a car. The only question that remained was: What kind of vehicle had they purchased? The thought of what their collective minds would come up with made Skye shudder.

May took her place on Skye's left. "Close your eyes."

Skye was way ahead of her mother's orders. The problem was: Could she bring herself to ever open them again?

Vince stood behind her and whispered in her ear, "It's not as bad as it might seem at first."

Skye heard the tarp being pulled off as Charlie yelled, "Ta-dah!"

She forced herself to look. Her mouth dropped open and little sounds came out, but no words. The car was bigger than Charlie's Cadillac, painted a bright turquoise, and . . . and it had fins. She moaned.

Charlie took her hand and led her toward the vehicle. "I'll bet you don't know what a gem me and your daddy found for you."

Skye shook her head, unable to produce a coherent utterance.

Jed declared, "This is a genuine 1957 Chevrolet Bel Air."

When Skye still didn't respond, May poked her in the side. "Your father has been working on this car for you since December. It was a wreck when Charlie discovered it in old man Gar's barn."

"I knew what a beauty was hidden beneath the rust and rags," Charlie said, using his sleeve to wipe a smudge off the hood.

Jed relinquished his grip on Skye's arm and popped open the hood. "See that? Everything's like new. This'll run forever. They don't make 'em like that anymore."

Skye peered at the engine. It was clean enough to eat from. She looked at Vince with raised brows. He shrugged and leaned against his Jeep.

"Here, sit behind the wheel." Charlie opened the driver's door, and May shoved Skye inside.

"Wow," Skye finally managed to say. "This leather is so soft." The front bench was mostly white with broad aqua stripes running down both edges, a double band down the middle. The seat was wide and comfortable.

"Take it for a spin," Charlie urged, handing her the keys.

"It's really big and bright. People will talk."

Charlie stuck his thumbs in his red suspenders and puffed out his chest. "If you ain't makin' waves, you ain't kickin' hard enough."

"Ah, well." Skye located the ignition and slid the key in the slot. "Vince, why don't you come with me?"

He grinned. "Sure."

Skye handed Charlie her house keys. "You guys go in and have some coffee or something. We'll be right back."

The car was so big that it took her a while to get used to driving it, and instead of talking she concentrated on keeping it between the lines of the road. When she reached a straight stretch, she said, "How in the world did they come up with this? And why didn't you warn me?"

Vince laughed. "They're getting too smart. They didn't tell me until this morning. Mom and Dad came over after eight o'clock Mass. They know you always go at ten." He put his arm across the back of the seat. "Mom was driving their car, and Dad had this one. They told me to meet them at your place at eleven. Charlie was already there when I arrived."

"What am I going to do?" Skye searched for a place to turn the huge car around.

"What *can* you do? They'd be crushed if you turned it down."

Skye pounded the wheel and almost ran the Bel Air into the ditch. "But I want to pick out my own car. I'm thirty-one years old, and I've never chosen my own vehicle."

"So?" Vince was not as into independence as Skye was. He was happy to have Jed mow the lawn in front of his shop once a week, and he was thrilled that May brought him lunch every day.

"It's not right that they spend so much of their money on us," Skye said. As they drove down Basin Street, people waved at them as if they were royalty.

Vince had perfected the princely motion and was waving back. "Hey, we get it all when they die anyway. At least when they give us presents, they get to share our pleasure."

Skye narrowed her eyes. They were almost back at her cottage. "What do you get out of all this?" Vince was too eager for her to accept this gift. He had to have an ulterior motive. Besides, their parents would never spend this kind of money on her without also getting Vince something nearly as valuable.

Vince looked straight ahead. "They promised me a new set of drums."

"I thought you quit playing in high school."

"I always kept a set to mess around on, but these are the best you can buy."

Skye turned the Chevrolet into her drive, and cut the ignition. "It's not like they wouldn't buy you the drums if I turned down this car."

Vince hopped out and headed inside. "That's not the point. The point is, how can you say to Dad, 'Sorry, I don't want the gift you worked four months restoring'? And how can you say to Charlie, 'I don't want the car you found for me'? He gave old man Gar's son the secret location of his favorite fishing spot to get this car for you."

Skye pursed her lips. "This is my new car, isn't it?"

Vince nodded as he opened the cottage door for her.

She turned and took another look at the Bel Air. "Well, I always wanted a convertible."

Monday morning brought the April showers made famous in the poem. Skye scowled into her closet. What to wear, what to wear — the age-old question that haunted women of every age, shape, and profession.

She felt in the mood for black, but would that be fair to the kids? Pastels were out in this weather. The sage-green outfit she'd bought last spring on sale at T.J. Maxx would be perfect.

After feeding Bingo and herself breakfast, Skye donned her tan trench coat, grabbed her purse, and ran for the Bel Air. It was nice to have her own transportation again. And she felt better now that she had convinced her folks and Charlie to accept the check from the insurance company, when it came.

Still, this was hardly the Miata she had pictured herself buzzing around town in. She just hoped the roof would stay up. It had a tendency to fall down whenever she hit a bump, and the only way to raise it again was to pull over and tug on it by hand.

The elementary school was already humming when she arrived. Teachers were discussing the weather and whether they should plan to have recess inside or outside today. The kids were talking about their weekends. And the phone was ringing with parents calling to ask questions they could have answered for themselves if they read the weekly newsletter.

Skye signed in unnoticed, grabbed the messages from her box, and headed toward her office. Since she had lasted a second year in the job, the elementary school had been forced to ante up the space they had promised her when she was first hired.

It had been given grudgingly, was not much bigger than a voting booth, and outside the door, in the hallway, was the milk cooler that had occupied that room before Skye's tenancy. It rattled and shrieked, scaring many of the kids Skye was trying to work with. But, she was quick to remind herself, at least she had a private office all to herself — except on Tuesday and Thursday mornings when the speech therapist used it.

Skye hung her coat behind the door, celebrating another small victory. It had taken months to hound the custodian into putting up that hook. She stowed her purse in the desk drawer and opened her appointment book. Her morning schedule included observing a first grader, therapy sessions with two second graders, and testing a kindergartner.

She grabbed the first grader's file and made her way to the classroom. Twenty minutes later, she was noting the number of times the child had left his seat without permission when there was a knock on the classroom door. It was Fern Otte, the secretary, who motioned to Skye.

Grabbing her pad and pencil, Skye left the room as unobtrusively as possible. Several kids whispered good-bye and waved to her, undoing her effort.

As soon as the classroom door closed behind Skye, Fern whispered, "Hurry, there's a problem in Mrs. Kennedy's room."

"What's wrong?" Skye followed the secretary.

"I can't explain. Hurry."

Caroline Greer greeted Skye at the door. "Another crisis, I'm afraid," she said.

The third-grade classroom was in an uproar. Most of the kids were seated, but the noise level would have registered well above "acid-rock band" on the meter.

Skye frowned. Caroline was a great principal. Two emergencies in one year, let alone within days of each other, were unheard of for her.

"Give me the big picture first," Skye requested.

"Shauna" — Caroline pointed to a little girl standing by the teacher — "had a disagreement with Cassie over a dance recital they're both in next weekend."

"And?" Skye waited for the other shoe to drop.

Caroline motioned for the teacher to join them. "Mrs. Kennedy, please give Ms. Denison the details."

"Cassie sits in front of Shauna. I was at the blackboard writing out math problems when I heard the girls start to argue. I shushed them."

"Then what happened?" Skye asked, worried because she didn't see the other girl anywhere.

"I turned back to the board, and all of a sudden I heard a scream." The older woman grabbed a piece of paper and fanned herself. "I turned around, and Shauna was holding a huge pair of scissors in one hand and Cassie's hacked-off braid in the other."

"Oh, my." Skye hadn't seen that coming. "Where's Cassie?"

"In the bathroom with my student teacher. She refuses to come out." Mrs. Kennedy paused. "Cassie, that is, not the student teacher."

"I'd better talk to Shauna first."

"You can use the room next door," Caroline Greer whispered to Skye. "That class is on a field trip." In her normal voice she said, "Shauna, this is Ms. Denison. You need to talk to her about what you did to Cassie."

Shauna walked between the adults, out of her classroom and into the next one. Mrs. Greer left them alone.

Skye pulled up a couple of chairs. She urged Shauna to sit and followed suit. "Tell me what happened."

A stubborn look settled on the little girl's face, and she crossed her arms. "My mom said I should have had the lead in the recital, and that Cassie's mom was sleeping with our dance teacher. That's why she got the lead, not me."

"Uh-huh." Skye wasn't sure if the girl understood what "sleeping with" someone meant. "How did you feel about that?"

"I told my mom she should sleep with the teacher, too. Then I could have the lead."

"And what did your mom say to that?" Skye still wasn't sure if Shauna knew what she was saying.

"Mom said she wasn't a lizzy bean so that wouldn't work."

"Did you know what she meant?" Skye asked hesitantly.

Shauna shook her head. "Not really, so I figured if Mom wasn't going to sleep with my teacher, I'd better make Cassie give me the part myself."

"So you and Cassie argued about that this morning?"

"Right."

"And that's why you cut off her braid?"

The girl twirled one of her own long curls. "Not exactly."

"Then why, exactly?" Skye asked.

"Mom said that it was too bad we both had long hair, because if Cassie didn't, our teacher would have to let me be the lead."

"Oh?" Skye made encouraging noises to continue.

"Yeah, so I took the scissors my mom uses to cut flowers and put them in my backpack, and when Cassie said she wouldn't give me the lead in the recital, I took them out and cut off her braid." Shauna looked straight at Skye. "It was easy, like snipping one of my mom's roses."

"I'm still not sure how cutting off

Cassie's braid will get you the lead," Skye said.

Shauna flipped back her waist-length hair and stood. "Because we're doing *Rapunzel*, silly."

Chapter 11

Hook, Line, and Stinker

The rest of Skye's morning was taken up by *The Case of the Third-Grade Barber.* Both mothers were summoned, and a great number of preposterous accusations were exchanged. The issue was somewhat resolved with Shauna's three-day suspension and a quick call to Vince, securing Cassie an immediate appointment to have her hacked hair styled. But Cassie's mother was still unhappy until Skye contacted the dance teacher, who reassured everyone that Cassie would continue to dance the role of Rapunzel, wearing a wig. Shauna would not take part in the recital in any capacity.

Because of the problem at the elementary school, it was nearly one o'clock by the time Skye reached the high school. As usual, her schedule was shot, and she was trying to play catch-up. For once, the guidance office was unlocked and empty. After stashing her raincoat, Skye grabbed her calendar. Who or what was first?

She had missed two appointments — one with a girl who had been referred to her for impulse-control problems. The teen was making a lot of progress and was nearly ready to be dismissed from counseling. A missed session wouldn't hurt her.

The other appointment was with a young man whose grades were mysteriously dropping after a lifetime of straight As. Skye had originally suspected either depression or substance abuse, but after several meetings she didn't see any evidence of either. He claimed he didn't like the teachers, and Skye was ready to believe him. As Freud said, sometimes a cigar is just a cigar.

Damn! Skye had almost forgotten the meeting with Homer and Charlie scheduled for two o'clock. Charlie wanted to discuss formulating a crisis plan. While Skye agreed they needed one, she didn't have time to deal with it just then. But she had no choice. The bosses had spoken. She'd better find the folder of plans she had collected from other schools. Why recreate the wheel when you could ride someone else's tricycle?

"Ms. Denison?" A voice crept through the door. "You busy?"

"Come on in, Justin. I'm free until two." It was best to tell kids up front what the timelines were; otherwise, they might think you were ending their session arbitrarily.

Justin slunk in and poured himself into a chair. His dull brown hair hung straight in his eyes, and his pasty skin had blossomed with acne. He was not a candidate for King of the Prom, and it was evident from his demeanor that he knew it.

"Hi, were we scheduled for today?" Skye asked. She didn't remember seeing his name in her book.

"No. Want me to leave?"

"No. I was worried that I had forgotten an appointment, that's all," Skye reassured the skittish boy. "How are things going?"

"Okay." He shrugged. "I've been thinking about Lorelei."

"Oh?" Skye wondered where this was leading. Justin usually didn't voluntarily talk to her, or think much about others.

"Yeah. Nobody's acting sad she's dead." A troubled look passed over his normally expressionless face.

"And that bothers you?" Skye asked evenly. If Justin suspected she was interested, he'd close up tighter than a Tupperware container.

"Doesn't seem right. The only ones that

are acting sad are the ones that didn't really know her. The ones that saw her as a princess, not a real person." Justin slouched farther down in his chair. "Her so-called friends were nice to her, to her face, and now that she's dead, it's like they hated her."

"That must be very confusing." Skye ventured a guess.

"Yeah, well, it's not right." Justin avoided her eyes.

"Unfair, right?" Skye tried again.

He nodded. "She wasn't like the rest of them."

"In what way?"

"The other kids in that clique are all body Nazis."

"And she wasn't?" Skye didn't have a clue as to what he meant, but she often had to keep the kid talking while she figured out the newest slang.

"No. She was always on a diet and talking about exercising, but she wasn't hard-core. She wasn't a fanatic who looked down on anyone who didn't work out like a maniac. She'd even gained a little weight in the last couple of months."

"How do you know that?" Skye casually slipped in the question, hoping he wouldn't notice her interest. "You're a freshman and she was a senior. You'd hardly ever see her."

"I was helping her with her Spanish."

"You speak Spanish?" Skye glanced at his file. "I don't see you signed up for freshman Spanish."

A trace of color seeped into his cheeks. "Once I got a video game, and the instructions were all in Spanish, so I got a Spanish-English dictionary and translated. Then I started to watch the Spanish-language TV and it just sort of came to me. I got an ear for it or something."

"That's amazing. I've never met anyone who taught himself another language. I'll bet you could use that, and your talent for writing, and become a foreign correspondent for a newspaper after you finish college."

Justin froze, his face deadpan.

It was obvious she had gone too far, gotten too enthusiastic. She quickly backed up and tried a less personal topic. "But how are you still hanging around with that group?" Skye couldn't picture Justin with Troy and Chase, let alone Zoë.

"Long as I don't say anything, they don't even notice me."

"You said they're acting like they hated Lorelei. What do you mean?" Skye was relieved he was still talking to her after her gaffe.

"Zoë wants to *be* Lorelei. She wants her part in the play, her boyfriend, and the Miss Central Illinois title."

"Sounds like Miss Zoë's life has vastly improved with Lorelei out of the way." Skye made a note. "Surely Troy is sad."

"No! He's happier. It was weird; they weren't actually together these last few months, but they weren't really broken up either. It was almost like he didn't want to be her boyfriend anymore, but she was making him somehow." Justin sounded near tears. "Now he's flirting with the other cheerleaders."

"Really?"

"The only thing on his mind is who he'll take to prom."

Skye was so amazed that Justin had shown some emotion that she made another mistake and appeared eager. "Do you know anything about Frannie Ryan?"

His face closed once again, and he shook his head.

She backpedaled quickly. "Do you want me to let you know when Lorelei's wake will be?"

Justin shrugged. "If you want. I got class. Can I go?"

"Sure, let me write you a pass."

After Justin left, Skye sat back and thought about the conversation. He was full of surprises. Counseling him was like driving through hairpin turns — blindfolded, without any brakes.

It was nearly two. Skye picked up her folder and headed toward the principal's office. Charlie was already there when she arrived. He and Homer were laughing. That was a bad sign. It meant the men were getting along, and she would get stuck doing all the work.

"Sit down." Charlie patted the chair next to him. "I was telling Homer about your new car."

"Charlie says it's a real beauty. I'd love a ride."

Skye had never seen the principal appear so excited about anything. His eyes were actually sparkling. "Sure, anytime."

Homer turned to Charlie and asked, "Does the Bel Air have its original engine?"

Charlie went into a lengthy explanation. Skye's mind wandered. Would this be her fate, being saddled with a car that only old men admired? At this rate, she'd end up dating one of Charlie's cronies.

It was over between her and Kent. She

just hadn't told him yet. She had asked her cousin about his supposed affair with Lorna Ingels, and Gillian had said he had been seen with Lorelei's mother on a couple of occasions. Once someone saw her sitting in his car at the gas station while he was inside paying. Another time they were spotted driving in the direction of Joliet. Gillian said he and Lorna had always had an explanation, which was why she had never mentioned any of this to Skye.

Even before Lorelei's death, Kent's narcissism had begun to grow tiresome. It hadn't bothered her that he was dating other people, but to hear that he was having an affair with a married woman — that was beyond her tolerance limit. Thank goodness she had never slept with the creep.

Too bad things hadn't gone better between her and Simon yesterday. How could she have been so stupid as to ask him about the autopsy, knowing his disapproval of her playing detective?

She shuddered and tried to refocus by calling the men back to the reason for the meeting. "So, Charlie, you wanted to talk about a crisis plan. Do you have something in mind?"

Charlie smoothed back his mane of white hair. "Yeah, I want it on paper so we can follow it step by step, like a recipe. If something like this girl's dying ever happens again, damned if we're going to be caught unprepared."

"Here are a couple of plans from surrounding schools." Skye handed the men stapled sheaves of paper.

Charlie flipped through the pages, but Homer barely glanced at his copies.

Charlie was the first to speak. "Why don't you take the plans you have, and the outline the co-op gave us, and put them together as they apply to our district?"

"Charlie, should we start something like this without the superintendent's input?" Homer asked anxiously.

"I talked to him this morning, and he gave it his blessing." Charlie looked at Skye. "Any questions?"

"Yes. Look, without a social worker I'm already doing double duty. This should be done by a committee, or if not that, at least by the co-op coordinator. He would be more aware of what outside resources are available."

The two men turned to each other. Skye didn't see whatever signal passed between them, but Charlie said, "Not the co-op coordinator. He doesn't know the school. We're all busy, so just fit it in when you can."

"Okay, but I'm up to my neck right now. I've got to start annual reviews soon. The coordinator isn't doing them this year. I got a message from his office that they're all mine."

"I don't know why we have to meet each year with every parent of every child in special education," Homer grumbled.

"Because it's a state and federal law, and it gives us a chance to review progress and plan for next year."

Charlie stood. "Do the best you can. Try to have it to me by the first Tuesday in May, for the next school-board meeting."

Skye twisted the Bel Air's rearview mirror toward her and dug around in her tote bag for her makeup kit. The constant drizzle had transformed her smooth pageboy into a mass of waves. She yanked her wide-toothed comb through the ringlets and shoved a headband into place. After she applied lipstick and blush, she was ready to face Wally. Maybe today would be the day he forgave her.

His shift officially ended at three, but now that he was in the process of a divorce, he usually hung around longer.

Her mom was sitting behind the counter as Skye pushed through the glass door. May buzzed her through to the back. "What's up?"

"I came to talk to Wally."

"Good luck. According to Thea, he's been a bear all afternoon. I haven't seen him since I've been on. He hasn't had the good manners to come out of his office and say hi."

Before Skye could respond, a male voice spoke from the doorway. Wally stood with his arms crossed and a frown on his face. "May, I would prefer that you not allow your relatives behind the counter. If you look in your handbook, you'll see it's against the rules."

Skye was shocked. If anything, he seemed more angry now than he had been last summer, when she went against his wishes and behind his back. Was it her or was he just having a bad day?

She finally said, "Sorry, Chief Boyd. It won't happen again. But I did want to speak to you about . . ." Suddenly her mind went blank. What was it she wanted?

May quickly filled in. "You want to know about Lorelei's autopsy and when the body will be released."

"Thanks, Mom." Skye smiled. That's one of the nice things about living in a small town. Even if you don't know what you're doing, someone else probably does. "So, can you fill me in?" Skye asked.

"No."

"What?" Skye couldn't believe what she had heard.

"I said no. You have no right to that information."

"I see." Skye could feel her temper rising. She'd wanted to yell at Wally for a long time. The only thing that had stopped her was that he was in the right. She *had* betrayed his trust.

"Good." He had been standing in the doorway between the dispatcher's office and the interrogation room. Now he moved toward the other door leading to the stairs.

Skye followed him. "So how am I supposed to help the kids deal with Lorelei's death if I don't know what really happened, or even when she'll be buried?"

He shrugged. "That's not my problem."

"No, it's mine and the community's." Skye tried to speak evenly.

"You just want an excuse to nose around and play Sherlock Holmes."

"That's not true." She shushed the small

voice inside her head that told her she might be lying. "If this isn't handled right, we could have a rash of suicides in response to Lorelei's death." Skye knew she was exaggerating, but it was possible. It had happened. She had read about it in the literature.

"I think all that crap about grieving and the seven stages and all that is just hooey you shrinks thought up to make a lot of money," Wally said, looking straight into Skye's eyes. "And I think you get a kick out of running around and being important and *saving* everyone."

Skye's lips thinned with anger. "What did you say?"

"You get a thrill out of being the center of attention. Your true reason for wanting to know this stuff is that you're nosy." His tone dripped with contempt. He tried to brush past her and go up the stairs.

She stepped into his path and threw her words at him like stones, wanting to hurt him back. "Ah, that explains your unreasonable hostility. Counseling didn't work for you and Darleen, did it? So, of course it can't be worthwhile for other people. Then you'd have to admit you failed as a husband."

His eyes blazed dark fire, and he grabbed

her by the upper arms. Time froze, then with a curse he moved her out of his way and stomped up the stairs.

She heard his office door slam, and she slowly turned and went back into the dispatcher's office. What was wrong with her? Was she deliberately destroying any chance she had for a relationship with a man to whom she was attracted? Why had she intentionally poked and prodded at all his vulnerabilities? What had she been thinking?

It was plain that May had heard every word of the argument. Mother and daughter looked at each other in silence. May nodded to a chair, and Skye sank into it gratefully. Her knees were oddly weak, and her head was throbbing. She hated losing her temper.

"So," May said, "is that smoke coming out of your ears from the bridge you just burned?" Her mother wasn't much into comforting people.

Skye wasn't sure whether to laugh or cry. "Was that as bad as I think it was?"

May nodded.

"Why did I let him get to me like that?" Skye buried her head in her hands.

"He sure knew the right buttons to push." May tugged on her ear. "Of course, you were right in there, jabbing at his sore spots, too."

"Is he right? Am I only involved in this investigation to make myself feel important?" Skye looked down at the tissue she was shredding.

"Probably a little. That's human nature. But you're also doing it because you like to help people." May reached over and lifted Skye's chin. "Even when you were little you were always the one who wanted to help. You used to iron for Grandma, and wrap all of Aunt Kitty's Christmas presents, and you were always the one who insisted we stop at the nursing home to visit your great-grandma."

Skye sniffed. It wasn't like her mom to say something that nice. "I think I just learned an important lesson."

"What?"

"It takes years to build up trust, and only a second to destroy it." Skye shook her head. "I don't think Wally is ever going to forgive me."

"That may be true. But if he doesn't, is he the kind of man you'd want — even to be friends with?"

May's insights sometimes surprised Skye. "No, I guess not." She got to her feet. "I suppose if he can't see why I had to talk to those survivalists alone, then he doesn't and won't ever understand me."

"That's right, honey. And you don't want a man like that."

Skye nodded and got back to business. She whispered in May's ear as she hugged her, "Can you get a copy of the autopsy?"

May shook her head, and whispered back, "No, the creep has it locked in his personal safe, and I don't have the combination."

"Rats. Have they said anything about releasing the body?"

"Not in front of me." May made a face. "They're keeping it all very hush-hush. The file isn't even in the cabinet, and there's nothing in the computer."

"I wonder what the big secret is." Skye's brows drew together. "We know she died from an overdose of pills, and we're pretty sure they weren't self-administered, so what are they keeping from us? What does that autopsy show?"

May shrugged. "I'll talk to the other dispatchers and see if they know anything."

"Good idea." Skye walked around to the other side of the counter. "I'll think of a way of seeing that autopsy report yet," she vowed.

Chapter 12

By Look or by Crook

Bingo yowled in protest when Skye flung off the covers and jumped up. He looked at her with accusing eyes, as if to say: What are you doing getting up, I haven't ordered you to fix my breakfast yet.

Skye had followed her normal school-night routine and gone to bed at ten. It was now a little after eleven, and she had yet to fall asleep. She couldn't stop thinking about Lorelei.

Charlie had called around six, wanting to know her progress in solving the murder. She'd had to admit she wasn't getting very far in her investigation. And since Wally was keeping her in the dark, she had no idea if the police were doing any better.

The faster these thoughts crowded into Skye's mind, the faster she pulled on clothes. But after she had finished dressing, she didn't know what to do.

She sat on the edge of the unmade bed and stroked Bingo, who had forgiven her

213

earlier indiscretion and was curled up by her side. She petted in time with his purrs, nearly lulling herself into the sleep that had eluded her earlier.

Just as she was about to nod off, it hit her. She had to see the autopsy report. Otherwise, she had no idea what direction to go. Obviously, something in that report was important.

How could she get ahold of the document? Too bad she didn't know any safecrackers. She was pretty good with locked doors, but she'd never get the police department's safe open by herself.

There was only one other place where a second copy of the autopsy might be found: Simon's office. As the coroner, he'd keep a copy for his records. Since he had no clerical staff and wouldn't worry about anyone snooping, the report probably wasn't even locked up. So how could she get into the funeral home and take a look?

She could pretend someone in her family had died, and she needed to make arrangements. No. He'd never leave her alone long enough. Could she talk Simon's assistant, Xavier, into letting her in, to "surprise" Simon? That was a bad idea on two counts. Xavier might get into trouble, and he knew that she and Simon were no longer a couple.

Skye wandered over to her dresser and stared in the mirror. She looked at the black jeans, black sweatshirt, and black shoes she had put on. Unconsciously she had selected clothes appropriate for breaking into the funeral home.

Grabbing a dark baseball cap, she tucked her hair underneath. She hoped breaking and entering wasn't getting to be a habit with her. Previously she'd searched a condo on the Gold Coast and a bungalow on the South Side of Chicago, but she'd sort of had permission for those two intrusions. So this was the first time she was truly going to do something illegal. Did that make her feel better or worse?

In the kitchen, Skye rummaged through her junk drawer. She retrieved a heavy-duty flashlight, a pair of surgical gloves from one of the first-aid kits the school nurse passed out every year, and a thin piece of celluloid she had confiscated from a student attempting to open a locker that wasn't his.

As she closed her front door, Skye was struck with how distinctive the Bel Air really was. Not the ideal vehicle with which to commit a crime.

While she drove toward town, she thought about where she could stash the Chevy while she burgled the funeral home. "The Purloined Letter" popped into her head. She'd hide the car in plain sight.

She pulled into the back of the used-car lot on Stebler and tucked the Chevy in among the other vehicles. From there it was only four blocks to Reid's Funeral Home. The streets were empty, and most of the houses looked as if their occupants were asleep. Skye shivered; the temperature had dropped back into the forties, and she could smell rain in the air. It was a cold spring.

She was a block from her destination when the barking started. It wasn't the yapping of a cute little fur ball; it was the full-throated woofs of a large breed such as a Doberman or German shepherd. This was a good part of town, but old habits died hard, and many residents felt safe only with shotguns beside their beds and big dogs in their yards.

Skye quickened her pace and tried to pinpoint where the growling was coming from, and whether it was getting any closer. The house she was passing was surrounded with chain-link fence. Suddenly, the source of the barking roared around a corner and threw itself at the metal barrier. Skye started to run, which further inflamed the Rottweiler.

Looking back over her shoulder, she could see the porch light come on. A man dressed only in long johns appeared on the front step holding a rifle. "Hey, what's going on out there?" The man squinted past the pool of light and into the darkness.

The dog barked for a few more minutes, then gave up. Skye kept running until she reached Simon's house. His windows were dark. Skye waited for her breathing to return to normal, then moved on.

Across the street, the front of the funeral home was brightly illuminated. She crept toward the back, where Simon's office was located. It was shrouded in darkness, and she shivered again, this time not from the frigid air. She looked around. No one in sight. She pulled on the latex gloves.

When she thumbed on the flashlight she noticed the time on her watch. Ten minutes to twelve. Maybe this wasn't such a good idea. Breaking into a mortuary at midnight seemed pretty stupid.

Skye shook her head. This was real life, not some scene from a horror movie. There was nothing inside that could hurt her. Still, images of the living dead danced in her head, and she had to force herself to aim the light at the lock and slip the celluloid into the crack.

Nothing happened. What was she doing wrong? Maybe she should have used her trusty Swiss Army knife. The locks usually popped right open when she applied its thinnest blade to the bolt. The kid had told her that what he called a " 'loid" worked better, but she didn't think so.

Before she could try again, a hand descended on her shoulder, and she let out a muffled scream as she whirled around.

She couldn't believe her eyes. "What are you doing here?"

Justin Boward slouched in front of her, a smirk on his face. "I live back there." He pointed across the backyard of the funeral home, toward the small white house that stood behind it. "I saw you with my night-vision binoculars. What are *you* doing here?"

This was not a good situation. Being caught breaking into a funeral home by a student ranked right up there among the top five reasons to be fired. What could she say to make Justin think this wasn't what his eyes told him it was?

He continued before she could come up

with a plausible excuse. "Say, I know what you're doing. You're investigating Lorelei's murder. Cool."

His demeanor had changed from a cat who had caught the canary to something close to admiration. She tried to wiggle out of the situation. "Well, no, ah, I'm just trying this out for a book I'm writing."

Something shuttered closed behind his eyes, and Skye could see that lying had been a mistake. She tried to ease around the boy, thinking that retreat might be the best choice.

His words stopped her. "I hate it when adults lie to me." His face was expressionless in the flashlight's glare. "My parents do it all the time. My dad is never straight with me about his health. And my mother would rather lock herself in the bathroom and cry than tell me what's really bothering her."

Skye's counseling instincts kicked in. "That must make you feel left out."

He nodded.

She thought she saw a tear on his cheek, but it was too dark to tell.

Justin continued in a cold voice. "That's why at school I make it a point to know about everything. Nobody will tell you anything directly, but if you hang around and listen, you find out stuff."

"Does that help you feel more in control?" Skye couldn't believe she was having a therapy session at midnight outside of a funeral home.

"Yeah. Someday the other kids are going to figure out I know all their dirty little secrets, and then they'll realize I'm one of those bad things that happen to good people."

"I don't think so." Skye took a chance and contradicted Justin. "I think you're one of the good people, not one of the 'bad things.'"

Hope, doubt, and denial chased across his face. Finally, he crossed his arms, and said, "So, are we breaking in here or not? And don't give me that crap about research for a book."

"No, *we* are not breaking in. *We*'re going home." Skye realized it was time to call a halt to the whole idea.

Justin bent down and picked up the celluloid she had dropped. "Then you don't need this."

"Neither do you. Give it here." She held out her hand.

He turned his back on her and inserted it into the door near the bolt. "This is how you open one of these types of locks."

At the same time that the latch clicked and the door swung open, she heard another sound — footsteps crossing the street. Skye immediately switched off the flashlight and pushed Justin inside. She followed, quietly closing the door behind her. Unable to see in the utter darkness, she put her lips to what she hoped was the boy's ear, and whispered, "Hide. Someone's coming."

She counted her blessings that at least Justin was one of the smartest kids she had in therapy. Without a word he silently faded away. Obviously his night vision was superior to hers.

Skye put up her hands to feel her way, trying to visualize where she was from previous visits to the funeral home. She thought she was in a tiny back hall and that Simon's office was the first door to her right. She felt an opening at the same time she heard a key rattle. She slipped quickly inside the room, closed the door, and pushed the button to lock it.

She knew immediately that this was not Simon's office. She must have gotten turned around, but it was too late to leave now. A light went on in the hall, and she heard footsteps pass the room she was hiding in.

Something wasn't right. Where was she? There were only two choices, and neither one was a winner. She was either in the room where they prepared the bodies or she was . . . Her hand encountered cold metal, then smooth satin. *Oh, shit. I'm in the casket-display room.* Her heart started to beat rapidly. Swallowing a scream, she forced herself to think rationally. *There's nothing in here that can hurt me.* She eased herself to a sitting position on the floor and tried to calm herself. *Just because it's midnight, and I'm locked in a room with a bunch of coffins does not mean that Dracula is out there sharpening his fangs.*

She had never liked scary movies, but her Uncle Dante had loved them. Every Saturday night her parents would drop her and her brother off for Dante and Olive to baby-sit. And every week he would force them to watch *Creature Features*: two horror movies back-to-back, ending at midnight. Vince tried to help calm her fears, sitting next to her and holding her hand, but it was never enough. Because when she went to bed she was alone, and that's when all the monsters came out to get her.

At a conscious level, she knew it was ridiculous for a grown woman to be frightened of vampires and werewolves, but down deep inside she was still the eight-year-old girl who had been terrified by those TV images. Skye still had occasional bad dreams starring the cast from those flicks.

She had to get her mind off where she was or she'd go crazy. Concentrating, she thought of Justin and said a prayer that he was okay, that he had managed to slip back outside and was at home this very minute. She'd never forgive herself if something happened to that boy because of her stupidity.

Skye stiffened. Someone was jiggling the door and cursing. She heard a key chain being taken from a pocket. She stood up. What was she going to do? The door would open any minute. The key was shoved into the lock. Before she could talk herself out of it, and as quietly as possible, she climbed into the nearest casket and eased down the lid.

I'm definitely going to scream or throw up. Maybe both. She tried to lie still and silent, but she could almost feel hot breath on her neck. No way would she be able to handle being closed in for long.

The situation reminded her of when she was six, and her cousin Hugo locked her in her grandmother's hope chest. They had been playing hide-and-seek, and instead of finding her, he had turned the key and left her. She had screamed and screamed, but the chest was in the closet and no one heard her. Luckily, Vince missed her and forced Hugo to tell what he had done.

I'm going to faint. Skye tried to quiet her breathing. Bad move; now she could hear every rustle of the satin and every creak of the metal. Was that something gnawing on her ankle?

I can't stand this. This is like my worst nightmare come to life. Maybe that's it. Maybe I'm dreaming.

She couldn't hear anything. How would she know when it was safe to come out? Or worse yet, what if the lid wouldn't open? Skye felt the hysteria building and couldn't control it. When they finally found her in this thing, she'd be either stark raving mad or dead.

Without warning, the top was flung open, and light flooded in, blinding her. She shrieked, thinking for a moment that some chainsaw-wielding maniac was after her.

She vaguely heard a shout, "What in blazes?" before she lost what little control she possessed.

Screaming, she fought the arms that reached for her. Despite her struggle, she felt herself being lifted from the casket.

A familiar, soothing voice said, "Skye, it's Simon. You're okay, sweetheart. You're fine." He patted her back and smoothed her hair until she calmed down. He handed her his handkerchief and waited for her to wipe her eyes and blow her nose.

Skye took a deep breath and focused on the gentle concern radiating from Simon's features. "Sorry," she hiccuped. "I don't know what came over me." She reached up and stroked his cheek. "I was convinced you were Norman Bates. Isn't that stupid?"

Instead of the response she hoped for, the mask she had grown to recognize descended, and Simon said, "What in the hell are you doing inside a casket, inside my funeral home, at midnight?"

"Would you believe a scavenger hunt?" Her voice was shaky.

His expression darkened. "You have two minutes to tell me the truth, or I'm calling the police. Even your precious Wally would have trouble finding a reason not to arrest you this time."

What could she say? "Well, um, I couldn't sleep."

"So you thought a casket would be more comfortable than your bed?"

"No, don't be silly."

His eyebrows shot into his hairline, and Simon said through closed teeth, "That's not the attitude I'd take right now if I were you."

Skye quickly tried another tack. "I've been missing you."

"And you got confused between my house and the funeral home?" Simon's tone remained unamused.

"No." Skye tried to refocus his attention. "What are *you* doing prowling around here at midnight?"

"I own the place."

"True. I didn't say you didn't have a right to be here. I just asked why?"

"You'd ask the Pope whether he were celibate after he heard your confession for murder, wouldn't you?" Simon allowed a fleeting look of admiration to cross his face.

"Maybe. If I had a good reason. So, why are you here?"

"Because I left the book I was reading in my office, and when I couldn't sleep, I decided to come get it. As I crossed the street, I saw a light bobbing around the back door. I've had trouble with kids and vandalism before, so I decided to investigate. Then I heard something thumping in the casket-display room. And you know, the sad thing is, I wasn't even that surprised when I opened the lid and saw you." He raised a brow. "Satisfied?"

"Yes." Skye edged toward the door. "Sorry about all this. I was in the neighborhood and —"

He cut her off with a snarl. "Just tell me the truth for once."

"Okay. Fine." Skye had run out of both excuses and patience. "I wanted to see Lorelei Ingels's autopsy. Wally is being stupid about the whole thing, and I knew you'd never let me look at it."

"This is Wally's and my fault?" His voice rose.

"In a sense, yes." Her fear had been replaced with exasperation. "If you men would just cooperate. It's not like I haven't helped the police out before. Without me, they would never have figured out who killed Honey Adair or my grandmother."

"So, now you want me to make a copy of the autopsy and send you on your way, so you can solve this crime for us, too?" A pulse became visible in Simon's temple.

"That would be a step in the right direction." How far could she take this before he exploded?

"Get out of here before I lose my temper, as well as my mind. I'm not calling the police, only out of respect for your family." Simon took her arm and led her to the door. "If I ever catch you doing something like this again, I will press charges."

He thrust her outside, but didn't release her. "One more thing. How did you learn to pick locks?"

Skye forced a carefree smile, not willing to let Simon know how bad she really felt. "Hey, if I waited to get keys to the rooms at school, I'd never get anything done."

Simon made a growling noise deep in his throat, stepped back inside, and closed the door in her face.

Skye took a shaky breath. Now, if only Justin were okay. She didn't dare try and get back inside, and there were no windows to peer into. Her only choice was to see if he had made it home.

She walked toward the house he had pointed out earlier. What should she do? She couldn't exactly ring the bell and ask for him.

As she approached what she hoped was his window, she heard, "Psst, over here."

Skye turned around. The only thing she

could see in the pitch-black backyard was a tree house.

Justin's face appeared in the doorway. "Up here, Ms. D."

"Come down," she half whispered.

He grinned. "No, you come up. My parents might hear us down there."

"As long as you're okay. I've got to get going anyhow." Skye turned. "I'll see you at school tomorrow."

"Ms. Denison."

She turned back. "What?"

"I think you might want to see this right away." He held up a sheaf of papers.

"What's that?"

"Lorelei's autopsy. I copied it while you and Mr. Reid were yelling at each other."

She sighed. She was way too old to be climbing trees.

Chapter 13

Tryst for the Mill

Lorelei had been pregnant. Not even two months along, but definitely with child. So that was the big secret. Skye could see how the police would want to keep that quiet. It pointed the finger at a whole slew of new suspects. Troy Yates, the boyfriend, jumped right to the top of the list. And maybe her pregnancy explained why her parents were so against the autopsy.

The document contained nothing else of interest. Lorelei had been a healthy eighteen-year-old. No cause of death was listed. The medical examiner was waiting for the results of the toxicology tests.

Skye suspected that Justin was lying when he claimed he hadn't had time to read the report. He had handed it over too easily. He'd either read the packet of papers or made another copy. But that was an issue she'd have to deal with another time.

It was after two by the time Skye got to

bed. When her alarm rang at six o'clock, she hit the snooze button. She kept hitting it until seven, when Bingo added his vocal displeasure to the cacophony, and she swung her legs over the side of the bed. Another day without her morning swim. This had to stop. She needed to get back into her routine.

She was supposed to be at school by seven-thirty. No way could she call in sick. First of all, there was too much to do as the school year neared its end. Most importantly, today was PPS at the junior high. No one missed the Pupil Personal Services meeting without a really good excuse — like death. If you weren't in attendance, you were the one assigned all the crappy duties.

Too tired to care what she looked like, Skye pulled on the first thing she grabbed from her closet — a knit pantsuit that, although extremely comfortable, bagged at the knees after a few hours of wear. She swept her hair back with a long clip, shoved her feet into flats, and ran out the door.

She was five minutes late arriving at the junior high school, and the principal, Neva Llewellyn, commented as she handed Skye a stack of message slips. "Looks like you had a hard night."

Neva and Skye were on friendly terms, but the principal was a perfectionist and expected everyone else to be flawless also. Tardiness was one of her pet peeves.

Skye skidded to a halt. "Sorry." She never was a morning person, and less than eight hours of sleep made her cranky. Less than five hours made her downright crabby. "Bad morning." She had to be careful or she'd say something snippy she'd regret later. "I hope I haven't kept you waiting."

Neva raised an eyebrow. "Do you have appointments this morning before PPS?"

"I've got kids lined up to test. I need to get the reevaluations finished so I can get started on annual reviews."

"Go get settled, but before you start, come talk to me," Neva ordered.

Skye tucked her purse in her desk, prepared the room and materials for the first child she would evaluate, then sat down and leafed through her messages. One from Charlie stated the wake for Lorelei Ingels was being held that afternoon and evening. He wanted her to be there in case a student needed her help, and also to continue her investigation. The funeral would take place the next morning. Charlie again suggested that her presence was required.

A note from Homer said almost the same thing, although no snooping was mentioned.

After giving Ursula Nelson, the junior-high secretary, a pass for the student she wanted to test when the first bell rang, Skye knocked on the principal's door.

Neva had redecorated when she took over from the last occupant, and the office had gone from utilitarian to tasteful. Skye seated herself in a Queen Anne chair and faced Neva across a gleaming wooden desk, breathing in the pleasant odor of vanilla that wafted through the air from a small bowl of potpourri tucked away on a butterfly table next to the ivory wall.

Neva straightened the sleeve of her flax-colored suit and leaned forward. "I don't like it."

Skye's heart jumped, but she forced an unperturbed look on her face. "What?"

"The way the co-op coordinator has thrust his work onto us."

"You mean the annual reviews?" Skye hazarded a guess.

"Yes, that's *his* job."

"That's what I said, but the superintendent backed him up."

"The old boys' network, no doubt."

Neva tapped a perfectly manicured nail on the desktop.

"Probably, but to be fair, the coordinator is assigned to three other school districts."

Neva ignored Skye's comment. "So now we have to do all the paperwork, make the appointments, and run the meetings?"

"That's what I was ordered to do. I was told to pick the dates with the special-education teachers, fill out the forms, send them to the co-op, where the secretary would type them and put together the file. Ursula would receive the packages and call the parents. If they couldn't make the appointment, the whole process would start over."

"That's ridiculous." Neva stood up. "I'll look into it."

Skye rose, too. "You might mention that since I have to do a ton of reevals, write the reports, and attend all the annual reviews, I'll have to stop the counseling sessions at the end of this month, instead of continuing until the end of the year."

Neva frowned as they walked out the door together. "That isn't right."

"No, it isn't, and I'll have to do it in all three schools." Skye started down the hall, but stopped and said over her shoulder, "We really need a social worker. The board's got to raise the beginning salary so we can attract one. I can't do my real job the way it should be done because I'm always trying to make up for missing staff members."

The morning went quickly. Most kids were very cooperative when tested. A lot even seemed to like the one-on-one attention and praise. One of the last tasks Skye had the student attempt was a written language sample that consisted of a short essay. During this time, Skye usually started to score the measures already administered, but today she was distracted and let her gaze wander over her office. She remembered the fight it had taken to obtain this space, when she had first come to work for Scumble River Junior High.

The room had originally been a janitor's closet, and on damp days she could still smell the peculiar combination of bleach and mildew. Skye had covered the egg-yolk yellow walls with travel posters. Since she had no window, she had created a faux one using old curtains and a poster of a forest scene.

Her battered desk doubled as a testing table because the office was too small to accommodate both. She sat on a metal folding chair, and when she brought in a second chair for a student to use, there was no way to get to the door without crawling over something or somebody.

Still, it was her own space. She didn't have to share it or beg for a room every time she came to the building. Many school psychologists would see that as a luxury.

Her student finished writing and pushed the form toward Skye. "It's not very good."

"Did you do the best you could?" Skye found this to be a better response than a meaningless "I'm sure it's fine."

The boy nodded.

"Well, I know you worked hard for me this morning, and I really appreciate your effort and concentration." Skye reached into her drawer and pulled out a fistful of pencils and pens with team logos. "You may choose one for doing such a good job."

The student hesitated, then selected a pen with the Chicago Bulls insignia. "Thanks. Will I see you again?"

"No, we finished everything this morning." Skye filled out a pass and handed it over. "You can go back to class now. Bye."

After the boy left, Skye straightened everything up, grabbed her PPS binder, and headed for the rest room. One of the first lessons she had learned as an intern was never to enter a meeting with a full bladder.

Skye reached the high school at twelve-fifteen and caught Trixie just as she was on her way to lunch. Skye grabbed a salad from the cafeteria, while Trixie fetched two sodas from the machine in the teachers' lounge. They settled in the guidance office to eat and catch up.

"What did you think of that pageant last Saturday?" Trixie asked, biting into an Italian beef sandwich that she had brought from home.

"Interesting. But I hear this coming Saturday's will be even more so." Skye forked a piece of lettuce into her mouth. "It's for the older girls. The one Lorelei would have competed in."

"Mmm." Trixie swallowed another huge bite. "Speaking of Lorelei, have you found out anything new?"

"Not really." Skye was extremely tempted to tell Trixie about Lorelei's pregnancy, but decided it wasn't either ethical or smart to share that information — considering how Skye had come across it. "But that reminds me, I wanted to ask you about the cheerleader meeting last Wednesday, the day of Lorelei's death."

"We all got together to discuss replacing a girl who had moved."

"Did you pick someone?"

"No, we couldn't agree." Trixie frowned. "We all have an equal vote, and it's too much power for the girls to have."

"I heard what happened to Frannie Ryan." Skye was curious as to Trixie's view of that incident.

"That was a disgrace. I'm going to change the selection process next year." Trixie was silent as she crunched on potato chips. She finally asked, "What are you doing about it? The murder, I mean."

"Wally's blocking me, and Simon won't help, so I'm talking to the kids and trying to find excuses to nose around." Skye pushed away her barely eaten salad. The lettuce tasted slimy. "I need a reason to hang around Lorelei's group on an informal basis."

"Like cheerleading practice?" Trixie took a Ding Dong from her bag and peeled back the foil.

"Like cheerleading practice." Skye eyed the chocolate cake and Trixie's size-four figure. Life was not fair, Skye decided, as she settled for the saltines that had come with her salad. "Need an assistant coach?"

"Know anything about cheerleading?" Trixie licked frosting from her upper lip.

"Nope."

"Perfect. We meet tomorrow after school." Trixie got up and threw away her trash. "Wear sweats or a leotard."

"Really?" Skye rose and dumped her garbage, too. "I have to dress? This sounds suspiciously like gym. I hated gym."

"If you want to hang out with the girls and get them comfortable enough to talk in front of you, you'll have to make the sacrifice."

"Wonderful." Skye thought of how attractive she looked in sweats. A leotard was out of the question.

"Deal with it," Trixie said, and shot out the door.

Skye checked her watch. She had just enough time to talk with Homer before she ran home and changed for the wake. Charlie's note had said it was being held from two to four and six to eight.

Homer was in his office surrounded by stacks of test papers. He waved Skye inside. "Yeah?"

"Just wanted to ask you about Lorelei's funeral and wake. What is the school doing?"

Homer eyed her as if she were posing a trick question. "We sent flowers," he answered cautiously.

"Good. But are we allowing students to leave school? Are we offering transportation to the funeral home?"

"Well, I didn't find out about the wake until late last night. The parents didn't notify us. Surprise, surprise. So, we'll let kids with notes from their parents go today."

"How about if tomorrow we provide a bus to the funeral?" Skye held out her hand like a traffic cop. "There are a lot of good reasons to do this. For one, we can control the amount of time the kids are gone from school. Doing it my way, they'll be gone for a couple of hours, max."

"But more will go if we make it too convenient."

"Maybe. Does it matter? Teachers can't really move ahead in the curriculum anyway with half the kids gone."

"Okay. You write the note and make sure it goes home with all the kids tonight. Anyone wanting to go to the funeral has to have it signed to get on the bus tomorrow." Homer looked mournfully at the piles of work on his desk. "I've got to get these Iowa Achievement tests sorted and in the mail today."

"Sounds like a plan." Skye stood in the doorway. "I'll give the letter to Opal to type, make copies, and hand them out. Then I've got to go home and change, if you want me to attend the wake this afternoon. It starts in less than forty-five minutes."

Homer nodded, but didn't look up from the instruction sheet he was reading.

Skye tugged on her skirt. The hem barely brushed the top of her knees. She hesitated in the funeral-home foyer halfway up the steps and stared at herself in the mirrored wall. The black suit jacket skimmed her hips, and the shorter hem showed off her shapely calves and ankles. She had vowed not to drape herself in yards of polyester and hide just because she weighed more than *Cosmo* said she should, but every once in a while she lost her nerve. Especially when she was fairly certain she'd have to face an old boyfriend or two before the day was over.

If she got really lucky, all three of her latest emotional disasters would show up today — the two who had recently become angry at her all over again and the third she hadn't quite got around to formally breaking up with yet.

Clutching her tiny black handbag, Skye made herself walk through the double glass doors. The smell of flowers hit her full force, and she took a step backward, sneezing. Once she recovered, she signed the guest book and joined the short line of people waiting to pay their respects.

It was slightly after two, and the visitation had just begun. From her place in the back of the line, Skye studied the Ingelses. Today Lorna looked every one of her fortysomething years. The faint lines that earlier had been well hidden by makeup now bracketed her mouth and furrowed her forehead. Her lips, no longer moist with lipstick, were cracked and dry. There could be no question that Lorna's grief was genuine and devastating.

Allen stood next to his wife, sober in a charcoal gray Armani suit. His face revealed no emotion, but Skye noticed an occasional tic near his left eye and the constant clenching of his right fist.

Linette stood apart from both her parents and her sister's casket, half-hidden by a huge floral arrangement. Skye was trying to interpret the ten-year-old's expression when she noticed she was next in line.

"Mrs. Ingels, you have my deepest sympathy."

Lorelei's mother nodded, tears leaking from her red-rimmed eyes. "How could she do this to me?"

Skye thought fast. Was this the stage of grief where the survivor became angry at the one who died? "I'm sure she didn't want to leave you."

Before his wife could respond, Allen took Skye's arm and propelled her down the line, saying, "Thank you for coming."

Skye found herself facing Linette as the girl stepped deeper into the flowers. She tried smiling at the girl. Linette took another step back, a look of cold arrogance on her face.

If she ever decided to get her doctorate, Skye decided she'd use this family for her dissertation. Their reactions were totally out of the norm.

Skye looked around. Troy Yates was slouched on a chair in one corner. How convenient. She'd wanted to talk to him today at school, but hadn't had time. "Hi." Skye slid into the seat next to him.

Troy sat up straighter. "Hi."

"Are you okay?"

"Yeah." Troy pulled at his necktie. "It's just that people don't really understand."

"Oh?" Skye scooted closer so she could lower her voice. "In what way?"

"Lorelei and I had pretty much broken up. We just hadn't told everyone yet. We were going to wait until after the prom."

"Why?" Skye asked. "You both could certainly have found other dates."

"She already had."

"What?" Skye was confused.

Troy's fair skin reddened. "Well, the thing was, she was already seeing someone, but he couldn't take her to the prom because we were up for king and queen. You know, senior couple. Lorelei really wanted to win."

"She told you she was dating some other guy and you still planned to take her to the prom? That seems above and beyond the call of niceness."

The teen squirmed. "Well, ah, she never actually told me. Zoë let me in on the big secret."

"Secret? Who was this guy?"

Troy shrugged and didn't respond.

Skye could tell she'd never get an answer to that question, so she tried another. "When did you guys really stop being together?"

"Valentine's Day." Troy studied his hands. "I bought her a big heart-shaped box of candy, and she got real mad at me."

Skye was confused. "Was she hoping for something else?"

"No, but she accused me of trying to make her fat, so no one else would want her."

"That is one of life's mysteries, you know," Skye said, trying for some humor.

"What?"

"How a two-pound box of chocolates can make a woman gain five pounds."

Troy didn't smile back, and Skye quickly added, "Were you jealous that she cared if anyone else would want her?"

"Not then. A little, after Zoë told me about the other guy."

"And you were still going to take her to the prom."

Troy frowned. "We'd been together since eighth grade. I didn't want to hurt her."

Skye said good-bye to Troy and wandered to the other side of the room. Interesting. Troy *could* be the father, but the date of conception would have been close to the time they broke up.

If, that is, Troy was telling the truth.

Chapter 14

Mean with Envy

If not Troy, then who was the father of Lorelei's baby? The new boyfriend? What was the big secret? Was he someone she couldn't be seen with in public?

A commotion at the funeral-home door drew Skye's attention away from her speculation. Standing just inside the room, arguing in whispers, were her twin cousins, Ginger and Gillian.

Skye moved toward them in time to hear Ginger say to Gillian, "I will not be nice to Lorna Ingels. You be a hypocrite if you want to, but I'm not doing it."

"Hi, Skye." Gillian acknowledged her cousin before tightening her grip on her twin's arm. "Just say you're sorry for her loss. You are sorry Lorelei is dead, right?"

"Hi, Gillian, Ginger," Skye said softly, not wanting to interrupt their conversation.

"Hi, Skye," Ginger echoed before a mutinous look descended on her face. "Of course I'm sorry. But that woman had Linette compete in a pageant three days after her other daughter was murdered. She's no more in mourning than my dog is."

"You're probably right," Gillian replied, guiding her twin toward the front of the visitation room, "but since when does Scumble River give points for sincerity?"

As her cousins moved off, Skye remained by the door pondering what she had just heard. Lorna and the whole pageant scene really caused some strong feelings among those involved.

The afternoon hours crawled by. As far as she could see, most of the people who came were older, and many seemed to have only distant connections with the family. They went through the line, and then stood at the back and chatted with each other, treating the wake like any other opportunity to socialize.

Troy and Zoë were the only two students present. He sat quietly in the back row, alternately studying the ceiling and his shoes. Zoë's mother had a firm grip on her daughter's arm as they occupied the third row without speaking.

It was a relief when the grandfather clock struck four and Skye could leave. So far she had been able to avoid Simon, and neither Wally nor Kent had put in an appearance. She had two hours until the next round.

The weather had grown colder while Skye was inside the funeral parlor. She hurried toward her car, flung herself inside, and backed the Chevy out of its space. She adjusted the instruments for heat and waited, anticipating a flood of warm air pouring out of the dashboard openings.

Nothing happened. She continued to drive, but only cold gusts emerged from the car's vents. The air stream was still near freezing when Skye approached her driveway. Great. She'd have to find a mechanic who worked on old cars. Or she could mention it to her mom, and her dad would take care of it.

At least her house was toasty, she thought as she walked through her front door, smiling. Wait a minute. She hadn't set the thermostat this high before she left. Someone had been here. A burglar or May? Skye voted for her mother.

How many times had she told her folks that the key she let them have was for emergency use only? Still, a tiny smile remained on Skye's lips. Was that a roast she smelled?

Skye shared the beef dinner with Bingo as she admired her freshly cleaned house. She was fighting a losing battle — her need for independence versus her parents' need to take care of her. The note May had left said it all: "I know Charlie is asking you to go to all the visitation hours today and the funeral tomorrow, so I went shopping from your list on the fridge, cleaned a little, and cooked. Hope you're okay. Love, Mom."

What seemed only seconds later, Skye was stretched out on her bed when the high-pitched beep of her alarm cut through her dream of the beach and a tall dark stranger. Groggily, she forced open one eye. Quarter to six. She had managed to squeeze in an hour of sleep. Time to freshen up and get back to Reid's Funeral Home.

She dug out a black velvet-covered headband in an attempt to tame her chestnut curls. A quick dab of blush, some eyeshadow to highlight her best feature, her emerald green eyes, and she was ready to go. She certainly wasn't looking her best, but at least she wouldn't scare small children — she hoped.

A line had already formed when she

pushed through the doors of the funeral home. Skye knew many if not all of the faces. Most were students and staff.

She made her way to a sofa situated off to the side of the row of folding chairs and prepared to intervene if anyone needed assistance. Simon was seated in the very back corner at a small desk. He appeared to be going through papers, but his sharp gaze swept the area every few minutes.

Everything was quiet. Skye watched Farrah Miles, Caresse Wren, and Zoë VanHorn go through the line. All three cheerleaders had tears running down their cheeks, but their mascara remained intact. Score one for waterproof makeup. They found chairs near the back, brought out mirrors, and began to chat as they repaired the nonexistent damage to their faces.

Next through were a group of teachers. Many of them had swollen eyes and sobbed audibly as they faced the coffin. Skye watched them, trying to gauge whether she could help comfort them.

One of the teachers approached her, and Skye steered the woman toward a small parlor off the main area, settling her into a chair. Nearly a half hour passed by the time Skye and the teacher finished talking.

After the woman left Skye headed back

to the visitation room. The line now stretched out the door and contained many people she didn't recognize. She settled back on what she now thought of as her sofa and crossed her legs.

Skye was watching the front, so she nearly missed an argument in the back corner, opposite where Simon had sat earlier. Her attention was finally caught by voices hissing at each other. Turning to look, Skye saw Kent Walker involved in a deep conversation with a woman she didn't recognize.

Skye rose and strolled nonchalantly in that direction. She got close enough to hear the woman whisper, "You're just lucky I'm not going to your principal. I know all about you and Lorna."

Kent's head came up and met Skye's stare. A chill ran down her spine at the look of loathing he gave her. He grabbed the woman's arm and urged her outside.

The evidence was piling up. Kent really had been having an affair with Lorelei's mother. Skye wondered if he'd been sleeping with anyone else, and once again counted her blessings that none of his bedroom conquests had included her.

Skye moved to follow Kent and the woman, but a hand came down on her arm. She jumped.

Simon spoke before she could. "You're awfully jittery lately. One might even think you were up to something you weren't supposed to be."

She shook off his hand and started after the other couple. He caught up with her in one easy stride. "Leave it alone." He paused, and a look of distaste crept over his features as an unpleasant thought seemed to cross his mind. "Unless, of course, you're jealous and intend to fight for your man."

Skye wrinkled her nose. "That isn't it. They're arguing. I want to make sure the woman is okay."

"She'll be fine."

"How do you know?"

"Because I sent Xavier out to patrol the grounds. He'll break things up if they get out of hand."

"How? Pardon me for stereotyping, but Xavier's the personification of a ninety-pound weakling. What could he do?" Skye questioned.

"You of all people should know how dangerous it is to judge by appearances. Xavier is tough. He studied martial arts when he was a medic in Vietnam."

"Oh." For a moment Skye was caught without an answer. "What do you mean, me of all people?" Was he referring to her weight?

"A psychologist." He raised a brow, and a tiny hint of sarcasm came through his voice.

"Oh, yeah." Skye wasn't sure how to break away, or if she really wanted to now.

They continued to stand close together. Not touching, not saying anything, until Skye noticed Simon's eyes widen.

She turned to see what had stolen his attention from her, and murmured, "Oh, my."

It was the Doozier family. Leading the group was the family patriarch, Earl. Tattoos covered most of his body; he usually wore only shorts so everyone could enjoy them. Today he had taken the seriousness of the occasion into consideration and wore a pair of tiger-striped sweatpants and a T-shirt with the saying: 24 HOURS IN A DAY . . . 24 BEERS IN A CASE . . . COINCIDENCE?

Following him was his wife, Glenda. Skye blinked. She could swear that the woman's black halter jumpsuit was made of rubber. It caused her chalk-white skin to look corpselike. Her poorly dyed blond hair was arranged in an elaborately teased hairdo.

Two boys and a girl fidgeted next to the adults. The children's sullen expressions matched Elvira's, who brought up the rear.

"I should probably go do something about that." Skye nodded toward the brood.

"What?" Simon asked. "They aren't causing any problems."

"No, I meant make sure they get through the line all right," Skye hurried to explain. "I'm afraid the Ingelses will hurt their feelings. Or that they'll feel awkward. Or someone will make a remark."

"Besides, you're dying to find out what they're doing here," Simon said, cutting to the chase.

"I am a little curious," Skye admitted, "but I really don't want their feelings to be hurt. That family has helped me more than once."

"So, go over there."

"Well, here's the tricky part." Skye smoothed her jacket. "Ah, I'm on great terms with Earl and the children, but Glenda's a little ticked at me."

"Why?"

"When I first moved back to town, she and I had words on proper parenting."

"At a school conference?"

"Not exactly," Skye acknowledged. "At

my brother's hair salon. The little ones were throwing rocks at Vince's glass sign, and I made them stop."

"And?"

"And Glenda didn't think I should have interfered. And some things were said."

"Interesting dilemma." A smile lurked at the corner of Simon's lips.

"Oh, well. Maybe she won't recognize me. Nothing ventured, nothing gained." Skye moved off in their direction, muttering to herself, "Whatever she does to me I'm in the right place; I'm already at a funeral parlor."

Skye approached Earl. "Hello, Mr. Doozier. Nice to see you again."

The thin man smiled, revealing missing teeth. "Miz Denison. What you doing here?"

"Sometimes kids get upset at wakes, so the school asked me to hang around in case any of the students need help." Skye slid a glance at the woman. "Hello, Mrs. Doozier."

"Don't think we met," the blonde answered.

"Baby, this is the lady from the school that me and Junior helped when her car went in the river a while back," Earl explained.

"Oh." Glenda, losing interest, turned to stare at two women whose heads were bent close together as they gossiped in low voices and occasionally sneaked peeks at the Dooziers.

"How about you and your family?" Skye asked. "Did you know Lorelei or her folks?"

"Nah, nothing like that." Earl pointed to Elvira, who was trying to ignore the whole situation. "You know Elvira here found the body. So it was only right we pay our last respects."

"That's very nice of you." Skye patted his arm, then regretted the gesture. Touching the tattoos was like touching the scales of a snake. "How is Elvira related to you?" She worded the question carefully, well aware of the Dooziers' reputation for inbreeding. Often fathers, brothers, and uncles were all the same people in that family.

"She's my youngest sister. Our folks done passed on, so she lives with us."

They had almost reached the front of the line. Skye moved between the two adults, and when their turn came, she said, "Mr. and Mrs. Ingels, this is Mr. and Mrs. Doozier. Their sister is the one who found Lorelei and tried to get help for her."

Earl pumped Allen Ingels's hand. "Sorry 'bout your little girl. When they find out who did this to her, you need any help, you call me. I'll bring my shotgun and my dog. We'll get that son of a —"

"And this is Elvira Doozier," Skye hurriedly interrupted, bringing her forward. "The girl we were talking about."

As Elvira looked at the Ingelses, her hostile, pierced, tattooed demeanor subtly softened. "I'm real sorry."

Allen nodded and moved back half a step, subtly distancing himself from the group.

"Thank you." Lorna took Elvira's hand and gazed intently into her eyes, as if seeking the answer to an ancient mystery. "Are you happy?"

Skye wondered what Lorna meant. Did she think her daughter had committed suicide?

Elvira's expression became uneasy. "Yes'm. Most of the time." She withdrew her hand and backed away.

"Good." After a moment Lorna said, "Thank you for coming." She turned to the next people in line, her brittle control firmly back in place.

As the Dooziers and Skye moved on, Earl announced, "I gotta use the can before we go."

"Me and the kids'll be waiting in the Regal," Glenda told her husband.

Earl nodded and went in search of relief.

Skye glanced at her watch. It was only seven-thirty. People were continuing to pour through the door. The scents of flowers, perfume, and sweat were closing up her sinuses. She needed a breath of fresh air.

Outside, the night was cool, and she wrapped her arms around herself as she gazed up at the moon. From where she stood on the sidewalk, she could hear the murmur of voices inside.

She was about to go back when Earl Doozier stepped through the doors. He had managed to spill water down his front, soaking the small potbelly that hung over his waistband.

He caught Skye staring at him and grinned. "When you've got a tool as good as mine, you have to build a shed over it." He patted both his upper and lower bulges for emphasis.

Half of her wanted to laugh, but the other half fought for a more dignified response. Before she could react either way, Glenda appeared out of nowhere and grabbed Earl's arm. "Too bad all that shade stunted your prize tool's growth."

Skye could hear the couple arguing as they walked to their car. She decided to return to the visitation, where it was relatively safe.

The line had finally stopped growing, and only a few stragglers remained. Skye glanced around. It was nearly eight, and there was no one left whom she knew. Time to retrieve her purse and go home.

She had left her handbag in the parlor off the visitation area. She made her way to the little room, but her purse wasn't there.

Shit! Where could it be? Surely, no one would steal it during a wake. Maybe it had slipped. Skye got on her hands and knees, and crawled between the chair and sofa. Still no sign of her bag. Could it have been kicked behind the couch?

She inched toward the wall and spotted it wedged between a sofa leg and the wood molding. As she reached for the clutch, she heard voices. People were standing in the doorway and didn't realize she was there.

Before she could speak, a voice she recognized as Mrs. VanHorn's fake Southern drawl said, "We are not canceling Saturday's pageant."

Lorna Ingels answered, "We'll see about that. I've made several calls, and everyone agrees the Miss Central Illinois contest

259

should be eliminated this year, and the title awarded posthumously to Lorelei."

"That's a bunch of crap. No one wants that but you. It wouldn't be fair to the other girls."

"Especially Zoë, who would finally have a slim chance at a real title." Venom oozed from Lorna's words.

Skye decided to wait quietly rather than embarrass the two women and herself by revealing her presence.

"If we should cancel Miss Central Illinois out of respect, why was it okay for Linette to compete for Junior Miss Stanley County last weekend?" Priscilla asked belligerently.

"That was entirely different. It had nothing to do with Lorelei, and it wouldn't have been fair to Linette to penalize her for her sister's death," Lorna replied smoothly.

"Well, it isn't fair to all the girls who have been getting ready for the Miss Central Illinois pageant for months. Not to mention the money their parents have spent," Priscilla retorted. "Anyway, they've never awarded an honorary crown in the history of the pageants, and no matter how many stupid calls you make, it isn't going to happen now."

"Never say never," Lorna said, as Skye

watched her feet move toward the door.

Priscilla followed. "What do you mean by that?"

"I have a call in to the governor," Lorna announced.

"So?"

"Didn't you know, dear? She's Allen's distant cousin."

Priscilla's reply was cut off as the woman moved away from the door. Skye crawled from her unintended hiding place, clutching her purse and thinking, *Isn't that an interesting tidbit?*

Chapter 15

Gasp at Flaws

Skye rolled her shoulders as she supervised the loading of the bus that would take the students to Lorelei's funeral. It had felt wonderful to get into the pool this morning before school, but after having missed a week's worth of morning swims, her muscles were protesting. She squinted into the ten o'clock sun. Wednesday had dawned clear and warm, with predicted temperatures in the seventies. It was the nicest day they'd had so far that spring. Too bad they'd be spending it at the cemetery.

The kids were subdued as they climbed the bus steps and found seats. Skye's gaze strayed to Troy, who had claimed the back bench. Zoë sat on his right and Farrah on his left. Both girls competed for his attention. Was he the father of Lorelei's baby? He certainly would have had a lot to lose if she had lived and insisted on having the child. Would Notre Dame have honored Troy's scholarship? It was a Catholic university. There might very well be a morals clause.

Rumor had it that Troy was desperate to get out of Scumble River, and Skye could certainly empathize with that desire. If he had been the father of Lorelei's baby, and her family exerted enough pressure, he might have been stuck in his hated hometown forever. Maybe he made up the story about Lorelei's other boyfriend.

"Ready to go?" The bus driver leaned through the open door and directed his question to Skye.

"Two of the chaperons aren't here yet. We'll wait a few minutes, then I'll go look for them."

"I got to be back for the kindergarten run at eleven-thirty."

"Okay." Skye went back to her musings, while keeping an eye on the school doors. Zoë and her mother had a lot of motive. She had never seen two more ruthless people. With Lorelei out of the way, Zoë could not only take over as "queen of the school," but she could also win some real money on the pageant circuit.

The quiet spring morning was assaulted by the clamor of the bell announcing that second period had begun. Trixie and Kent hurried out of the school and toward the bus.

Kent gave a mock salute as he and Trixie mounted the steps.

Skye climbed aboard after them and settled next to Trixie, saying to the driver, "Okay, we can leave now."

Kent had taken the empty seat next to Caresse, and soon the girl's giggles rang through the nearly silent vehicle.

The teens remained quiet through the brief ceremony at the church. They filed off the bus at the cemetery without talking, and stood in a semicircle around the open tent that had been erected over the grave.

Skye stood between Justin and Frannie. Both adolescents' presence worried her. While the boy's attendance was most likely due to curiosity and a desire to miss class, much the same as many of the kids who were there, the girl's participation was a little more ominous, considering her avowed hatred of Lorelei.

Justin said softly to Skye, "Did the copy of the autopsy give you any clues?"

Skye looked around uneasily. No one seemed to be paying attention to them. "We can't talk about that here."

The boy stiffened, his feelings obviously hurt. "Sure, just wondering."

His ability to form relationships was so fragile that in spite of her better judgment,

Skye told him, "You were a big help. But I want your promise you won't ever copy someone's private papers again." She ignored the tiny voice of conscience that was calling her a hypocrite.

Justin ducked his head in what Skye hoped was a nod of agreement. She heard him mutter, "Too bad it didn't include the tox screen."

Skye shot him a censorious look before moving away.

Homer and Charlie, who had come by car, made their way over to where Skye was standing.

Charlie whispered in her ear, "Any leads?"

"I've gathered a lot of information," she whispered back. "Lots of people with motives."

"Good." He gripped her hand. "Nothing that makes the school look bad, right?"

"No, not really, I guess." Skye wondered if the school would look bad if it turned out that Lorelei's boyfriend or best friend had killed her. Deep down, she was afraid the school would look bad whoever was found guilty, because the public would expect the school to have been clairvoyant, to have prevented Lorelei's death no matter what.

Skye's attention was drawn back to Frannie and Justin, who were whispering together. Frannie had a strange expression on her face. Skye thought the girl looked half scared, half satisfied.

Something Simon had said last night bubbled to the surface of Skye's thoughts. If Frannie's father, Xavier, had been a medic in the military, he probably knew about pharmaceuticals. Could Frannie have gotten her father talking and figured out what to give Lorelei to kill her? Or maybe Xavier got tired of the cheerleaders tormenting his daughter and took matters into his own hands.

The minister concluded the graveside ceremony by inviting everyone to say the Lord's Prayer. As she murmured the words, Skye's glance was drawn to Kent. He and Priscilla VanHorn stood some distance from the main crowd, and from the angry look on his face, Skye doubted they were praying.

She sighed. She knew she had been putting off talking to Kent. It would no doubt be awkward, especially since she had found out it was highly likely that Mrs. VanHorn's allegations were true — he probably was sleeping with Lorna Ingels. But did that give him a motive to murder Lorelei?

People were filing past the casket. Lately it had become the custom to take a flower from one of the floral arrangements at a funeral as a keepsake. Most of the kids were behaving appropriately, and Skye was only half-aware of their movements when she spotted Justin Boward reaching again and again into a spray of pink roses. When he plucked out the sixth blossom, several adults started buzzing and pointing.

Homer grabbed Skye's arm and hissed in her ear, "Stop that boy right now. Next thing we know all the kids'll be stripping the grave of every last flower."

She rolled her eyes but complied with the principal's demand. Something that would seem unimportant to most people, like taking a few extra roses, was a capital offense within the school system.

Skye cut Justin out of the herd as quietly as a sheepdog separates a lamb from the flock.

When they were well away from the others, she said, "You'll have to put those back. It's inappropriate for you to have taken so many."

The boy clutched the roses, reverting back to silence.

Skye took a breath and started again. "Maybe you didn't know, but the custom is for everyone to take only one flower, as a remembrance."

He shrugged. "It doesn't matter. Whatever I do is wrong."

Skye felt her heart sink. It was one step forward with this kid and two steps back. What had happened in his short life that had so thoroughly stripped him of his self-esteem?

She led the boy farther from the others. "Now, I know that's not true. But I also know that what I think doesn't matter. It's what you believe that counts." She stole a look at his face. It had relaxed a little. "Something I try to remember when I have negative thoughts about myself is that it takes a long time to become the person we want to be. It's not a road we can race down, but one we have to walk every step of the way."

Justin nodded slightly. "Didn't mean to do anything wrong."

"I know that."

He sniffed. "I saw everybody taking flowers, and my mom loves roses, and I just thought no one would miss a couple extra. She's been real sad lately."

"Okay, here's what we do. Give me the flowers, and I'll put them back. Then after school we'll go and get some nice fresh ones at Stybr's Florist. Okay?"

He nodded and thrust the bouquet into her arms. Skye walked back to the casket. Nearly everyone had left, heading back to town for the funeral luncheon. She quickly tucked the roses into one of the vases and hurried to the bus.

The students had already boarded, and their mood was now more relaxed. They had an air of having completed something, and now they were moving on.

Skye sat and listened as the bus inched its way forward, caught in a line of vehicles trying to exit the single-lane road.

One of the younger girls said to her seatmate, "Lorelei was so perfect. She was beautiful and smart and really, really nice to everyone. She reminded me of Princess Diana. Why do all the best people die?"

One of the senior girls turned and skewered the freshman with a look. "Lorelei was a real bitch. And it just galled me to see how she fooled all you children."

Another senior girl turned in her seat and joined in. "Yeah, all you saw was the Miss Goody Two-shoes act. You didn't see the dirty tricks she played to stay on top."

The first senior said, "I was doing Humorous Interpretation for the speech team. I'd finaled both my freshman and sopho-

269

more years and was sure I could win my junior year, but Lorelei decided she wanted to do Humor, and Miss Cormorant just shoved me into Prose."

"I know the feeling," another girl added. "I had a part in the musical, and during one of the rehearsals my lines got some laughs, and Sleeping Beauty wasn't the star for a minute and a half. Suddenly, my character had no dialogue."

Skye let the words whirl around her. It seemed as if Lorelei had fooled the teachers and the younger students, but the girls in her own class had seen her inner self. Instead of being Sleeping Beauty, maybe Lorelei had been the evil fairy.

That explained the lack of true grief Skye had witnessed while working with Lorelei's so-called closest friends. She had thought that the incident with Frannie not making cheerleading because of Lorelei was an isolated one, but it sounded like it was the norm.

The bus reached the main road and started to pick up speed. Skye twisted in her seat and tried to hear what Lorelei's clique was saying. Zoë was draped over Troy, whispering in his ear. He wore a goofy grin. Skye caught his eye and frowned, shaking her head. He pulled slowly away and said something to the girl. She shot Skye a malevolent look. Skye would take odds they hadn't been talking about Lorelei.

Caresse and Farrah were seated together, and Skye zeroed in on their conversation. "She was an angel. One time I broke my nail right before the big game, and she glued it back on for me. She even touched up the polish with her very own bottle."

Farrah nodded. "I know what you mean. Around Christmas I was gaining a little weight and she helped me. She took me aside and told me no one likes fat girls, and I'd better start doing what she did or I'd be as big as Fat Frannie."

Caresse looked horrified and asked in a breathless tone, "What did you do?"

"I did what she told me, of course." The teen shuddered. "Can you imagine getting like Fat Frannie? She must take a size twelve, maybe even a fourteen." Farrah patted her nonexistent hip. "I'm happy to say the Lorelei weight-loss plan put me right back into a size four."

Caresse shook her head. "You're satisfied with that?" She took out a mirror. "I'd just die if I got higher than a two."

"I really don't want to go to the funeral

luncheon," Skye repeated.

"Why not? You got to eat anyway, and it gives you a good excuse to psychoanalyze what people are saying," Charlie said, leaning both hands on her desk.

Skye smiled to herself. No matter how many times she explained, Charlie never quite seemed to understand what a psychologist could and couldn't do. He was convinced she was a cross between Houdini and Miss Marple.

She patted his hand. "You're going anyway, so you nose around and tell me what you find out."

"Do I look like a goddamn people person? No one's going to tell me anything."

Skye snorted. Yeah. Right. Like Charlie wasn't the best manipulator in the state. "I've got so much work to do. I've got thirteen more kids to test at the elementary school, four at the middle school, and a couple here. And starting May first, I have eight annual reviews scheduled every day for the rest of the year. On top of that, there's that crisis plan you've ordered me to develop."

"If you run out of time, we'll pay you to finish up during the summer."

Skye paled at the threat to her summer

vacation. "I've already agreed to work at the recreational club again this summer."

"We'll talk about that later," Charlie hedged. "Right now we should get going, or we'll miss most of the meal."

"You go ahead. I'll join you if I have time."

"Skye, sweetheart, I'm saying I really would like you to come along." A strange look crossed his face. "I've been having these pains."

Skye flew around the desk and guided him to a chair. "Pains? Where? How long? I'll call 911."

Charlie's blue eyes started to twinkle. "In my butt, from people hounding me ever since you found Lorelei's body."

Skye insisted on driving her own car to the luncheon, hoping she could sneak out early and get some testing done at the grade school in the afternoon.

The Ingelses were Lutheran, and since the Lutheran church had no hall, they'd been forced to make other arrangements. They had decided to have the funeral meal at the new country club, located halfway between the towns of Laurel and Scumble River.

As Skye turned into the long drive, she

saw golfers on both sides. All were in carts. So much for golf as a chance to exercise. She wondered how come so many people weren't working on a Wednesday in the middle of April. Then again, the lush, green gently rolling hills spoke of privilege and not working a nine-to-five kind of job.

She noticed several of the golfers had stopped to stare at her. What was going on? Had she forgotten to button something? Was her car on fire? Car, that explained it. A 1957 Chevrolet Bel Air at a country club probably stood out like a bikini at a church social. She fought the urge to sink below the dash and resolutely drove on.

The clubhouse was faced in cream-colored brick and sported huge floor-to-ceiling windows. Skye parked and hurried inside. To the right, the golf shop and offices ran the length of the building. The opposite wing was set up for the lunch.

The delicious scents of garlic and ginger wafted over Skye as she entered the banquet room. Against one wall was a salad bar, pasta and stir-fry station, and dessert table. Extremely unusual fare for a Scumble River funeral.

Skye wondered briefly what the Ingelses had done with all the food contributed by their neighbors and friends. Probably given it to the housekeeper.

Circular tables for eight were scattered around the room. Most people had already arrived, and many were grouped around the portable bar set up at the back of the room. Skye adjusted the sleeves of her navy blazer, made sure her white blouse was tucked in, and tugged down her skirt before joining the throng vying for a drink.

She was always a little nervous in this type of crowd and setting. It reminded her of the bittersweet time she'd spent in New Orleans, engaged to a wealthy young man, before her life collapsed and she found herself back in Scumble River.

A handsome man smiled at her as she joined the people milling around the room. "Hi, I don't believe we've met. I'm Troy Yates."

For a second Skye was taken aback, but she quickly figured this man had to be the father of the Troy Yates she knew. "Hello, I'm Skye Denison. I believe I know your son. I'm the psychologist at the high school."

"Right, right. You've talked to Troy Junior a couple of times since Lorelei died, right?"

"Yes." Skye wanted to know what this

guy did for a living and how he was connected to the Ingelses. "He's a nice boy. Very popular."

A strange look crossed the senior Troy's face. "Well, yes, in the sense that his peers like him, but he was faithful to Lorelei."

"I'm sure he was." Skye tucked that odd response away for later examination. "He and Lorelei must have made a striking couple."

"Troy was devoted to Lorelei. He would have never even considered dating another girl." A hand descended on the man's shoulder, and he jumped.

Allen Ingels stood there with a forced smile on his lips. "Glad to hear it, Yates. Wouldn't want to find out Junior had hurt Lorelei in any way."

"No, of course not, Allen." The senior Yates shook his head. "Troy would never do anything to cause Lorelei any pain."

Except possibly make her pregnant, thought Skye.

After Allen Ingels moved on, Skye asked Troy Senior, "Are you and the Ingelses friends? Is that how the kids got together?"

"Well, ah, yes and no. I work for Allen. I'm the bank's manager. Lorelei and Troy met at school." The man's handsome face was flushed. "Excuse me. Time for a refill."

So, both Troy and his family had a lot to lose if Lorelei's baby turned out to be his. Skye picked up a soft drink from a passing waiter's tray and moved to another knot of people.

"Ms. Denison, nice to see you. I wanted to thank you for all your help when Cassie was attacked by that hellion."

Cassie? Ah, she remembered her now. This was Mrs. Wren, the mother of the third-grade girl whose hair was cut off. "You're more than welcome. Is Cassie alright now?"

"It was a tremendous loss, but your brother did a wonderful job. Luckily she has a classically beautiful face and can wear any hairstyle." The woman leaned closer as if to impart a secret. "We decided to go with ringlets, and I think it's going to work. Since all the girls have long straight hair, she stands out from the crowd."

"I'm so glad." Skye was never sure how parents would take things. A few were grateful for her assistance, but most resented the need for it. "I can't imagine why the other girl thought it was okay to do what she did."

Mrs. Wren leaned even closer. "It's the mothers. They tell the daughters it's okay to do anything to win the title, get the part, dance the lead." She took a sip of her martini. "I've seriously considered taking both Cassie and Caresse out of the competition."

"Really?"

"Yes, but I decided against it. I mean, why make my girls quit? Unlike many of the other children, they really have talent and a good chance to make it professionally."

"I see your point," Skye said. Every mother thought her child was special.

"Lorna Ingels is a good example of the type of mother I was talking about." Mrs. Wren looked around, and must have decided it was safe to go on. "Lorelei was bad enough, but she had a soft spot and would at least help out her friends. That Linette is downright scary. She'll do anything to get ahead. And you know, at her age it's got to be the mother behind it."

"Is Cassie in the pageants with Linette?" Skye fought to contain her excitement. This was important information.

"No, she didn't like beauty pageants as much as dance, and her agent didn't think they were all that advantageous, since she was already getting commercial spots," Mrs. Wren bragged.

"So, what has Linette done to ensure that she wins?" Skye asked, getting back to the subject that most interested her.

"Mmm." The woman narrowed her eyes. "Well, she spies on the other girls, then tells on them."

"That must be pretty annoying."

"And she steals parts of their costume or makeup or equipment."

"Why doesn't she get kicked out for that?" asked Skye.

"No one's caught her so far, but we know she's behind it." Mrs. Wren took another slug of her drink. "Once, she passed out chocolates that had Ex-Lax mixed into them. Most of the girls had to miss portions of the pageant. Some even had accidents on stage. It was awful."

"Surely she was disqualified that time."

"Nope. She was smart enough to eat some herself and claimed the box of candy had been an anonymous gift." The woman leaned even closer and a wave of gin breath washed over Skye. "But I noticed that Linette didn't eat hers until after she had competed, so she didn't miss any of the pageant."

"That sounds pretty devious for a ten-year-old." Skye backed a few feet away. "How did you decide it wasn't her mother behind the sabotage?"

"Lorna usually had an alibi for the time the incidents took place." The woman pursed her lips. "Of course, they probably work together." Mrs. Wren finished her drink and looked toward the bar. "I need another. Excuse me."

Skye spotted Charlie sitting at a table with some of his cronies. She was getting hungry, so she filled a plate from the food stations and brought it over to where they were seated.

The owner of the real-estate agency was speaking. "A murder in the town's school is not good for property values. I haven't sold one house since the Ingels girl was killed. You need to do something, Charlie."

Mayor Clapp joined in. "Yeah, it isn't a good image for this town. We pride ourself on having safe schools."

Skye decided it was time to interrupt when Charlie's face turned redder than his suspenders. "Hi. Mind if I join you?"

The men moved over to make room for her. An extra chair was snagged from an adjacent table.

As she seated herself, Charlie said, "What's that stuff you're eating?"

"Mixed green salad, angel hair pasta

with sun-dried tomatoes and olive oil, and a vegetable and tofu stir-fry." Skye paused with her fork halfway to her mouth. "Want some?"

"Hell, no," Charlie bellowed. "I didn't climb to the top of the food chain to be a vegetarian."

"Eating a meatless meal every once in a while does not mean you're a vegetarian," Skye said, exasperated. "And being a vegetarian is not a contagious disease. Consuming a portion of tofu won't make you allergic to steak."

Charlie frowned and got up from the table. "Very funny. I'm getting some dessert. Unless they've done something weird to that, too."

Chapter 16

If the Clue Fits

It was close to two-thirty before Skye was able to break away from the funeral lunch. She was already on her way to the grade school when she remembered her plan to attend cheerleading practice that afternoon. Looking down at her suit, she realized she needed to go home and change, again. Making an abrupt U-turn — not an easy maneuver in a car the size of Rhode Island — she turned toward her cottage.

After putting on black sweatpants and an orange University of Illinois T-shirt, Skye fed Bingo and headed to school. The dismissal bell was ringing when she arrived, which meant she had a few minutes before she needed to meet Trixie.

The main office was crowded and noisy with teachers and students getting ready to go home. Skye emptied her mailbox and ducked into the empty health room to skim her messages. Most were from parents or staff, and nothing was marked urgent. She'd return the calls tomorrow.

One slip of yellow paper caught her eye. It was from Thea, the daytime police dispatcher. What could she want?

Skye reached for the phone. "Thea? Hi, it's Skye."

"I can't talk now. Call me back in ten minutes."

"Thea, what's going on?" Skye figured her mom had found out some important information on the murder and wanted Thea to tell her about it ASAP.

"Call me back," Thea repeated.

"Okay. Look, Thea, sorry I can't call back then, because I'll be coaching the cheerleaders." Skye spoke quickly, sure Thea was about to hang up. "Tell Mom I'll stop by after practice."

"No —" Thea started to speak. "Sorry, got to go. Bye."

That had been weird. Skye chewed on her lower lip. What was up with Thea? She'd stop by the station after practice and find out. Right now it was time to learn some new cheers.

She found Trixie and her merry band of cheerleaders in the girls' locker room. "Hi."

"Hi, we'll be out in a minute. The girls are just changing." Trixie was dressed in a plain white leotard and sweatpants. "Let's wait in the gym. The process takes a while."

The two women settled themselves on a bleacher.

Skye asked, "How's Owen doing?"

The question about her husband brought a scowl to Trixie's face. "How would I know? It's spring. He's getting the machinery and fields ready for planting. He's up before dawn and doesn't drag his butt home until after dark. The only way I know he's still living in the house is that the dishes of food I leave in the oven are empty when I come back."

"Yeah, it's a tough time of year. Dad and my uncles are the same way."

"I'm beginning to think there isn't a good time of year for farmers. Owen was always a hard worker, but now that we — and the bank — own the land, he's obsessive." Trixie popped off the bench.

"He'll be better in a month or so," Skye said, following her.

"I doubt it. Hey, did you hear this joke? How many men does it take to screw in a lightbulb? One. He just holds it up there and waits for the world to revolve around him." Trixie stuck her head in the locker room. "Five-minute warning."

Skye was still snickering as the cheerleading squad filed out. They wore warmup suits of silver and black, and carried matching pom-poms. The back of each jacket was embroidered with a black widow spider.

Skye stiffened. The pom-poms. It wasn't a piece of tinsel that Wally had found on the gym floor. It was a strand from a pompom. Had it been there from the last cheerleaders' practice? Or had it been clinging to the clothes of the killer?

Trixie's voice interrupted Skye's thoughts. "Most of you know Ms. Denison, the school psychologist. She's going to help me out today."

The nine girls started talking.

"Quiet." Trixie continued, "I'll take the junior varsity and Ms. Denison will take the senior squad."

Skye grabbed Trixie's arm and whispered fiercely in her ear, "I don't know what to do."

Sotto voce, Trixie said, "Just have them run through their routines."

"I don't know their routines. I was never a cheerleader."

Trixie shrugged. "Have them do cheers one, five, seven, and ten. Watch their timing, their smiles, their voice levels. Just have them do it again and again until it looks perfect."

Skye took the scrunchie from her wrist and put her hair into a ponytail. She was already starting to sweat.

Her squad, which consisted of Zoë, Caresse, Farrah, and a raven-haired girl she didn't know, had gathered at the end of the gym nearest the stage. They were doing stretches and talking.

Skye sat on the steps to the stage and listened. Zoë was saying to the unknown teen, "Boy, Tara, you've really missed it. Why didn't you go to the funeral today?"

Tara answered, "Hey, I just got back into town at noon. I only came to school at all so I could come to practice."

Farrah joined them. "How was California?"

"Wonderful."

"I can't believe your parents let you take two weeks off of school to go on vacation with them," Caresse interjected.

"They don't like going during the regular spring break. Too many college kids, and the prices are all doubled," Tara said, then lowered her voice. "Plus, Dad had a job interview, but no one is supposed to know. He doesn't like the way things are going at the bank."

Skye perked up. Something funny at the bank. Could Charlie be right about Allen Ingels being involved in something fishy?

Caresse, obviously not interested in something as mundane as jobs, asked, "Did you meet any movie stars?"

Skye got up from her perch. If the teens wouldn't talk about anything interesting, they'd have to practice. "Okay, girls, please take your positions for cheer number one."

"Aren't we going to elect a new captain?" Caresse asked.

"I'll ask Mrs. Frayne about that later," Skye answered.

Zoë put her hands on her hips. "I should be the captain. I got the most votes after Lorelei."

"I'm sure Mrs. Frayne will do what's fair."

Zoë shot Skye a poisonous look. They practiced for half an hour, then took a break. The girls dug out water bottles and towels from their tote bags. Trixie and Skye sat on the bleachers and supervised.

Skye explained to Trixie Zoë's concern over who would be captain. Trixie answered, "We need to hold tryouts for two new members of the squad anyway, and I'm not electing a new captain until we have a full team."

"Zoë seems certain she'll be it." Skye kept one ear tuned to the girls, but they were discussing prom dresses, not Lorelei.

"She may. Most of these girls are fairly impressed by the superficial."

"Well, to be fair, most teens are. It's one of those lessons they have to learn before becoming grown-ups." Skye paused. "What worries me after meeting their moms is that they don't have good role models at home."

"Are you going to the pageant Saturday?" Trixie asked, bringing up a tangential subject.

"I want to, but I haven't thought of a good reason to be there."

"No more convenient cousins, huh?" Trixie teased.

"No. None of my relatives have girls entered in the Miss Central Illinois contest. I asked Gillian if she thought I could get away with just hanging around backstage on my own, and she said the security guards would throw me out."

"Sounds like you'll have to just go sit in the audience."

"I suppose. You want to come along?"

"Love to, but my in-laws are spending the weekend."

"Maybe Mom's not working," Skye said.

"She'd probably enjoy going."

Trixie unfolded herself from the bleachers and stood. "Okay, girls, let's give it another half hour."

Skye moved off to watch her squad.

After the girls finished and returned to the locker room to change, Trixie said to Skye, "Now's the time to eavesdrop. All that physical activity really gets them going."

"I hate to go in there while they're showering and dressing. That was one of my major gripes about PE — being watched by a fully dressed adult while I was naked." Skye shuddered. "I swear Miss Lake was a ghoul or something. She was so grotesque."

"Oh, I remember her," Trixie replied. "That was one of the good things about moving. My new PE teacher sat in her office and monitored us by how loud we got." Trixie grinned. "It was the quietest locker room I've ever been in." She paused for effect. "Which is how I discovered if you sit by the vent in the PE office, you can hear just about everything that's said in the locker room."

"Cool." Skye headed in that direction. "Do the girls know?"

"No."

Skye settled into the office chair she had positioned next to the vent and listened, resolving to forget immediately anything she heard that wasn't relevant to Lorelei's death.

At first the girls chatted about clothes, makeup, and music, but finally Skye heard: "I can't believe none of the adults have caught on that Lorelei was sleeping with a teacher."

"You mean . . . ?" This voice was too low for Skye to hear the rest of what was said.

"No, she means . . ." a different girl whispered, and Skye missed who they were talking about.

The shower came on and Skye couldn't hear anymore. She was half out of the chair, trying to get closer to the vent, when the door slammed open. The glass rattled as the frame banged into the wall. Skye's heart skipped a beat, and her breath caught in her lungs. Her eyes widened as Wally strode into the office, a pained expression on his face. He spoke without inflection. "Get up."

She rose as if in a trance. The pulse in her neck felt as if it were beating at ten times the normal rate. "Wha— ?"

He gently swung her around and cuffed her before she could complete the word.

Then he spoke the dreaded words, "Skye Denison, you're under arrest for theft. You have the right to remain silent."

Part of her listened to Wally recite the rights that were familiar to anyone who watched TV cop shows, while the other part noticed that Trixie had rounded up the girls and was leading them more than a gossip's length away.

"Wally, are you crazy? How can you do this to me? What's going on?" Skye protested.

The chief ignored her questions, marching her out the side door and into the back of his squad car. She wondered how many people were watching and felt her chest tightening. This was humiliating. He buckled her into the seat belt and got into the front seat. She leaned as far forward as she could and tried again to ask what was going on.

He cut her off. "We'll talk at the station."

What had she done? The short ride was excruciating. What was happening? Her emotions ranged from outrage to fear, and back again.

Wally parked the squad car in the police garage and after unbuckling the seat belt, eased her from the vehicle. He remained silent. Sheer black fright swept her as he marched her through the station.

He grunted to the dispatcher as they passed by. "Call the county jail for a matron."

He deposited her in the coffee/interrogation room and locked the door behind him. Icy fear twisted around her heart. She had never seen Wally this way. And to drag her out of school in handcuffs — this was bad, this was very bad. Skye tried to retrieve the anger she had initially felt over her treatment, but she was too scared.

Then it dawned on her. The dispatcher was some woman she didn't know. Where was her mother? She was supposed to be working. Why had they gotten rid of May? That frightened her most of all.

Finally, she forced herself to focus. What did they think she'd done? Theft. What had been stolen? Should she call a lawyer?

After what felt to Skye like the longest wait in her life, Wally walked back into the room. He motioned for her to stand, and directing her with a hand on her upper arm, led her up the stairs and into his office. The decor had not improved since her last visit. It was still drab with faded blue linoleum, a metal desk, and vinyl-covered chairs. The smell of stale tobacco was finally fading, but even after several years of a smokeless occupant, traces lingered. A silent matron sat in a corner with a notepad.

Wally and Skye both settled into chairs. By this point, Skye was beginning to feel numb.

The chief flipped open a file and said, "A theft was reported this afternoon."

"And you're accusing me?"

"That's right. You're my primary suspect." Wally spoke like a machine, and he looked as if he had a migraine.

"This is ridiculous," sputtered Skye.

"It's a serious crime."

"Oh, my God." Skye was beginning to feel nauseous. "I'd better call my attorney."

The chief nodded. "That might be a good idea. But if you do, we have to sit here until she arrives. In fact, you could end up in jail, waiting to hear about bonds and things like that once you get a lawyer involved."

Could he really do that? Skye felt a shiver of panic run up her back. "But I haven't done anything!" She fought to calm down. "Why do you suspect me?"

"Because the stolen object is something others would have limited interest in."

She searched anxiously for the meaning

behind his words. "What was stolen? What would only I be interested in?"

"Your innocent act is really good," Wally said disdainfully. "You know what was taken."

"No, no I don't," Skye replied in a small, frightened voice. "What was it?"

"A copy of Lorelei Ingels's tox report was stolen from the coroner's mail today." The chief's lip curled. "Simon Reid returned to the funeral home after Lorelei Ingels's services at approximately twelve-thirty. He retrieved his mail from the box at that time and glanced through the pile, noting it contained an envelope from the forensics lab. He put the mail on his desk and went about his business. At approximately two o'clock he went to get the envelope. It was gone. After questioning his assistant and calling the lab, he phoned me."

Skye wondered if Simon had mentioned her midnight adventure at his funeral home and decided she'd better act as if he hadn't. "That's it? You're accusing me of this crime just because I had motive? Others have motive, too, you know. Lorelei's killer for instance."

Wally's sighed. "We do have other evidence."

Skye felt a flicker of apprehension. "What?"

"A witness driving by saw a female of your general build, with brown wavy hair, coming out of the funeral home at close to one o'clock this afternoon."

"What do you mean, my 'general build'?"

Wally's eyes dropped. "Not thin."

"Fat."

"That wasn't what the woman said." Wally didn't look up.

This seemed to embarrass him, but she wasn't about to let the matter pass. "What exactly did she say?"

"She said she saw a big girl coming out of the funeral home."

"She used the word 'girl'?"

He consulted his notes. "Yeah, but the lady was about ninety. Anyone under sixty would be a girl to her."

"I see. And she said brown hair?" Skye asked.

The chief nodded.

"Well, I can see you have never really looked at me. I have chestnut-colored hair."

"Look, try to wiggle out of this any way you can, but the description fits you." Wally crossed his arms.

Skye straightened her spine and assumed a dignified pose. "Perhaps, but you said the report was stolen between twelve-thirty and two o'clock. Probably closest to one o'clock."

"Yes."

"I have an alibi for those times." Skye took her first deep breath since he'd accused her of the crime. "I was at the Thistle Creek Country Club for Lorelei's funeral lunch. Several parents spoke to me, as did Charlie."

Diverse emotions battled for prominence on the chief's face — relief among them. "Give me those names."

After she listed everyone she could remember speaking to, Wally said to the matron, "Escort her to the coffee room. Do not let her talk to anyone, including yourself."

Skye's relief was so great she felt a silly hysteria creeping over her. If her hands hadn't still been cuffed, she would've saluted Wally. "Yes, sir."

In the other room she sat staring at the coffeemaker and the soda-pop machine. *Who did steal that report?* She prayed it wasn't Justin. If he did it, she was morally to blame. But if the witness was right, it couldn't have been the boy. Who else would want the tox report — aside from the murderer, that is?

The dispatcher's voice penetrated Skye's thoughts. "The chief says to take the cuffs off of her and bring her back upstairs."

Wally was slouched back in his chair, looking relaxed, when she entered his domain. He spoke to the matron. "Thanks for your help. You can go now."

Skye fought to keep her voice normal. "So, do my alibis check out?" She wasn't sure if he was in a better mood because he had cleared her or because he had found more reason to think she was guilty.

"Yes, lucky for you, you and your car seem to be quite memorable."

"Can I go?" Skye asked, rubbing her wrists.

"Yes." Wally leaned forward, appearing a little less confident. "Look, I know you've probably been snoo— investigating, so since I was wrong about you stealing the tox report, I'm going to give you one 'get out of jail free' card."

"What are you talking about?"

"This is your chance to fill me in on anything you've discovered that you think I should know, *and* it's your chance to ask me some questions."

She thought quickly. "In other words,

you have diddly-squat on the investigation, and you want to see if I can give you a lead."

He retained his newfound affability, but there was a distinct hardening of his eyes. "If that's how you want to interpret my generous gesture, you're free to leave."

"I'll take that as a yes." Skye hated having to back down. She knew she was right about his motives, but May had taught her a long time ago not to bite off her nose to spite her face. Besides, Wally had just screwed up royally, and she wasn't about to let him forget it. She smiled and said, "Here's what I want: For every piece of information I give you, you answer a question for me. Deal?"

He nodded.

"Also, you call Homer and the superintendent, and tell them I've been completely cleared."

He nodded again.

"Okay. Let's see, what have I found out? One, Lorelei was far from the saint the teachers seem to think she was. Many students are not sad that she's gone."

"Anyone in particular?"

Skye frowned. She had to separate what the teens had told her during counseling, which she couldn't reveal, from what she had overheard. "Zoë VanHorn benefits greatly from Lorelei's death." She couldn't mention Frannie, as her revelation had been with the expectation of confidentiality. And she couldn't mention Troy because she wasn't supposed to know of Lorelei's pregnancy.

"Interesting." The chief made a note. "What's your first question?"

"Were you ever allowed to search Lorelei's room?"

"No, we're still trying to get a warrant."

"Okay, info number two. Mrs. Ingels and Linette both have reputations for being willing to do anything to win a beauty pageant." Skye crossed her legs.

"That has no bearing on Lorelei's murder. No question for you."

Her lips thinned. "Be that way. How about Mrs. VanHorn? She's bound and determined to have Zoë take over everything that Lorelei had. I've heard her threatening the director of the musical and Mrs. Ingels. And you may not realize how much money is involved with the pageants those girls compete in."

"I'll accept that as relevant. What's your second question?"

"Have you searched Lorelei's school locker?"

The chief sighed. "No, we're still waiting for a warrant for that, too."

"Third, I overheard a bunch of Lorelei's closest girlfriends talking about the teacher she was sleeping with. I didn't get a name because you arrested me at just that moment."

"We didn't have any hint of that." Wally looked a little sheepish. "Too bad you didn't hear who it was."

"Yeah." Skye decided it wasn't a good idea to pursue that line of thought. "There are only so many male teachers, which narrows it down." Skye paused, remembering what the little girl who cut off the other kid's braid had said. "Or, maybe the teachers weren't necessarily male, and not necessarily from the school. She had a lot of dance, voice, and drama teachers, too."

"Very interesting. Question three?"

"How are people's alibis holding up?"

"Without the results of the tox screen, we haven't been sure how long whatever she was given takes to work. But according to the medical examiner, she could have been given the doctored drink at any time and consumed it hours later. That means no one has an alibi."

Skye had one more question, but couldn't think of anything else to trade.

She tried passing speculation as information. "Last, the Ingelses are a strange family. The little sister is spooky. She reminds me of the girl in that movie, *The Bad Seed*."

"You think the little girl might have killed her sister?"

"No." What she really wondered was if Mr. Ingels had been molesting Lorelei and then turned to Linette. But it would be irresponsible for her to suggest such a possibility without some evidence. "But maybe her parents think so. Maybe that's why they're fighting so hard for you not to search Lorelei's room. Maybe they're afraid there's some proof." Or maybe Mr. Ingels was hiding his own sins.

"Interesting, but pure conjecture. No question."

"Okay." Skye suddenly remembered her discovery during cheerleading practice. "How about this? That piece of tinsel you found in the gym the day Lorelei died — it's probably part of a pom-pom."

Wally made a note. "Thanks. Next question?"

"Did you ever find out what the bottle with the pill fragments originally contained?"

"No, we've looked in all the stores in

Scumble River, Clay City, Brooklyn, and even Laurel. Nothing matches." The chief stood. "I'm sending someone to Kankakee tomorrow."

Skye got up, too. "Good luck finding out who stole the report. I assume another is being mailed — as we speak."

"No. I just made Simon a copy of the one I received. The lab sends the reports to both of us."

Damn! If she had known that, she could have used one of her questions to get the results of the tox screen. She tried the casual approach. "What were the results?"

The chief smiled, not fooled for a moment. "Sorry, you've used up all your questions for today."

She didn't bother to suppress her loud groan. Oh well, maybe his victory would improve their relationship.

Chapter 17

Keep a Watchful Lie

Considering everything, Skye felt surprisingly pleased as she went down the police-station stairs. True, being arrested had been a terrifying and humiliating experience, but now she and the chief were even. How could he remain ticked off at her after he had wrongly accused her of committing a crime? To add to her sense of well-being, she had been able to share her information with Wally, so he couldn't accuse her later of hiding evidence, plus she'd gotten answers to some of her questions. Too bad she messed up and didn't ask about the tox-screen results. But all in all, not a bad few hours' work. Good thing she tended to see the glass as half-full and not half-empty.

She glanced at her watch. Past seven. Maybe she should have suggested to Wally that they get something to eat. She'd check with the dispatcher to see what time he went off duty when she asked about her mother's whereabouts.

Almost whistling, she pushed open the dispatch door and smiled at the unfamiliar woman sitting behind the radio panel. "Hi, I'm Skye Denison, May's daughter. I thought she was on duty tonight. Do you know what happened?"

"No, they don't tell us part-timers much. Just got a call about three to come in." The woman indicated the phone. "Want to call your mama?"

"Thanks." As she dialed, Skye asked, "Do you know when the chief gets off work?"

The dispatcher started to answer, but her radio blared to life and she held up a finger indicating just a minute.

Meanwhile, Skye's call went through. "Mom, why aren't you working?"

"Hello to you too," May said. "I got a call this afternoon saying the schedule had been screwed up, and I wasn't on until tomorrow. Why?"

Interesting. Obviously Wally had finagled to keep May off-site. He'd learned something since the last time he had dealt with their family, when he had tried to interrogate her brother, and Skye and her mother had foiled his scheme by getting a lawyer there pronto.

Skye told May what had happened. Her

304

mother was not amused, and Skye almost pitied Wally. A verbal bloodbath would almost certainly take place tomorrow afternoon when May came on duty. Before hanging up she invited May to go with her to the pageant on Saturday. May said she'd consider it.

As Skye finished her call, the dispatcher asked, "You were asking about the chief?"

"Right."

"I think he was supposed to be out of here a half hour ago." The woman pointed to the window that opened onto the waiting area. "That lady's been waiting at least that long for him."

Skye felt a twinge in her chest as she stared at the person the dispatcher indicated. Seated on the vinyl sofa was Abby Fleming — school nurse, Vince's ex-girlfriend, and one of the most beautiful women in Scumble River.

It had been a long day. Skye resisted the desire to tell Charlie about her false arrest and have him yell at the chief, but she did phone Trixie. She was the one person who would listen to her woes without trying to fix them.

Toward the end of their conversation, Skye tried to be magnanimous, and said,

"Well, maybe Wally has learned something from all this. Now he'll have to admit how easy it is to do something against your common sense in the heat of an investigation."

Trixie wasn't convinced. "Men always think what they do is fine, but heaven forbid us women make mistakes."

"I think it's a sign of progress that he's dating again," Skye commented, closing her eyes in pain as she forced herself to utter the words.

Trixie snorted. "A hard-on does not count as personal growth."

Trust Trixie to get to the heart of the matter. Skye laughed so loud she scared Bingo, who hid under the bed for twenty minutes after she hung up.

Sleep came in snatches, punctuated by horrible dreams. Finally, at five, she gave up and got out of bed. Her head felt fuzzy, and it took an effort to walk across the room. She dug through her dresser drawer for her swimsuit and pulled it on.

After packing what she would need to wear for the school day, and feeding the cat, she slid into the Bel Air. The aqua car made her feel as if she should be wearing a formal gown and tiara, and waving to the crowd along a parade route.

Skye tried to swim three or four mornings a week, but the Lorelei crisis had interrupted her routine. When it was cold she swam at the high school before the day started. In the summer she used the Scumble River recreational club, a lake formed from a reclaimed coal mine.

Today she was earlier than usual and felt a chill run up her spine as she entered the empty building. There hadn't been a single car in the lot — even the janitor hadn't arrived yet.

A few years ago, when the district received some money from a neighboring nuclear power plant, they added a pool to one side of the gym. Instead of using the funds for new books or more teachers, the school board had been hoodwinked by a fast-talking salesman and a group of parents with their own agendas. It was the one time in anyone's memory that the board had voted against Charlie. Allen Ingels had supported the pool. Because of this, Skye always had mixed feelings when she used the facility.

The only entrance to the pool was through the locker rooms. Today she slowed as she entered the girls' side, daunted by the lingering memory of being dragged out in handcuffs. Her face reddened, and she cringed at the thought that she would be the focus of gossip du jour.

A picture on one of the cheerleader's lockers distracted her. Skye leaned in for a better look. It was a head shot of a girl, presumably the locker's owner. Skye wondered what that was all about. She'd have to ask Trixie.

The scent of chlorine overpowered the smell of sweat as Skye unlocked the door to the pool. Dropping her belongings on a chair, she eased out of the sweat suit she wore over her maillot and slipped into the water. The cool liquid washed her cares away.

She knew she shouldn't swim alone, which is why she didn't dive or go into the deeper areas. Instead she swam laps until she was tired, then floated on her back.

A second after she heard a splash, she felt a wave. She was struggling to stand when a blond head popped up beside her.

"Kent! You scared me to death. What are you doing here?" She treaded water as she tried to move back into a shallower area.

His smile appeared forced. "Long time, no see. I thought perhaps you were avoiding me. So when I noticed your car, and remembered you mentioning swimming in the morning, I decided to join you. Hope I'm not intruding."

You just happened to have a bathing suit in your car? Right. As to his intruding, this wasn't the time or the place to tell Kent Walker what she really thought of him.

"I guess we've both been distracted." Kent ran his hand up and down her arm.

She let the water move her out of his reach. "Every time I've seen you, it seems Priscilla VanHorn has been with you. Or some other female parent."

"I never would have thought you were the jealous type." His voice held a hint of smugness.

"I'm full of surprises." *And you're overdue for one of them.* Skye moved away even farther from him. "I want to do a few more laps."

As she swam, she considered the situation. It was time to tell Kent they were finished, that she knew about Lorna. But before she did, she had a few questions for him regarding Lorelei's death and his affair with her mother.

Using the ladder, she climbed out of the pool. She had always lacked the upper body strength to boost herself up on the side using only her arms.

After gathering her stuff, she stood at the

edge, and said, "Come for dinner tonight and we'll talk things over." She forced herself to sound friendly. Her plan was to lull him into a false sense of security before she interrogated him.

Kent swam over to the side. "Sorry. I'm tied up tonight and tomorrow with rehearsals for *Sleeping Beauty*. How about Saturday?"

"I'm going to the Miss Central Illinois pageant with my mom on Saturday. How about Sunday at six?"

"Six, Sunday night, sounds good. See you then." It would be a dinner Kent would not soon forget. Surprisingly, Skye hadn't felt the betrayal she would have expected from finding out the man she was dating was sleeping with a married woman. What she felt was stone-cold anger. Kent Walker was going to pay.

While Skye showered, she thought about Lorelei's murder. She finally had some facts now that she had seen the autopsy report and talked to Wally. The teen had been given a bottle of something that contained crushed pills of some sort, which seemed to have caused her death. Two things Skye needed to know: Who gave Lorelei that drink, and what type of pills were they?

Finding out what that bottle originally contained might help. Sometime over the weekend she would drive to Bolingbrook and visit the Meijer Superstore. If that megamart didn't have the brand, no one would.

She also wanted to take a look at the school's visitors' sign-in sheet. Odds were that Wally had already checked it out, but she might spot something he hadn't noticed. Not that she thought a murderer would voluntarily comply with school policy, but signing in was one rule that the secretary strictly enforced. Opal had been known to chase people down the hall if they failed to stop in the office and leave their signatures.

Skye continued mulling over the murder as she finished applying her makeup and stepped into her dress. What else was she missing? There was no lack of motives. Fear of what Lorelei's pregnancy would reveal or require. Jealousy of what Lorelei had and others wanted. Hatred for things Lorelei had done.

But how could Skye find out whose motive was the strongest? A child's room could tell you a lot, but then, so could her locker. There was no way to search Lorelei's room, but getting a peek at her locker should be a piece of cake.

Skye slid on a pair of pumps and grabbed her tote bag. School would start in ten minutes, and she wanted to be in the main office when it did.

On her way, she hurriedly deposited her belongings in the guidance room. She had just greeted Opal when the first bell rang. Immediately the poor secretary became inundated with students. They swarmed the counter while the harried woman wrote passes, collected money, and checked permission slips.

The staff lined up to empty their mailboxes, photocopy one last paper, and look something up in the files. Amid this confusion, no one noticed Skye slide the master key to the lockers into her pocket. She'd be fine unless some kid couldn't get his door open and Opal tried to find the key. But it was April, and even those who were not the sharpest pencil in the cup should remember their combinations by now.

Skye headed nonchalantly back to her room. All she needed was to get into the locker banks at a time when the hallways were empty. How difficult could that be?

"Ms. Denison, Ms. Denison. Do you have a moment?"

Skye jerked back from Lorelei's locker and turned to face the art teacher. "Why, of course, Ms. Lowe. I was, ah . . . just looking for my earring. I dropped it this morning." Skye's hand went to her ear and she palmed the pearl stud she wore.

"I'll help you look."

"No, that's okay. I can do it later. What did you want to see me about?"

The art teacher fiddled with a stack of papers she held. "I'd like you to take a look at some drawings that disturb me."

"Sure." The woman looked as if she had just stepped out of *Glamour.* Skye had to fight the urge to tug at her skirt and check her hair.

In the art room, the teacher spread out six large sheets of paper. "I asked the kids to take a word as their trademark, and use it in a logo."

"Wow, what a neat idea. Ever since I started working here I've admired what you have the kids do."

"Thanks." The art teacher brushed an imaginary fleck from her red designer suit. "I was trained in New York."

Before she could stop herself, Skye blurted, "How did you end up in Scumble River?"

The woman smiled enigmatically. "If ru-

313

mors are true, you and I might have taken similar routes." Tapping a picture with a polished red nail, the art teacher continued, "Do you find these at all disturbing?"

Skye leaned in for a closer look. Most were obvious in their attempt to be shocking. The kids had drawn weapons, people exploding, and the occasional swastika, but one picture in particular seemed different, more unsettling.

The artist had taken the word "self" and put it in front of a mirror. The original "self" was colored in pretty pastels and had flowers and hearts intertwined with the letters. The reflected word was done in thick black marker. Jagged pieces had broken off the letters, and drops of crimson were splattered on the mirror surface.

"The others are fairly typical for certain adolescent types," Skye said, "but who did this one?"

The teacher turned the paper over and peeled away a flap. "I have the kids cover their names, so my grading is not tainted by my personal opinion of that student."

"That's a great idea." Skye was sincere in her praise, but anxious to know the identity of the anguished artist.

"Lorelei Ingels," the woman read, then pressed her hand to her chest. "Oh, my. Maybe if I had graded these earlier, Lorelei would be alive today."

"No," Skye said sharply. "That's not how it works. Besides, Lorelei did not commit suicide, she was murdered."

"Right. I forgot for a moment."

"Could I borrow this for a while? I'll try making a copy, and then I'd like to show it to the police."

"Sure. Thanks for looking at them." Ms. Lowe opened her door just as the bell rang.

Skye glanced at the clock in the guidance office. Nearly time for the dismissal bell, and she had already been foiled three times in her attempt to open Lorelei's locker in private. As soon as the kids left, the janitors would be everywhere, emptying trash cans, vacuuming floors, washing marks from the walls. She'd have to wait until tomorrow to try again.

Once again the office was busy, this time with students who were collecting materials that had to be taken home. The hubbub allowed Skye to slip the master locker key back on its hook undetected. She had one more mission to accomplish

— take a look at the sign-in sheets — then she would call it a day. As soon as Opal turned to answer the phone, Skye scooped up the book and took it into the health room.

As she sat down at Abby's desk, an image of the nurse and Wally on a date flashed through Skye's mind. She cringed, then firmly pushed that thought away. She leafed through the pages until she came to a week ago Wednesday.

Almost all the names were those of parents, including Mrs. VanHorn, Mrs. Ingels, Mrs. Wren, and Mrs. Miles. The cheerleader moms must have had a meeting that morning. She'd have to ask Trixie about that. There had been a couple of delivery people, and a service person for the copying machine, but no one out of the ordinary.

Feeling defeated, Skye left school. As she turned out of the parking lot, Skye realized that she had forgotten to check her box for messages. She hesitated, but the car in back of her honked, and she drove on. Surely if there was something that needed her immediate attention, she'd have been told about it by now. The principals were not shy in making their needs known.

Coming to that conclusion, she headed

toward the police station to drop off Lorelei's drawing. Neither Wally nor May were on duty, so she wrote a note, put it with the picture in a manila envelope, and handed it to the dispatcher to give to the chief. Next she stopped at the grocery store to pick up ingredients for Sunday night's dinner. She was going to make all the dishes she knew Kent would loathe. She selected a cheap bottle of burgundy. Kent insisted that a meal wasn't a meal without a good glass of wine. This would not be a *good* glass of wine.

One of the few things she liked in Scumble River was her cottage. Besides nice clothes, it was her one extravagance. The rent was almost double what most houses in the area went for. She leased it from a couple who had built it as a weekend river retreat, then divorced before it was complete. Each refused to let the other have it or sell it, so they rented it to Skye. She hoped that if they ever reconciled, it would be the same year she could afford to move out of Scumble River.

Anticipating company, even Kent, made her look at the cottage with new eyes. As she entered the tiny foyer, she appreciated the antique coat tree with attached bench seat, which opened to provide storage.

To the left was a small kitchen. It was just big enough for a two-person table if it were shoved against the wall. Skye put away her groceries and went into her bedroom to change clothes. It had been another long day. It was time to relax, pet Bingo, and give herself a chance to process all that she'd seen and heard.

Friday morning had whizzed by like a kid on a skateboard. It was nearly one by the time Skye was able to take a break. She grabbed two cans of soda from the machine in the teachers' lounge and headed to the library.

Trixie was helping a small group of students find books on various occupations for the vocational unit of their health class — the closest thing to career counseling the teens got at Scumble River High School.

Skye held up the can of Pepsi and motioned with her head to a small room off the main IMC area. The librarian nodded and held up five fingers.

Trixie's office was crammed with a copy machine, desk, and boxes and boxes of books. Skye cleared an orange plastic chair and settled in. She popped the top of her Diet Pepsi and took a swig, wishing she had remembered to bring a Diet Coke from home.

Trixie bounced inside and closed the door. "Hi, how's it going?"

"So-so. Just when I think things have calmed down, something else happens."

"This is a tough situation."

"True. Hey, I've got a question for you. Did the cheerleaders' mothers have a meeting here at school the morning Lorelei was killed?"

Trixie dug through her desk drawer and pulled out her calendar. After flipping a few pages, she said, "Yes. The cheerleaders met before school and their moms met first period. We discussed fund-raising."

"Was anyone missing?"

"They were all there except for Tara's mom. Her whole family was out of town."

"Did any of the moms handle the pom-poms?"

"I think they all did." Trixie scratched her head. "Yeah, we handed them around while they were waiting for the cheerleaders' meeting to end. We were talking about buying better ones when we upgraded the uniforms."

"How about the cheerleaders, did they work with the pom-poms that morning?"

"No. It was a meeting, not a practice."

"Did any of the moms come in contact with Lorelei?"

Trixie shrugged. "Maybe. At one point they were all in one room together."

"So, Mrs. VanHorn could have had a pom-pom strand clinging to her, which transferred to the doctored bottle of juice, which she had an opportunity to hand to Lorelei?"

"Sure, but so could anyone else."

Friday afternoon was productive. Skye saw a couple of her regular counselees, made arrangements for the first round of annual reviews, and returned calls. At four-thirty she packed up several files and the pile of papers she had grabbed from her box that morning but never gotten around to reading, and headed home. She had big plans for her Friday night — a pizza, a bubble bath, and a new Margaret Maron mystery.

It was time to relax. The week from hell was finally over.

Chapter 18

Not a Boast of a Chance

Saturday morning at exactly five to seven, Skye maneuvered the Bel Air into her parents' driveway. The white pea gravel shone like a sea of pearls as she guided the huge car toward the red brick ranch house.

It was obvious that her father had cut the lawn only yesterday. The acre of grass spread as smooth as a putting green to the edge of the cornfield.

She hadn't been out to visit in a while and was almost afraid to look and see what the concrete goose was wearing. A quick peek revealed a pink fur bunny costume, complete with ears and a powder-puff tail. Skye vowed to try once again to talk her mother out of dressing the lawn statuary.

Before she had fully stopped the car, May was climbing into the passenger seat. "Let's go, you're late."

Skye put the Chevy in reverse. "Why're you in such a hurry?"

"I promised your dad's cousin I'd take

pictures when her granddaughter competes, and I don't know when she's on."

"It doesn't start until nine, and it's only an hour's drive to Bloomington." Skye gave up trying to explain, knowing that to her mother, "late" meant you were less than fifteen minutes early. "Which cousin is this?"

"One on the Denison side. Her mom and your dad's father's first wife were half sisters."

Skye didn't follow the genealogy, but asked, "What's her name?"

"The cousin's name or the granddaughter's name?" May rubbed her arms. "It's chilly this morning. Turn up the heat."

"The heater doesn't work." She handed her mother an afghan. "The granddaughter, what's her name?"

"Farrah Miles."

Skye felt a mild shock run through her. No doubt about it, she was definitely related to too many people. "I never knew they were our relatives."

"Someone was recently working on a family tree and discovered the connection. It's over a hundred years old."

"Mom, could you kind of keep this quiet?"

"Why?" May narrowed her eyes. "They

seem like nice people. Nothing to be ashamed of."

"It's not that. It's just that Farrah is mixed up with the Lorelei Ingels crowd and . . ."

"And she's a suspect."

"Sort of," Skye admitted.

"Okay. But it's not as if I'm the only one who knows."

Skye shrugged. A secret in Scumble River had about as much chance as a weed in her father's lawn. "Do your best."

For the rest of the way they chatted about family matters and the latest Scumble River gossip. The drive itself was routine: a straight shot down Interstate 55, passing little towns with unusual names — Dwight, Odell, Pontiac, and Skye's favorite, Towanda. Meticulously kept farmhouses and fields being readied for spring planting constituted most of the scenery. Even with the highway smells, the air was fresh, with only an occasional trace of hog to remind them what was around the next bend.

As they neared the exit for Jumer's Hotel, the pageant location, the scenery changed from farmland to college town. Once Skye made the turn, she would never have guessed that crops would soon be growing less than a mile away.

They parked in the hotel's lot and hiked across the asphalt to the elaborate entrance. Jumer's had been built to resemble an elegant French château, but the furnishings looked truer to the owner's original German roots. The lobby was full of heavy, carved wooden furniture, elaborate artwork, and tapestries.

Skye was relieved when May spotted a Miss Central Illinois pageant sign. She had been half-afraid that Lorna Ingels would get the governor to call off the contest and award the crown to Lorelei posthumously. Obviously that hadn't happened. Abby had said that it was highly unlikely since the state government had nothing to do with the pageants, which were all privately run.

Part of the contest was already over. On Friday, the preliminary competition had been held. Today were the finals. The crowning would take place on Sunday. After purchasing tickets, Skye and her mother moved farther into the convention area. Older teens and young twenty-somethings scurried up and down the hall, usually followed by their mothers. One of the pair was often screaming or crying.

Skye found the room where the first round of the finals was being held and guided her mother to a front-row seat. They had ten minutes to spare. She wondered if any of the girls from Scumble River had made the cut.

According to the program, the girls were judged on intelligence, poise, personality, beauty of face and figure, grooming, and speaking ability. Prizes ranged from five-hundred- to twenty-thousand-dollar scholarships.

Having seen the little girls compete, Skye was prepared for the spectacle of the older teens. May was not. Lights dimmed, and the emcee climbed onto the makeshift stage.

He welcomed everyone, and said, "Our first round today is Modeling. Points will be awarded for beauty, grooming, and personality. Our first contestant is Caresse Wren."

May gasped and clutched Skye's arm. "Do you see what that girl is wearing?"

Caresse wore formfitting black satin pants that rode low on her hips and were connected to her skimpy halter top by silver laces. Over this was a chiffon bolero jacket trimmed in marabou.

"Prepare yourself, Mom," Skye warned. "That may well be one of the milder outfits. You should have seen what the little kids wore last weekend."

"Do you mean the twins let their daughters expose themselves in public like this?"

"They did last weekend."

May sputtered. "I always knew those girls were a few feathers short of a whole duck, but I didn't realize they were dumber than a box of hair."

"Lots of people do this."

"I wonder if Minnie knows about it." May had a gleam in her eye, and Skye knew that her aunt, her cousins' mother, would be informed by this evening.

As more and more contestants came onstage, it was all Skye could do to contain her mother's comments. Most of the teens wore incredibly titillating outfits and paraded around as if they were dancing at a "gentleman's club."

When Farrah Miles was finally announced, Skye held her breath, afraid that if she were dressed too provocatively, May would charge the stage. Luckily for everyone, the girl wore a relatively modest yellow sundress with a matching hat and jacket. She still looked ten years older than her actual age, as did the other contestants, but the hooker quality was muted. May happily snapped several pictures for Farrah's grandmother.

The next round was Talent. Most of the girls seemed to do some variation of song, dance, or gymnastic routine, though a few performances were truly unique.

May whispered to Skye, "Whoever let that poor girl come out here and pack a suitcase for her talent should be horse-whipped."

"Or forced to watch that first girl, over and over," Skye said, agreeing with her mother. "The one who showed the video of herself doing tractor drills."

"True." May crossed her arms. "When's lunch?"

After a quick meal in the hotel restaurant May and Skye hurried to the conference theater for the Interview competition. It was the longest segment and often the one that separated the winners from the losers.

Skye scanned for seats in the already-full auditorium. She spotted two near the front and took her mother's arm. May was still complaining about the prices at the restaurant.

As the women sat down, the lights dimmed. The emcee came out, and after a brief spiel he introduced the judges. There were five. Charlie and Abby were the only two Skye recognized.

Skye perked up when she realized that Zoë VanHorn was the first contestant. She came onstage dressed in a shocking-pink-and-black suit. The pleated skirt barely covered her derriere, and she wore nothing under the jacket.

The emcee approached her with a broad smile. "Good afternoon. Zoë, your question is: If you were given a hundred thousand dollars and had to spend it on yourself, what would you do with it?"

A murmur ran through the audience. This was a tough one. Almost anything the girl said would make her look bad.

Thirty seconds went by, and the emcee called time. "Do you have an answer for us, Zoë?"

Skye had never seen the teen at such a loss for words.

Zoë fumbled with her hair and tugged at her skirt, losing points for poise. Finally, she said, "I'd use it to go to college and medical school."

The audience let out its breath. An acceptable answer.

"What would you specialize in?" the emcee asked.

Zoë blurted out, "Plastic surgery. No emergency calls to interrupt my beauty sleep." She flashed a smile that seemed to say, see how clever I am, but no one laughed.

Skye heard Priscilla VanHorn's groan from three rows away.

Her daughter must have heard it, too, because she quickly continued. "Just kidding. Really I want to ah . . . help burn victims and others with deformities."

The emcee raised an eyebrow, but moved on to the other contestants without comment. The next girl was asked: Why did you enter this pageant? Others were given questions such as: What can you contribute to the Miss Central Illinois pageant organization? and Who are your heroes?

After the program ended, Skye and her mother were chatting with someone May knew as they made their way out of the theater. A commotion onstage caught Skye's attention, and she turned in time to see Priscilla VanHorn confront the emcee. Skye edged backward toward the front.

After a minute or so of intense whispering between Priscilla and the emcee, Skye heard, "That was an unfair question. None of the other girls were asked anything nearly as tricky."

The emcee replied, "As I've been telling you, I don't make up the questions. The judges hand me a sheet of paper with a list of the contestants' names and a question next to them."

Priscilla's face turned red. "I see. So one of the judges had it in for my daughter."

"I'm sure the process is completely random."

"And I'm Princess Grace. I need to talk to the judges."

"You can't do that, ma'am. Not until after they hand in their score sheets."

"Are you an idiot, or do you just play one on TV? It'll be too late by then." Mrs. VanHorn ran from the theater.

Skye debated. Should she follow, or try to notify someone? Finally, she grabbed May with the intention of running after Priscilla.

May didn't budge. "What in the world are you doing?"

"Hurry, Mom, I think she's going after the judges. If she murdered Lorelei, she might do some serious harm to one of them."

"Who?" May had still not moved.

"Zoë's mother." Skye was trying to shake off her mother's restraining arm so she could pursue the woman alone.

May started running, yelling over her shoulder, "When I asked Charlie to go to lunch with us, he said they had a room set aside for the judges. He pointed in this direction."

As they hurried along, Skye kept an eye out for an official. Of course, the halls were now deserted. Most contestants had retired to their rooms to rest before the night's Evening Gown competition, and the audience was probably in the bar.

Skye heard several people shouting before they rounded the corner. Security guards were holding Mrs. VanHorn by both arms, and she was swearing like a rap singer on an MTV video.

Charlie was sitting on the floor with blood coming from his forehead. Skye and May ran up to him.

May whipped a Wash'n Dri from her purse and ripped open the foil packet. "What happened? Are you alright?" She pressed the damp paper to his wound and ordered, "Skye, call 911."

Charlie stood up slowly. "I'm fine. It's just a scratch. Don't call an ambulance."

Skye put her fingers to his wrist. His pulse was rapid and weak. His color was pasty, and he was shivering. She turned to the guards still struggling with Priscilla VanHorn. "Can you get hold of Abby Fleming? She's another one of the judges, but she's also a nurse."

One of the guards nodded and spoke into his radio.

Skye led Charlie to a chair and checked his cut. The bleeding had nearly stopped, but his breathing was shallow and his pupils dilated.

She was trying to decide whether to go against his wishes and call 911 as Priscilla was led away by the guards, shouting, "Zoë had better win, or you ain't seen nothing yet!"

Abby finally arrived, complete with first-aid kit and blanket. She cleaned Charlie's wound, had him lie down with his feet raised, and then covered him up. She tried to talk him into going to the hospital but he repeatedly refused. Abby reluctantly agreed to check back in fifteen minutes and told Skye and May to keep an eye on him.

They all sat quietly until Charlie's breathing was back to normal and his color was returning. He said, "She came out of nowhere. Everyone else was already in the judge's room, but I stopped to use the toilet. She was screaming at me about her daughter's interview question. When I said there was nothing I could do about it, she started to claw at me, like a cat out of hell."

"How scary," Skye said.

"I couldn't do anything. I just froze. Men don't hit women."

"That was the olden days, Charlie," May said. "If a crazy woman comes after you, it's okay to smack her."

"You should have seen her, May. I've never felt such hatred. Not even when I was in the war."

"And all over a beauty contest," May tsked.

When they got the news that Mrs. VanHorn had been taken to the police station and Zoë had been disqualified, May and Skye decided to skip the evening gown competition and leave as soon as they were sure Charlie was fully recovered. Skye tried to talk her godfather into coming with them, but he insisted he was okay and wasn't going to ruin things for the other contestants. Abby said she would keep an eye on him and follow his car home.

As they walked through Jumer's parking lot, May said, "Do you remember the pageant I entered you in when you were six?"

Skye shuddered. "Too well. I didn't even make it through the first round. I decided then and there that since I couldn't sing or dance and I wasn't pretty, I might as well be dead."

May stopped abruptly. "It wasn't that you didn't win. I took you out after the first round because you seemed so scared. You couldn't even talk, you were so upset."

"But I thought . . ." Skye trailed off, surprised into silence. The things you learn too late.

They'd almost reached the Bel Air when Skye spotted Abby's silver Camaro. The bumper sticker read: SO FEW MEN. SO FEW WHO CAN AFFORD ME. The citizens of Scumble River didn't mess around with vanity plates, at seventy-five dollars apiece, when bumper stickers cost less than a buck.

Skye watched her mother ease herself slowly into the Chevy, her movements a far cry from this morning when she had bounced into the car. The attack on Charlie had been hard on the older woman, and for once she looked all of her fifty-seven years.

May was asleep before Skye exited onto the highway.

She woke as they took the Scumble River exit. "Sorry, I don't know what came over me."

"That's okay. It's an easy drive. Are you hungry? You didn't have much for lunch, and we seem to have missed supper."

May nodded. "How about getting some ice cream?"

"Sounds good."

A few minutes later Skye pulled into a local drive-in. She ordered her favorite — a marshmallow sundae. May opted for a banana split. As they ate, Skye contemplated telling her mother about Kent and her recent discovery.

Finally, she compromised. "I'm breaking up with Kent tomorrow night."

"Good."

Trust May to eulogize a six-month relationship in one word.

Chapter 19

Here, There, and Every Affair

After Mass Sunday morning Skye hurried toward her car while mentally listing everything she had to do that day.

"Skye, wait up."

She paused. Simon was hurrying toward her. His Lexus was one spot over from her Bel Air in the church parking lot.

"We need to talk about the youth committee."

"I thought maybe you were going to have me arrested again."

"That business with the tox screen was not my fault," he declared. "If I thought you were responsible, I wouldn't have called the police. I would have handled it myself."

Was that last sentence meant to be as sexy as it sounded? "Well, I guess that's good to hear."

"I didn't mention your midnight escapade with the coffin, so I don't know why Wally jumped to the conclusion you were the thief."

"Thank you." Skye felt her face grow warm. "I suppose I have pulled a couple of boneheaded capers, and I shouldn't blame either of you for suspecting me."

Simon slid his fingers up and down her bare arm. "You do go a little overboard once in a while."

"Yeah, I get too involved sometimes."

"I've been thinking about things, and caring too much isn't the worst trait for a girlfriend to have."

Skye's face flamed at the word "girlfriend." Was she ready to make up with Simon? What about Wally? She just wasn't sure. What response would keep Simon interested, but not lead him on? "What a sweet thing to say."

"Why don't we get together sometime next week, and talk about the youth committee . . . and other things?" Simon's voice dropped to a seductive tone on the last few words.

"That'd be great." Skye was stunned by his change of attitude, and a little distrustful. What was he up to? Had he heard about Abby and Wally and felt sorry for her?

"How's Friday?"

She slid into the car and closed the door. "Fine."

He leaned into the Bel Air. "Six, okay?"

"Sure."

"Good." He placed a sweet kiss on her lips and strolled away.

Skye couldn't believe how hard it had been to find someone to go to Meijer Superstore with her. Normally she would have gone alone, but she was still leery of the Bel Air and wanted someone along in case it quit running or she went in the ditch or something.

Trixie had her in-laws to entertain, and May was going with Jed to a farm auction. Charlie was still in Bloomington. When she'd called to check on him, he had said he was feeling fine, Priscilla VanHorn had been released by the police to her husband, and a girl from Clay Center had won the pageant title.

Skye finally telephoned Vince and was shocked to learn he was free. Skye looked over at her brother as they sped north on Interstate 55, and sighed. He was way too good-looking and charming to be wasting his life in Scumble River. His butterscotch-blond ponytail flew in the breeze, and his year-round tan enhanced the muscles on his forearms and thighs.

"Vince?" Skye asked.

"Mmm?" He adjusted his sunglasses and turned toward her.

"Why do you stay in Scumble River?"

He shrugged. "Why not?"

"Don't you ever want to see what it might be like in a bigger pond?"

"Nah." Vince leaned against the headrest. "See, Sis, you're never satisfied. You always want more. I figure right now I've pretty much got everything I want."

"You do?"

"Yeah. I own my own business. I date the most beautiful girls around, and I've got my family close by."

Skye struggled to keep the big car between the lines. "And that's enough for you?"

"What more could I want?"

"Maybe if you opened a salon in Chicago, you could do hair for the rich and famous."

"And maybe I could spend a lot of money on rent to cut the hair of people that I wouldn't like or be comfortable with."

Skye let his words sink in as she took the Weber Road exit and followed it until it curved left onto Naper Boulevard. "You don't want fame and fortune? You don't want to be someone?"

As she maneuvered the huge aqua vehicle into a parking spot, Vince patted her knee. "I am someone. I have a feeling fame and fortune aren't all they're cracked up to be." He bounded out of the car. "Besides, now that I'm drumming again, maybe I'll hook up with a band and we'll become the next teen craze."

Skye joined her brother, and together they walked into Meijer Superstore. She had never been there before, although she had heard a lot about the megamart. It was gigantic. People were stationed every few feet, holding red flags to direct customers to the correct section of the building. They looked like the flight crew on the deck of an aircraft carrier.

Vince went to price supplies for his shop. Skye followed the greeter's directions to the beverage aisle. Twin walls full of every kind of soda, juice drink, and specialty water made her gape. She had never seen so many different ways to say "fruit juice." She was midway down the second side when she spotted the bottle she had seen next to Lorelei's dead body. She picked it up off the shelf. It was clear with a rounded bottom, a slight indentation about a quarter of the way up, and a neck that appeared to have been twisted several times. The cap was gold.

Eagerly, Skye turned the label toward her. It was blue, and printed in yellow letters were the words SEA MIST. Right beneath were smaller black letters that said: "ginseng, astragalus & agave." To the right of those words was a sailboat and farther down was the single word VAPOR.

Besides Vapor, it also came in three other flavors — Shore, Star, and Blaze. She took one of each and went in search of the store manager. He confirmed her suspicions. Meijer's was the only chain in the Chicago area that sold the Sea Mist brand.

It was nearly five by the time Skye got home from the megamart. After putting away the Sea Mist and changing into slacks and a twin set, she immediately began preparing supper. The doorbell was ringing as she slid a tuna casserole into the oven. It had to bake for half an hour. She hoped Kent was starving.

"That color suits you. It must be *sky* blue," Kent said as he strolled into the foyer and pecked her on the cheek. Always well dressed, tonight he wore gray wool slacks and a matching silk shirt. Skye figured they cost more than her weekly salary.

"Thank you." She guided him into the

back half of the cottage, which consisted of an open area lined with floor-to-ceiling windows, intermixed with bookcases and a set of French doors. "How were rehearsals?" She wanted to keep the discussion away from their relationship until she had a chance to question him about Lorna.

"Fine. Zoë has more talent than I gave her credit for. She makes a fine little Sleeping Beauty." He settled into Skye's newest piece of furniture, a cream-colored recliner.

"Would you like a drink? I have soda, Sea Mist, wine . . ." She wanted to see if he'd react to the name of the drink found beside Lorelei's body.

Kent didn't appear to notice. "No whiskey?"

She shook her head.

"Damn, I could do with a whiskey. Wine it will have to be."

Skye's mouth tightened. She'd been taught it was impolite to ask for something the host didn't offer. "Coming up."

In the kitchen, she poured the cheap wine into a crystal goblet, put it on a silver tray, and carried it out to him. She watched closely as he took a healthy swallow.

"This is awful." Kent plunked down the

glass with such force Skye was sure it would break.

"Really? I'm so sorry." Skye played innocent. "And it's the only liquor I have in the house. Would you rather have a soda?"

He took another sip and grimaced. "No. I need a drink."

Skye saw her opening. "Has that VanHorn woman been bothering you again?"

"She's relentless. She wants her daughter to win. It doesn't matter if it's a quiz worth ten points or a national beauty pageant; Zoë must have it all." Kent drank steadily and Skye kept topping off his glass.

"Isn't that typical of most moms?"

"It's the length she and some of these women go to that's astonishing."

"I suppose some have even offered to sleep with you," Skye said casually.

He smirked. "It goes with the territory. Of course, I've always turned them down."

Skye moved into the kitchen to check on dinner.

Kent followed. She handed him the platter of Jell-O. He held it as if it were alive. "What is this?"

"Surely you've seen blue Jell-O before."

"But what's suspended inside?" Kent swallowed hard. "They look like . . ."

"Gummy worms. See how the Jell-O mold is sitting on shredded cabbage? It's supposed to look like a pond in the middle of the field." Skye bit the inside of her cheek to keep from laughing. "Go ahead and put the platter on the table by the French doors. I'll be right there."

She took the casserole and bowl of mashed potatoes in herself.

After they had helped themselves to the food, Skye continued, "What's your opinion of Zoë?"

"A mouthwatering little morsel with the morals of an alley cat."

"Why do you say that?"

"I hear the kids talk. She's slept with the entire football team, except Troy, and she's working on him." Kent took a bite of the entrée. "What the devil is this?"

"Captain's casserole."

"Huh?"

"Tuna with cheese, noodles, peas, and potato chips crumbled on top."

"You're kidding."

"It's an old family recipe." Skye fought to keep a straight face.

"What's this orange stuff?" Kent thrust his fork toward her.

"A cheese that is in the recipe."

"It looks like Velveeta."

"Yes, doesn't it?" Skye hurried with another question, hoping to get in a few more answers before Kent realized he was deliberately getting a miserable meal. "So, did Lorelei have a reputation for sleeping around like Zoë?"

"No, very different. She didn't seem to be that attracted to teenage boys. They called her the ice queen." Kent forked up some mashed potatoes. "Where's the gravy?"

"Sorry, no gravy. Here, try some butter. How about some pickled beets? They're Midwest soul food."

Kent shook his head and muttered, "I see why we've always gone out to eat."

"What?" she asked sharply.

"Just wondering what's for dessert."

"I'll get it. I'm sure you'll like it."

She returned carrying a full glass bowl.

Kent leaned forward eagerly. "Is that my favorite?" He took a big spoonful, put it in his mouth, and frowned. "That's not Tiramasu."

Skye pasted on a sad expression and allowed her shoulders to slump. "Not exactly. I had to use banana pudding for the custard and vanilla wafers for the lady fingers."

"Ah, Scumble River's grocery store

doesn't carry the real ingredients, I suppose."

Why had she ever dated this guy? Skye wondered. Her taste in men was truly atrocious. So far this week one had trapped her in a coffin, another had arrested her, and now this jerk had insulted her cooking *and* her hometown. It was dawning on her that whereas she felt free to denigrate Scumble River, she didn't like it when anyone else did.

She said coolly, all traces of her fake remorse gone, "That's not it at all. I just didn't think you deserved a good meal."

"What do you mean by that?"

Skye ignored his question. "I'll bet Lorna Ingels would serve you a meal more to your tastes. She seems pretty sophisticated."

To Skye's surprise, Kent allowed her previous comment to drop, and answered, "So she fooled you, too. She has a veneer of culture, but it doesn't go very deep, and she's always afraid of what might show through if she lets go."

"Really? What is her background?"

"Lorelei told me her mother grew up in the trailer courts. In fact, Lorna's mother still lives there." His mouth puckered in disapproval. "I think that's why she buys so many things."

Skye held her temper. This man badly needed to be taken down a notch, but she still had questions. "Is that so bad? The Ingels certainly can afford it."

"That's not what I hear. Lorelei said her parents always fought about money and that Allen claimed Lorna would put them all in the poorhouse."

"Lorelei sure told you a lot. You must have been close." Could Kent have been the teacher Lorelei was sleeping with?

He became interested in his glass of wine and shrugged. "No more than any other student."

Skye decided to let that obvious prevarication slide for the moment. "Do you know the younger daughter, Linette?"

Kent moved back to the lounge chair, leaving Skye sitting at the table by the French doors. "I've met her. She's like Lorelei, but without a conscience."

"Interesting observations. Perhaps you should have been a psychologist."

"No offense, but why would anyone want to spend her life listening to other people talk about themselves?" Kent held out his wineglass for a refill.

Skye grabbed the bottle from the table and headed toward the lounge chair in which Kent had flung himself, not noticing that Bingo had chosen to stretch out in the middle of her path. Her foot thudded into something solid, and she pitched forward. She and a shower of wine landed squarely in Kent's lap.

He sprang up, swearing, and dumped her to the floor. "My trousers! My new trousers."

That did it. The oaf hadn't even asked if she were alright. She struggled to her feet. Still no assistance offered by Kent, who was scrubbing the wine stain on the front of his pants with a hand-crocheted lace scarf he had grabbed from the end table. She snatched the doily from his hand and screamed, "This was my grandmother's, my dead grandmother's! Don't you dare use it for a rag."

Kent look dumbfounded for a moment, then retorted, "Look at my trousers. You'd better hope the dry cleaner can get the stain out or you'll have to pay for them."

Skye was about to tell him where he could stick his pants when a thought occurred to her. If she offered to clean them herself, she could go through his pockets and wallet. Maybe there'd be something interesting in them. Men seemed to like to collect trophies of their conquests.

Biting back the words she wanted to speak, Skye said, "Take off your pants, and I'll see if I can clean them. I have some really good dry-cleaner-strength stain remover."

Kent, still swearing, disappeared into the bathroom.

Skye checked to see that Bingo was okay, then found a terry robe she'd never worn and pushed it through the bathroom door to Kent. She certainly didn't want to see him in his Jockeys. He handed her his pants.

She took the offending article of clothing into her tiny utility room. It had space for a washer/dryer and ironing board, but little else. She threw the pants on a small counter and felt around in the pockets. She retrieved a wallet, fifty-six cents in change, a comb, and a handkerchief.

Skye put his personal items aside, and grabbed a bottle from the shelf. After following the directions, which included waiting several minutes for the solution to work, she turned her attention to the wallet. It contained a twenty and two singles, the usual credit cards, insurance identifications, and other paraphernalia.

The most interesting items were tucked

away in the "secret" compartment that everyone knows about. There Skye found a very interesting picture of Lorna Ingels dressed in nothing but a teddy and high heels. Aha, here was her proof. Kent was having an affair with a married woman. A woman whose daughter had died under mysterious circumstances.

Where had the photo been taken? Skye squinted. It wasn't Kent's apartment. The setting didn't look like any of Charlie's cabins, either, but it did have a motel-like look. Must be the Holiday Inn near the highway in Laurel.

What a sleaze. Imagine having sex with your student's married mom. She tried to stuff the picture back where she had found it, but it wouldn't go all the way in. Something was in the way.

She dug her fingers into the leather fold and pulled out a much creased piece of pink paper. Skye read:

Dear Kenny,

Our night of wild sex was totally awesome. I still haven't showered so that I can smell you on my body. I love the way you kiss every inch of my skin. Next time let's try some of those other things from that book you showed me. It was fun sneaking

350

*into your apartment dressed as a pizza de-
livery boy. What shall I wear next time?*

> *Love,*
> *Lorelei*

*P.S. Remember you promised to change my
grade to an A.*

Yech! Kent was slimier than she'd
thought. He had taken advantage of not
only the mother, but the daughter, too.
The thought of him having sex with one of
his students made Skye want to shoot him,
or herself, for ever having dated him.

Skye took a few deep breaths, trying to
calm herself and decide what to do. Should
she confront him? No. That could be dangerous. It was clear Kent could be the father of Lorelei's baby.

Finally, she decided she would keep everything, and tomorrow morning she
would make photocopies, then turn it all
over to Wally. Kent was going to pay for his
sins.

Right now she had to give the man
back his pants, pretend she didn't know
he was lower than a worm's belly, and
break up with him. An awkward situation
at best.

"So, Kent, as I was saying, considering

everything, it would be best if we didn't see each other anymore." Skye tried to get her soon-to-be-ex-boyfriend's attention long enough to dump him.

He nodded, seemingly mesmerized by the TV screen.

"That means no more dating." Her eyes strayed to the program that held him enthralled. Three men and a woman sat in a semicircle talking about e-trades, on-line this, and instant that. It sounded like Swahili to Skye.

Skye had emerged from the utility room with Kent's pants to find him sitting in front of her TV, engrossed in some Channel 11 special about stocks, bonds, and the Internet.

Kent nodded again, and said, "Fine. Good. Just let me catch the end of this."

She stepped in front of the set and snapped it off.

His head jerked as if she had slapped him and he leaped up from the chair. "What did you do that for?"

"Because I just broke up with you and I want you out of my house. Now."

"What do you mean? You can't break up with me. I do the breaking up."

"Sorry, too late." Skye grabbed his arm and pulled him to the foyer. She flung open the front door, pushed him outside, and threw his pants after him.

She dusted her hands together. "Good riddance, to bad rubbish."

Chapter 20

Rages of Sin

It was a typical Monday morning. Skye had been late getting to the pool, late finishing her swim, and now she was going to be late for her first appointment. *Damned panty hose.* Skye had already tried to put on two pairs of nylons and managed to run both of them. She knew it was because she was in a hurry. Inanimate objects could sense her need for speed, and once that happened, they refused to cooperate. She had one more pair of hose, which she kept in her desk drawer for emergencies, but she'd have to get dressed before she could retrieve them.

She had rushed to school determined to use the copier before anyone else arrived. She'd made copies of the picture and letter from Kent's wallet, secured them in the Bel Air's trunk, and dropped the originals off at the police station — all before her morning swim. Now, if her panty hose would just cooperate.

She finished buttoning her lime silk

blouse and was still zipping the navy skirt as she hurried into the hall. The teacher's bell had rung, and staff scurried up and down the corridor as she unlocked the guidance office. A quick check to make sure that Coach was not anywhere in sight, and Skye slipped inside, closing the door behind her.

The panty hose was still in its original package, and she carefully opened the cellophane. Inching her hand down the leg to the toe, she bunched up the nylon as she went. Skye placed her foot inside and eased the material on up. One leg on, one to go.

A knock on her door startled her, but she kept calm and answered, "Just a minute please."

She had started to repeat the process for the other leg when the door burst open. Homer took one look at her and stood with his mouth open. Skye froze with the nylon half up her calf, her skirt bunched around her waist, and her foot resting on the seat of the chair. Neither one of them seemed capable of speech.

Finally, Homer spoke, sounding as if he were strangling, "Skye, ah, Ms. Denison, ah heck."

"Homer . . . ah . . . could you give me a minute?"

The man didn't move.

Skye tried again, louder. "Homer, step out of the office for a minute."

"Ah . . ." The principal complied as if he were coming out of suspended animation.

She finished donning her panty hose and straightened her clothing, then let Homer back into the office. "Sorry. I had a run. Should have used the ladies' room."

Homer's face was still red, but he managed to say, "Never mind. We've got real trouble."

"What now?"

"The police have arrested Kent Walker for Lorelei's murder."

"Oh." She had figured they might when she gave Lorelei's letter and Lorna's picture to the dispatcher to give to the chief.

"It gets worse." The hair in Homer's ears quivered. "They found all kinds of smutty letters and pictures of him with her."

"Oh, my." Skye tried to act surprised.

"And to top things off, he's asked to speak to you. You're his one phone call. The police dispatcher is on hold."

"Wonderful."

As Homer slammed out of the office, Skye sat down at her desk and reached for the receiver. She punched the blinking light and said, "Skye Denison. May I help you?"

"Skye, honey, this is Thea from down at the police station. Your friend Kent is in a heap of trouble, and he's asking for you. Can you come right away?"

"Can't I just talk to him on the phone?"

"Well . . . you could, I guess, but Wally and the others have him in the interrogation room, and things are sounding pretty ugly." The daytime dispatcher was a grandmotherly type who wanted everyone, even the police and criminals, to play nice.

"But if I'm his one phone call, they have to let him talk to me."

"See, they haven't arrested him, they're just questioning him, so they don't have to give him a phone call yet." Thea hesitated before adding, "The thing is, he was yelling he wanted to call you, so I called you for him. The chief doesn't know I did it. But your friend was already bleeding. Looked like he hit his head . . . or something."

"I see. I'll be right there." The last thing she wanted to do was rescue the slimeball, but it wasn't right for the police to beat him up. She wouldn't actually help him, just go and check things out.

She stopped at the office on her way out and told Opal where she was going.

During the short ride to the police station, she wondered why she was doing this. Kent was no longer her boyfriend. And after reading that letter from Lorelei she knew he'd had an affair with her. So, why was she going? Was it because he was a teacher in her school, and she was afraid of the scandal? Charlie would certainly have a fit.

Or maybe deep down inside, although she knew Kent was a jerk, she didn't believe he was a killer. Feelings were running high in town, and she was afraid that something would happen to Kent before he ever got to trial. Not that Wally would do anything to harm him, but she didn't trust the other officers.

Thea greeted her with a wink as she entered the station. "Skye, what are you doing here?"

Skye went along with the charade and raised her voice. "A little bird told me you had someone here who might need my help."

"You can't go in there," Thea said as she pushed the button to let Skye through the door.

Skye lowered her voice. "So what happened?"

Thea spoke just above a whisper. "Late last night, someone called Wally at home and said they knew who killed Lorelei Ingels. The woman said the murderer was Kent Walker, and that if they searched his apartment, they'd find proof that Kent and Lorelei were lovers."

"Oh, my."

"Wally finally got hold of the judge this morning and got a warrant. He'd already seen the picture and letter you dropped off at six. About seven-thirty the chief, Roy Quirk, and a couple of guys from county went to your friend's apartment and searched it." Thea's eyes widened. "They found dirty pictures and love letters from Lorelei *and* her mother."

"Can I see the stuff they confiscated?"

"You're in luck. Your friend was making such a fuss when they brought him in, Wally just threw the folder on top of the cabinet." Thea disappeared for a few minutes, then returned with a large manila envelope and handed it to Skye.

Skye emptied the envelope onto the counter and began to look through the material. The pictures were similar to the photo in his wallet — Mrs. Ingels in various stages of undress in motel-room settings. She didn't read the letters. She was already too disgusted.

When the dispatcher finished with her

call, Skye handed her the envelope. "Thanks. What a scumbag. I should just let him face the music."

"Innocent until proven guilty. And he was bleeding," Thea said softly as she left to replace the envelope.

When the older woman returned, Skye said, "Can I talk to Wally?"

"He doesn't want to be disturbed." She shrugged helplessly.

"What do you think would happen if I forced my way into the interrogation room?"

"They'd throw you out."

Skye chewed on a fingernail. "At least I don't hear any shouting coming from in there." She inclined her head toward the closed door. "What did he say, exactly, when he asked for me?"

Thea closed her eyes and screwed up her face. "He said, 'I want to make a phone call.' And when they said no, he said, 'Tell Skye Denison I need to talk to her.'"

"Is that all?" Why had he thought she'd help him? Skye made up her mind. Time to turn the problem over to someone who could be neutral. "Can I use the phone?"

Thea shoved the instrument toward her. "Dial nine first."

Skye rummaged through her tote bag

until she found her address book. She flipped to the S section, ran her finger down the page, then punched in the number. "Loretta Steiner, please. Skye Denison calling."

A few seconds later a throaty voice reverberated from the receiver. "Denison, what's up? I just heard of a great new restaurant."

Loretta was a sorority sister of Skye's, and one of the best criminal lawyers in Chicago. She had defended Vince a year and a half ago, when Skye's brother was accused of murder. Since then the two women had gotten together for lunch every time Skye went into the city.

"Unfortunately, this isn't a social call. I need to hire you again."

"Who's dead this time?"

After Skye explained, Loretta said, "Okay, if the roads are clear I'll see you in ninety minutes, and if they aren't, who knows?" Illinois had only two seasons — winter and construction. Winter was officially over. The first orange traffic cone had been spotted.

Before Skye could hang up, Loretta asked, "Do you think he killed her?"

"No, but I don't have a good reason for thinking that, except I don't want to have an ex-boyfriend who's a killer. It's bad enough that he slept with a married woman and her daughter while we were dating."

"Did you take precautions?" Loretta demanded.

"No."

Loretta drew in a sharp breath.

"Because I didn't sleep with him," Skye finished.

"Oh . . . ah . . . that's good. Great." Loretta fumbled for a comment. "See you soon."

A tiny smile played on Skye's lips as she hung up the phone. She had never heard her friend at such a loss for words.

Then she frowned. *Wait a minute. Am I the only thirty-something woman who's not sleeping with every man she dates?*

Skye sat on the vinyl couch in the police-station entryway as she waited for Loretta. She had written Kent a note, telling him a lawyer was on her way, but she doubted Wally had given it to him.

She shifted in her seat and grabbed her tote bag, hoping that she had put her current mystery into it before leaving that morning. Her questing hand didn't feel the hard edge of a book, but did come across the sheaf of papers she had taken from her mailbox on both Thursday and Friday. She had sorted out the phone messages at school and returned most of the calls, but she hadn't looked at the rest of the documents.

Her eyes automatically scanned the memos before tossing them into the wastebasket. Most had nothing to do with her, but one stopped her automatic crumple reflex. It was from Homer, calling a meeting to discuss their school's low grade on the state report card. Their achievement scores did not stack up well against those of other, wealthier school districts. The last paragraph read:

We're going to keep having these meetings until I find out why no work is getting done around here.

Skye smoothed the wrinkled sheet and put it back in her purse. It would go in her scrapbook of silly administrator memos.

The last thing in her pile was an envelope that had already been ripped open. She turned it over to see if she could figure out why the seal had been broken, and froze. She stared at the piece of mail in her hand. It was addressed to Mr. Simon Reid,

Coroner. The top left corner bore the name of the forensics lab. It was the missing toxicology report. How had it gotten into her mailbox at school? More importantly, what should she do with it?

She glanced around. She was alone in the waiting area, but anyone could come through one of several doors at any moment. What to do? Hand it over to Wally, was the obvious answer, but someone had gone to a lot of trouble to get this to her. And Wally already had a copy, so she wasn't withholding vital information.

Okay, she'd take a quick peek and then give it to the chief. But she needed to preserve any fingerprints. Skye reached into her purse and retrieved her cosmetic case. Inside were tweezers, which she used to pull the report from the envelope.

A quick scan told her nothing. Most of the narrative did not use words Skye understood. The summary was a little easier to grasp. Lorelei had been given a fatal dose of dextroamphetamine. That sounded familiar. Skye made a note of the drug and the amounts found in the young woman's blood.

She was using the tweezers to return the report to its envelope when she saw a Post-it stuck on the back. Scrawled on the yellow square was:

Thought you should see this. Watson.

Skye was hoping Watson wasn't who she thought he was when Loretta arrived. Six feet tall and well muscled, with smooth mahogany skin and black hair that she wore in a coronet of braids, Loretta turned heads whenever she entered a room.

The two women hugged.

"Same police chief?" Loretta asked.

"Same everything."

"Okay, here's the plan. I'll demand to see my client. If your friend is swift enough, he'll confirm I'm his lawyer and everything will be fine."

"And if he's not too quick on the up-take?"

"We'll play it by ear." Loretta turned and rang the visitor's bell.

Thea answered, listened to Loretta, and went to get the chief.

He appeared a few minutes later, scowling. "Ms. Steiner, what brings you to our neck of the woods?" He glanced over her shoulder at Skye. "As if I couldn't guess."

"Chief Boyd, nice to see you again. I'm

here on behalf of Kent Walker. I understand you've been questioning my client without benefit of attorney."

"He's not under arrest."

"So he's free to go?"

"We've asked him to cooperate in our investigation."

"I understand that cooperation was coerced with a blow to the head."

Wally's face reddened. "He hit his head getting into the police car."

"Right." Loretta narrowed her eyes. "I'd like to see my client now."

After Loretta was ushered into the interrogation room to confer with Kent, who had readily agreed that she was his attorney, Skye returned to school.

Her first act was to put the tox report into a Ziploc bag and stash it in her trunk with the photocopy of Lorelei's letter. Skye had a bad feeling that Watson was none other than Justin Boward, and that the girl who'd been seen right after the original report was stolen was Frannie Ryan. She wondered when those two had joined forces.

Skye was trying to figure out how much of what she knew was confidential when Opal knocked on her door. Homer wanted to see her.

Skye had barely settled into a chair in the principal's office when he demanded, "What in the hell is going on? Did Kent murder Lorelei?"

"The police got a tip and searched Kent's house. They found dirty pictures of, and letters from, both Lorna and Lorelei. It appears he was sleeping with both mother and daughter. It looked to me like they were going to charge him with Lorelei's murder, so I got him an attorney."

"He understands the school isn't paying lawyer fees, right?"

"Why would he think they would?" Skye countered.

A shifty look settled on the principal's features. "I'm not sure, but we may've promised him that when we hired him."

Light was dawning. "You mean, you gave Kent an under-the-table deal — outside the teachers' contract?"

Homer half nodded, then seemed to catch himself. "I can't talk about that."

"You know, I always wondered how someone like Kent Walker, who hated being in Scumble River — let alone in the Midwest — ended up in our school. Any ideas?"

"What do you mean by that?" The hair in Homer's ears bristled. "I'll have you know we pass over a lot of good people to get to the ones we hire."

Skye bit her lip to keep from laughing. The sad thing was that Homer was probably right. "Okay, but it's still odd that someone who thinks he's so much better than the rest of us ended up teaching in Scumble River." After the words left her mouth she realized the description sounded strangely like her own situation. She reddened slightly and blocked that thought.

The principal leaned back in his chair. "It's a long story."

"My day's already shot. Go ahead."

"Kent's father owns most of the car dealerships in Massachusetts. Mayor Clapp met him at some convention or other that one of the auto manufacturers put on. They had some business thing going so they kept in touch."

Skye could imagine the type of deal Mayor Clapp would be involved in. "So . . ."

"So, this summer the mayor gets a call from Mr. Walker asking if he could find a job around here for Kent. Seems that he'd been living on the family money and got into some trouble, and the father wanted to teach him a lesson."

"I'll bet I can guess what kind of trouble

he got into," Skye interjected, thinking of the pictures she had seen.

"Anyway, Mayor Clapp asked about his qualifications. He had a degree in English and we had a maternity leave to fill."

"That clears up that mystery." It was beginning to seem to Skye that the Scumble River school district attracted more than its share of misfits from the education world, herself included.

"It's not good." Loretta Steiner glanced up from the menu. "There's a lot against him, and not much for him."

Skye gazed around the Feedbag before responding. It was nearly five, and the restaurant was filling rapidly. "What do they have on him?"

Loretta closed the giant laminated folder and put it aside. She used her fingers to tally Kent's guilt. "They have several witnesses who will testify that Lorelei and Kent had an intimate relationship. Almost her entire cheerleading squad saw them alone together in compromising situations outside of school at one time or another."

Skye took a sip of ice water. "I knew Lorelei hadn't been discreet, but you'd think Kent would know better."

"Sounds like she may have set him up —

wanted the other girls to see them kissing and such." Loretta signaled to the waitress, then continued after they ordered. "He lucked out in one respect. Everyone agrees Lorelei was past the age of consent."

"Maybe legally, but morally to have an affair with your student is plain sleazy."

Loretta shrugged. "It's pretty mild compared to the cases I often see."

"Thank God I never let him photograph me. Of course, come to think of it, he never asked." Skye took another gulp of water. "I think I've been insulted."

"You were obviously his cover, so no one would realize what he was really up to." Loretta grinned. "Besides, he's terrified of Uncle Charlie. He was afraid to try anything with you."

"I can't decide whether to be relieved or offended."

"The most damning bit of evidence is that they found a bottle of prescription diet pills in Kent's medicine cabinet."

Skye looked blank.

"They were prescribed to Lorelei," Loretta explained. "And they were the drug that killed her."

"Shit!" That was how Skye had heard of dextroamphetamine — a doctor had probably tried to prescribe them for her at some point in her life. "What did he have to say about all this?"

"Kent had an explanation for it all. Said that Lorelei had decided to stop taking the weight-loss pills and given him the bottle to keep so she wouldn't be tempted." Loretta shook her head. "He's using the old 'she came on to me' defense to explain why he was sleeping with his student."

"Well, not that I'm blind to the evidence against Kent, but I do think Priscilla VanHorn is an equally good suspect," Skye said.

"Who's she?"

"Her daughter was runner up to Lorelei in everything — school, cheerleading, and even at these beauty pageants they all seem to be participating in — so she had motive." Skye explained about the incident with Charlie at the last contest. "She certainly had the opportunity. Zoë and Lorelei were always together, so all she had to do was hand her a bottle of doctored juice. And means would be no problem. I wouldn't be surprised to learn that Priscilla and her daughter are both taking the same diet pills that Lorelei was."

"I'll keep that in mind if I have to try this case."

"That reminds me — the juice bottle they found next to Lorelei's body, did it have Kent's fingerprints on it?"

"No." Loretta frowned. "From what I gathered, that bottle had a variety of prints, but they were so smudged they were useless. But his prints were on the band-room doorknob leading into the backstage area."

"He could have used that entrance as a shortcut while he was directing."

"That's what he's claiming."

"So, how did you leave things with Kent?"

A tiny smile played on Loretta's lips. "He wanted to know if he should tell the truth to the police."

"What did you say?" Skye was curious as to what a top criminal attorney's advice would be.

"I told him that honesty is the best policy, but insanity is a better defense."

Chapter 21

Lock, Stock, and Farewell

Skye's Tuesday morning at the elementary school had run long so it was close to one-thirty when she pulled into the high-school lot. Two cars blocked the bus zone, illegally parked in front of the entrance. Both were big, black, and expensive.

As she climbed the steps, a police cruiser swooped in and skidded to a stop next to the other vehicles. Wally threw open his door, ignored Skye, and ran into the building. She followed close on his heels. He headed down the hallway and into the maze of locker banks.

They're going to search Lorelei's locker. Skye stood quietly just out of sight, tucked behind a row of lockers, and hoped that no one would notice her.

Mr. and Mrs. Ingels, a man in a business suit, and Homer stood huddled together. Wally stopped in front of the group, and asked Homer, "Have they opened it yet?"

He shook his head. "No, we're waiting for our lawyer."

The man in the suit spoke up. "Mr. and Mrs. Ingels have every right to clear out their daughter's locker."

Wally turned to Mr. Suit. "And you are . . . ?"

"Mr. Wingate, the Ingelses' attorney." The man straightened his tie. "We heard you have a suspect in custody."

"That's correct." Wally oozed charm and turned to Lorna Ingels. "So you can see, ma'am, why we need to examine what Lorelei had in her locker. It could provide us with more evidence against our suspect."

Skye was surprised by how bad Lorna looked. She had deteriorated further in the few days since the funeral. Although she wore a designer suit, the hem hung crookedly, and there was a stain on the jacket. The skin on her face sagged, and her champagne-blond hair hung limp. Within less than two weeks, her daughter's death had aged her ten years.

The woman looked helplessly at her attorney.

At that moment, the school's lawyer arrived. Skye had met Bob Ginardi last year when her grandmother died. He had been

374

involved in some financial impropriety with her uncle, but managed to wiggle out without any charges being filed against him. She couldn't wait to hear his take on the present situation.

Ginardi, Homer, and the chief huddled for a moment, then Wally announced, "Okay, this is how we're going to do this. The Ingelses' attorney will take each item out of Lorelei's locker, show it to us, and hand it to the Ingelses. Our lawyer will write the official inventory, and we'll all sign it. Objections?"

Mr. Ingels stepped forward. "Hell, yes, I object. This should be a private family moment. You've got your man. Can't you see how upset my wife is?"

The contrast between Allen Ingels's appearance and his wife's was startling. He was freshly shaved and barbered, and wore an immaculate tan suit. Even his oxblood loafers glowed with care.

Wally's voice was detached. "We're very sorry for the intrusion, but a suspect is not a conviction, and we need to stay on top of the situation."

Wingate whispered in Allen's ear, then turned to the group. "We agree."

Skye stepped farther back, to make sure she remained unnoticed, and quietly slid a piece of paper and pen out of her purse. She had wanted to search the locker herself and had never gotten the opportunity, but this was probably better. She could see what they found, but wouldn't have to worry about how to tell Wally if she found something important while conducting an unauthorized search.

Several minutes went by as books, papers, pens, pencils, makeup, and a sweater were taken out and examined. The last item was a small prescription bottle. Skye couldn't see the label from where she was hidden, but Wally read the name out loud. It was the same diet pills that had been found at Kent's, and the same drug that the tox screen listed as the cause of death. How many bottles of that stuff were floating around?

Back in the guidance office, after persuading Coach it was her turn to use the space, Skye consulted her appointment book. She was supposed to see several students that day, and she made sure to schedule Justin Boward and Frannie Ryan for the last period, although what she was going to do about them and the tox-screen report was a conundrum.

The afternoon dragged on and on.

Finally, the eighth-hour bell sounded, and Justin appeared at her door; Frannie arrived soon afterward.

Once both teens were settled, Skye said to Justin, "Dr. Watson, I presume?"

The boy didn't respond, but Frannie's face paled.

Skye tried again. "Justin, I appreciate the help, but you must never do anything like that again."

He stared at her without speaking. They were obviously back to the silent treatment.

She turned to the girl. "Frannie, why did you steal the report for Justin?"

The teen's face flashed from white to red. "It wasn't for him. I just wanted the whole thing to be over with, and he said you'd solve the murder long before the police ever would."

"Thank you, Justin. That's very flattering. But I don't want either of you to get into trouble by trying to help me."

Neither teen responded.

"Any ideas what we should do about this situation?" Skye looked from face to face.

Justin shrugged. "What situation? You're in the clear, and the cops have Mr. Walker. Why should we do anything?"

"For one thing, I don't think Mr. Walker

is guilty. And when they find that out, they'll start looking again."

Frannie sagged in the chair. "Even dead, she's the center of attention."

"Worse than that, Frannie," Skye said gently. "They have a witness who saw you after you took the report from Simon's mail."

Her sag became a slump. "What should I do?"

"Tell your dad and Mr. Reid what you did."

"That's bogus," Justin protested, standing. "She'll get into trouble, and it's my fault. I asked her to do it."

"Then I guess you'd better go with her," Skye said.

The teens grumbled, but made sounds of agreement as they stood and headed for the door.

"Justin, one more thing. The day Lorelei was murdered, when you went backstage looking for a bathroom, were you talking to Mr. Walker before I got there?" Ever since Loretta had told her Kent's finger-prints were on the band-room doorknob, Skye'd been wondering if it was his voice she'd heard talking to Justin that day.

The teen looked at the floor. "Yeah. He came in through that little door and took some stuff from his desk. He told me not to tell. Said it was just personal junk."

Skye nodded. Another part of the puzzle revealed. "Okay, you can go now. You are going to talk to Mr. Reid, correct?"

Frannie and Justin both nodded.

After making sure the pair was out of earshot, she picked up the phone, dialed, and said, "Simon, you're about to have company." After she had explained, and extracted a promise that he'd be firm but not mean to the kids, she hung up.

The bell rang, and moments later Trixie stuck her head into the room. "Is the coast clear?"

"Sure. Come on in. What's up?"

Trixie pulled up a chair and sat down. "Just wondering what's going on with the Sleeping Beauty case. First the star and now the director — do you think they'll go on with the show?"

Skye shrugged. "You heard about Kent?"

"Which version?" The brown curls on Trixie's head bounced in time with her tapping toe.

Skye summed up what had happened, then asked, "Have the cheerleaders said anything about him?"

"He's the main topic of conversation."

"What do they think?"

"Well, they all knew Lorelei was sleeping with him, but they were sworn to secrecy." Trixie grinned. "I find it hard to believe they actually kept quiet about the affair."

"Interesting. What else did they know?"

"Certainly not about Kent and Mrs. Ingels. They think that's just plain gross. Moms are not supposed to be having sex, especially with their daughter's teacher." Trixie made an oops face. "Oh, gee, I'm sorry. I forgot you dated him. You okay?"

"Fine. I really don't care, which surprises me." Skye studied her nails, but glanced sideways at Trixie as she said, "Maybe it's because I never slept with him."

Trixie nodded. "Or because you were just dating him to get back at the guy you really love."

Skye was stunned by the suggestion. "And who would that be?"

"That's the problem, isn't it?" Trixie met her gaze head-on. "Even you don't really know."

Skye slumped in her chair. Trixie was right. She wondered if she'd ever be able to let herself love someone again. Probably not until she faced her ex-fiancé. Since he had cleaned out their shared apartment and refused to see her, she had never really gotten to finish things with him.

Straightening up, Skye changed the subject again. "Hey, I remember something else I wanted to ask you."

"What?" Trixie started to gather her belongings.

"When I walked through the girls' locker room on my way to the pool the other day, I noticed a picture of Caresse Wren on her locker. I knew it was her locker, since they have the names on masking tape right on them. Why would she have her own picture on the outside of her locker?"

Trixie, standing in the threshold, giggled. "I asked that, too. She said she put the picture up so when she forgot her name, she could still find her uniform."

"Was she serious?"

"I was afraid to ask," Trixie said over her shoulder on her way out.

Skye slumped in her desk and tried to figure out what was bothering her. She picked up a pen and paper and started to jot down words and phrases as they came to mind. Time ticked by, and the school grew quiet.

Finally, she looked at the legal pad in front of her. She had been writing the word "locker" over and over. Why? The contents of Lorelei's locker had been unsurprising. Even the diet pills meant little since they were the teen's own prescription.

What message wasn't she getting? It was odd that Lorelei didn't have any pictures hung on the inside of her locker. Skye grinned, thinking of Trixie's story about Caresse Wren with the picture on the outside.

That was it! Cheerleaders had a second locker: one in the gym. Had anyone thought to look at Lorelei's cheerleader locker?

Skye sprang from her chair and rushed out the door. The halls were empty. Her heels clicked eerily on the faded linoleum, and a dank smell assaulted her nostrils, making her feel as if she were about to sneeze. Where had everyone disappeared to?

She looked at her watch. It was past six. Both staff and students were long gone. She pushed through the double doors and into the darkened gym. The humid odor was stronger in there, and the silence more pronounced. Goose bumps rose on her arms, and she shivered.

Without warning, her mind turned to all the scary movies and murder mysteries she had read. She jerked her hand back from the door to the girls' locker room. What if the killer were waiting on the other side? There wouldn't be anyone to hear her scream.

This was silly. No one could know she'd choose this day and time to come here. She had to stop reading suspense thrillers.

She took a deep breath and pushed. The door swung open without a sound. Complete darkness greeted her. She fumbled for a light switch and finally found it, flooding the room with glaring illumination. Lockers lined the walls and stood in rows that formed dark aisles. Benches were bolted to the floor, and a huge tiled shower took up a corner of the room.

The place smelled of chlorine from the adjacent pool, sweat, and stale perfume. Skye's footsteps echoed as she made her way to the section that held the cheerleaders' lockers. A dozen shiny aqua rectangles were set apart from the gray of the other lockers. Each held a piece of tape on which was written the girl's name, and a padlock.

Skye stared at the padlock. *Shit!* How would she get that opened? *Wait.* She moved closer. There was a slight gap. Lorelei's lock wasn't fastened. She swung the door open and peered inside but couldn't see anything. She reached in and felt nothing. The locker was empty. That was why the padlock was open. Someone, probably Lorelei's parents, had beaten her to the punch and already cleared it out.

She sank onto the wooden bench, out of ideas. After a moment her gaze was drawn back to the bank of lockers — two metal cubes across and six down. Lorelei's locker was in the top row, nearest the wall.

Skye squinted. The lockers were perfect squares, but the wall wasn't straight. A vee formed between the wall and lockers. She got up and ran her hand up the gap where lockers and wall joined together. It was a tight fit down near the floor, but widened bit by bit as her fingers moved toward the top. There she could fit her hand into the fissure all the way up to her wrist. The opening was deeper than she expected. Skye stretched her fingers as far as she could, but felt nothing. She needed a long, thin probe.

She looked around, then hurried into the gym teacher's office and returned with a hanger. After carefully unbending the wire, leaving the neck curved in semicircle, she inserted it into the cleft. After a few seconds, she felt the probe bump up against something. With a little maneuvering she was able to encircle the object with the hook and pull out her prize.

It looked like a book of poetry — slim with a flowered cover. Skye's shoulders slumped in disappointment. All that work for nothing. Idly she flipped it open. Instead of the poems she expected, handwriting greeted her. It was Lorelei's diary.

Skye wasn't surprised to see the volume. In the back of her mind, she had always suspected that one might exist. Ever since she had been at the school district, the kids had been taught to keep journals, starting in kindergarten. Many adolescent girls continued the practice in private.

She was torn. What should she do with her find? It seemed such an invasion of privacy to read what the dead girl had never intended anyone else to see. On the other hand, if it led to her killer, was there any other choice? Giving the diary to Wally seemed worse somehow. She wasn't sure that he would understand a young woman's innermost thoughts.

No matter what she decided, she had a sudden urge to get out of the building. After tucking the book in her pocket, she put everything back the way she had found it and turned off the light. She hurried out of the gym, grabbed her tote bag from the guidance office, and headed for her car.

The five-minute ride home was excruciating. Skye could feel the diary almost pulsing in her pocket. Bingo was waiting for her as she skyrocketed through the front door of her cottage. He insisted on being fed before she did anything else.

Finally, she could sink onto her sofa and open the book.

Chapter 22

Shroud and Clear

A sigh escaped Skye's lips as she closed Lorelei's diary. Talk about looks being deceptive. On the surface, this was a girl who had everything — beauty, brains, popularity, and a prominent family name. Yet in the teen's perception, none of it was enough. Skye clearly remembered the pain of her own adolescence and felt the agony behind each of Lorelei's paragraphs.

January 1: I told Mother today that I was quitting everything — the pageants, cheerleading, and especially the pills. I'm tired of the competition, tired of being judged by how I look, and tired of my so-called friends who would stab me in the back for a crown or a trophy. My life is nothing but one big lie.

January 2: Mother is still furious. After she kept me up all night screaming and crying, I finally caved and agreed to finish out the cheerleading season, perform in the play, and do one last pageant — Miss Central Illinois. But I won about the pills. As of today no more diet pills.

January 16: Mrs. VanHorn has been so nice. I'm a little surprised. I never thought she liked me that much, but she's really supported my decisions to quit competing. She says she wishes she could stop Zoë from feeling she has to be the best at everything. I love stopping by after school. Mrs. V is an excellent baker. Her chocolate chip cookies are to die for.

January 29: Zoë can't seem to make up her mind. One day she's cheering me on about my decision to quit all the activities and the next she's saying that we won't be popular if I don't do what I've always done. Plus Zoë is really grossed out that I've gained weight and went up a dress size. She's always after me to go back on the diet pills.

March 10: Okay, how much weight am I going to gain? None of my clothes fit, and Mother claims we don't have the money for a new wardrobe. She actually suggested I try throwing up if I wouldn't go back on *the pills. Today they took the measurements for the* Sleeping Beauty *costumes and it was humiliating. I could hear the snickers when they yelled out my hip size. Thirty-seven inches, my gawd, I'm almost as big as Fat Frannie.*

March 16: I can't stand it anymore. Mother has started to leave boxes of laxatives in my room. She monitors every morsel I put in my mouth. I hated to do it, but today I started taking the diet pills again. I had to. Even Kenny has stopped saying I'm beautiful. I thought because he was older, he'd be less obsessed by my being thin, but he barely wants to have sex with me anymore. I think breaking up with Troy was a mistake.

March 30: The pills aren't working as well as they used to, so I've doubled the dosage. Missed my period this month. An advantage of taking the diet pills I'd forgotten. I guess I was stupid to try and stop.

There was nothing about being pregnant, and Skye was convinced that the teen was unaware that she was going to have a baby. And if Lorelei didn't suspect, the father surely couldn't know, which eliminated motives for both Kent and Troy.

April 13: The pills don't seem to be working anymore. I'm still gaining weight. I measured myself this morning. I'm now officially fat. I'm a size eight. I've decided to take three pills at a time.

Skye took a deep breath. That was the last entry, the day before she died. Lorelei must have felt as if she were the bone, and everyone she knew was a dog trying to take a bite. Maybe she had killed herself after all.

No, Skye was almost certain that wasn't the case. The circumstances just didn't fit what she knew of teen suicide — no note, no giving away of personal items, and why would she crush the pills into her juice rather than swallow them whole?

The more she thought about it, the more she believed that the killer was Priscilla VanHorn, who had wanted to eliminate Lorelei from competing with Zoë — especially if the woman had found out Lorelei was taking the diet drugs again. It was clear from the diary that Lorelei was used to accepting food and drink from Priscilla. With Troy and Kent out of the running, Zoë's mother had the strongest motive.

She certainly had the opportunity — she had been at the school that morning, and very likely saw Lorelei in the hall. That left only means. The pills would be easy enough to get, but did she have access to that type of juice? Surely, she would have used whatever was handy.

The phone had rung several times while Skye had been reading, and she had let the machine take the calls. Now she dragged herself into the kitchen, poured a can of Diet Coke over ice, and punched the play button.

May's voice ricochetted off the walls. "Where are you? It's after nine on a school night. Are you okay?"

Charlie was next. "I heard they arrested Kent Walker. Call me right away."

The last call was from Simon. "Hi, thanks for the heads-up about Frannie and Justin. Xavier and I gave them a good scare, as you suggested, but we told them they could work off their 'fine' this summer around the funeral home. Sorry you were blamed for their crime. I'm looking forward to our youth committee meeting Friday."

His warm tone soothed Skye's frazzled nerves. She reached for the phone, but noticed it was after eleven. Too late to return his call.

Instead, Skye got ready for bed. She stretched out on the crisp cotton sheets and tried to relax. Bingo burrowed into the crook of her knees, purring. But instead of sleep, various ways of proving that Priscilla had killed Lorelei played in her head.

By 3 A.M. she was annoyed, by four concerned, and by five resigned to a sleepless night. Fighting fatigue, Skye got up, dressed, and headed to work. At least it was Wednesday. The week was half-over.

Once again, Skye arrived at the high school well before anyone else. Before her swim, she photocopied the diary, intending to give the original to Wally sometime that day. Her stack of evidence was growing. Too bad it didn't point to any one person.

The first bell had yet to ring, and already she had returned both Simon's call and her mother's. Boy, if a person could eliminate the need to sleep, she could really get a lot done.

She was dialing Charlie's number when he walked into her office and kissed her on the forehead. "So, did Walker kill her?"

"I don't think so." Skye craned her neck to look him in the eye. "Sit down."

"Can't. I've got lots to do this morning." Charlie ran his fingers through his snow-white hair. "Got to do damage control."

"Concentrate on the affair."

Charlie's face turned red. "But who did kill that girl?"

"I think it was Priscilla VanHorn." Skye sketched out her reasoning, telling him about her discovery of the diary.

"Not enough to get an arrest." Charlie paced the room. "Have you told Wally any of this?"

"No. Like you said, I don't have any proof."

"I'll drop the diary off, so you don't have to be involved with that."

"Thanks. I think Wally'll look at it with less prejudice if it doesn't come from me. How are you going to explain having it?"

"I had a hunch, came over this morning and looked, and there it was." Charlie moved to the door. "We really need to figure out something before this stuff with Kent Walker permanently damages the school's reputation."

I think it's too late to save our reputation. "It'd also be nice if he didn't go to jail for a crime he didn't commit."

"Yeah." As Charlie stepped out the door, his voice trailed back into the room, "I'm real worried about that."

The rest of the day was a total waste.

Skye was unable to concentrate on any of her duties or figure out what she should do next about Lorelei's murder. Finally, a few minutes before the final bell, she had a glimmer of an idea. The key to the murderer's identity was the juice bottle. It was so unusual that only one chain of stores in the Chicago area carried it. Which meant that odds were, the person in Scumble River who drank it was the killer.

So, if Skye went to the VanHorns' house and saw bottles of Sea Mist Herbal Enhanced Juice there, then Priscilla was the murderer. She knew finding the drink would never be enough to convict the woman, but she'd figure out how to do that once she knew for sure who the killer was.

Now, what excuse could she use to drop by? A smile crept across Skye's face. The Principal's Choice Award. It was given to the best all-around student who excelled in school, the community, and at home. Skye could say she was gathering information on the finalists.

As soon as school ended Skye drove to the VanHorn home. When she explained why she was there, Mrs. VanHorn welcomed her with open arms. "Come in, come in. What a pleasant surprise. I wanted to apologize for hitting your Uncle Charlie the other day at the pageant. I don't know what came over me."

"He understands. No harm done." Skye forced the words out of her mouth, wishing she could say half of what she really thought.

She followed the woman into an overdecorated living room. The walls were covered with pictures of Zoë and plaques she'd won — mostly for second place. A thick rose carpet showed every footprint as the women made their way to the furniture.

Mrs. VanHorn nearly pushed Skye into a puffy, chintz-covered chair. "Sit down. Can I get you something to drink?"

Skye hid her smile. Things were working out just as she planned. She crossed her fingers and said, "Why, thank you. I hate to be a bother, but I'm on a new diet, and the only things I'm allowed to drink are herbal enhanced juices. You wouldn't happen to have any, would you? I particularly like the ones Sea Mist puts out."

"Gee, I'm sorry. All we've got is Diet Pepsi, coffee, tea, milk, or regular old orange juice." She twisted the handkerchief she held. "I could run next door and see if they have any of that herbal stuff, while you look at Zoë's photo albums."

Skye felt a stab of disappointment. Either Priscilla VanHorn wasn't the murderer, or she was a lot smarter than she looked. "Oh, I couldn't put you out." To be absolutely sure Priscilla didn't have the juice, she needed a peek in the fridge and pantry. She was counting on the Scumble River code of hospitality, which said you must make every attempt to get the guest what he or she wants.

"Nonsense. It'll just take a second. Myrna owes me." Priscilla turned to leave, but said over her shoulder, "The photo albums are under the coffee table."

As soon as Skye heard the door close, she shot out of the chair. The kitchen was visible at the end of the hall. She hurried into it and flung open the refrigerator door. No Sea Mist. While she was at it, Skye checked the pantry and the attached garage. No herbal juice anywhere.

She sank back in the overstuffed chair just as she heard the front door open and Mrs. VanHorn's voice say, "Sorry, no luck. They didn't have any of that stuff either."

Skye thought quickly. She needed information on the Ingelses, and who best to give it than their number one rival? "That's all right. I appreciate the effort.

Looking at all these wonderful photos of Zoë, I couldn't help but notice Lorelei and her mother are in most of them."

Mrs. VanHorn frowned. "Lorna's so pushy. It wasn't enough that her daughter won all the contests, she couldn't even let poor Zoë enjoy her moments as finalist and first runner-up."

"It was mostly Lorna, not Lorelei, pushing into the spotlight?"

"Definitely. You know that poor, sweet girl wanted to quit, and her mama wouldn't let her." Priscilla sat back and sighed. "I suppose now Lorna will focus all her energy on Linette, poor child."

"I'd heard that Lorelei wanted out, but I don't understand why."

"Well, Lorelei wasn't naturally thin like my Zoë, and she was sick of the pills and the diets, but Lorna just insisted she maintain her size-two figure."

Skye tsked. "I wonder why it was so important to Mrs. Ingels."

"I heard an interesting story about that." Priscilla leaned forward. "Seems that Lorna was quite the beauty-pageant winner in her day. She won all the titles, up to Miss Illinois. And right before she was supposed to compete in that contest, she started to gain weight. Turned out she was five months pregnant. Because she was so thin, she often missed her period, so she had no idea."

Skye did the math in her head. If Lorelei were the child of that pregnancy, that would make Lorna only thirty-six and Skye knew the woman was older than that. "Did Lorelei have an older sibling?"

"No, Lorna miscarried that baby." Priscilla clasped her handkerchief to her chest. "So sad. No crown, no baby, and a marriage you've been forced into. Not a lot to count for your life's achievements."

It took an hour for Skye to extricate herself from Priscilla VanHorn's verbal grasp. She'd had to look at every album, award, and trophy, and promise to write a glowing recommendation for Zoë for the Principal's Choice Award before the mother would allow her to leave.

Now she sat at home, rubbing Bingo's chin and thinking furiously. If Priscilla VanHorn wasn't the murderer, then it had to be Lorna Ingels. Even though Lorelei didn't know she was pregnant yet, her mother might have suspected it due to the missed periods, and perhaps thought that Lorelei would go through exactly what she herself had. But was Lorna twisted enough to think she was saving Lorelei by killing her?

The furiously ringing phone aroused Skye from her reverie. Dumping Bingo onto the sofa, she raced the answering machine, and scooped up the receiver with one ring to spare. "Hello."

"Oh, Skye, thank God you're home. We need a favor."

Skye wasn't sure which twin was speaking. "Ginger? Gillian?"

"It's Ginger. Could you go get Iris and Kristin?"

"Now?"

"Yes! They're supposed to be picked up at six, which was perfect because we were supposed to get off work at five-thirty, but our cash drawers aren't balancing and the computer's going crazy and no one is allowed to leave the bank. We've tried everyone, and no one is home."

"Sure, I'll get them. Where are they?"

"That's just it. They're at Linette Ingels's."

How convenient. I need to look around that house for the juice bottle.

Ginger continued, interrupting Skye's thoughts, "Lorna gets so pissy if we're late picking the kids up from her house."

This was the first time Skye had ever

heard her cousin sound intimidated. She wondered why Ginger found Lorna so alarming. She looked at the clock on the microwave. It was ten to six. "Okay, I'd better go right now. I'll bring them back here until you get off work."

"Thanks. We owe you one."

Skye arrived at the Ingelses' house at one minute before six. Their Polish housekeeper answered the door, and Skye explained she was there to pick up the girls.

The housekeeper gestured her into the foyer and left the room. When she returned she said in heavily accented English, "Girls are watching video with Miss Linette. Tape will be over in ten minutes. You wait?"

"Sure, no problem." Skye looked around for somewhere to sit. "Are Mr. and Mrs. Ingels home?"

"No, they are out." The woman turned. "I need to watch dinner. You would like to sit in library?"

"I'll just sit in the kitchen and keep you company, if that's okay?" Skye was counting on the housekeeper's good manners.

A fleeting frown crossed the woman's forehead. "Sure, sure, this way."

The kitchen was huge, with stainless-steel appliances and marble counters. The housekeeper tried to steer Skye to an oak table that could seat twelve without crowding, but Skye edged her way to a stool at the counter, closer to the action.

The woman went to the stove and stirred something in a pot, then checked a pan in the oven. Turning back to Skye, she asked, "You would like drink?"

"Yes, thanks." Before the housekeeper could react, Skye hopped off her stool and scurried over to the fridge. "Go ahead with your cooking, I'll get it myself."

It felt awful to be so pushy, and Skye was a little ashamed of herself for taking advantage of the woman, but she was hoping the housekeeper wouldn't know how to say no to a guest.

Skye flung open the refrigerator door and peered inside. She needed to get a good look before the housekeeper stopped her. She scanned the shelves starting at the top. The bottom shelf contained row after row of Sea Mist Herbal Enhanced Juices.

The housekeeper loomed between Skye and the fridge. "I will get your drink. You sit, please."

"Okay, thanks." Skye had seen what she came for. "Could I have a Sea Mist please?

Vapor if you have it."

The woman took a bottle from the shelf and turned to the cupboard.

Skye rushed to stop her. "Ah, I'd prefer it from the bottle, please. No glass."

The housekeeper handed Skye the drink.

Skye broke the cellophane seal around the neck and twisted off the gold cap. Hearing the pop, she knew that it was safe to drink. As she sipped and watched the housekeeper cook, she scratched at the label to see if it would come off.

The woman's voice surprised her. "Ah, you are like Mrs. Ingels. She, too, always must try to peel off label of this drink. Then she break her nail and be upset. But she never learns. And I have mess."

As Skye made sure that Iris and Kristin were buckled into the backseat of the Bel Air, she kept seeing the rows and rows of juice in her mind. While she made the girls toasted cheese sandwiches and tomato soup for supper, she kept hearing the house-keeper talk about Mrs. Ingels peeling off the labels. So, when the twins finally picked up their daughters at nearly eight o'clock, what they had to say didn't register with Skye until they were almost out the door.

"Whoa!" Skye grabbed Ginger's arm.

"Did you say that there's a lot of money missing from the bank, and they can't find Allen Ingels?"

"You never listen to what we say."

"Sorry," Skye answered automatically. "Tell me again."

Gillian sighed. "Well, as we just said, at first, when our drawers didn't balance they thought it was a computer glitch. Then they started checking further, and all of a sudden Mr. Yates was rounding everyone up and questioning all of us individually."

Ginger jumped in. "From what we can guess and what we overheard, over a million dollars is gone from the accounts, and it could be more. And they kept calling and calling, but no Mr. Ingels anywhere."

"Wow!"

"Anyway, we've got to go." The twins and their daughters swept out of Skye's cottage, amid hugs and thank-yous.

Silence abruptly descended. Skye tried to figure out what to do with her knowledge. It was obvious she'd have to go to Wally, and how mad would he be that she had seen the diary?

The answer was obvious. The longer she waited, the bigger the chance that something else would happen. Even as she contemplated, the Ingelses could be leaving the country for someplace without extra-dition.

She grabbed the phone and punched in the police-station number. "Scumble River Police, May speaking. Can I help you?"

"Mom, me. Is Wally around?"

"No. You know he works days."

Skye bit her lip. There was no other choice. "Call him at home and have him meet me at the PD." She explained the sit-uation.

"I never heard a thing about the bank. Are you sure?"

"That's what the twins said."

"That's where all our money is. What should we do?" Suddenly May sounded weak and old.

"It's okay, Mom. Even if Allen Ingels did steal a lot of cash, everyone's money is se-cure. Remember the FDIC insurance?"

"Right." May gave a relieved sigh. "Let me call Wally on the other line. You hang on."

Skye could hear her mother lifting the receiver and talking. No fancy Muzak for the Scumble River police.

Finally, May came back. "He'll be here in five."

"See you soon, bye."

Skye grabbed her purse and headed out the door.

The night was chilly. She had finally managed to get the top to stay up on the Bel Air, but the heat still didn't work. Even so, she snuggled into the comfy seat and smiled. The car was growing on her, although she'd never get used to the fan club it attracted wherever she went.

Wally was waiting for her as she pulled into the police station's parking lot. "What took you so long?"

"Traffic jam," she answered with a straight face. By nine o'clock the Scumble River streets were empty.

"Very funny. So what's this about Allen Ingels and the bank? And how did you happen to read a diary that Charlie found only this morning?"

"Can we go inside? I'm freezing."

The chief opened the door and gestured her through. "Go up to my office. I'll be right there."

Skye waved to her mom on her way through, then lingered on the stairs, curious as to what Wally was up to. She heard him sending a patrol car to the Ingelses' to check for lights.

"Even if the lights are on, it doesn't mean Allen and Lorna are there," she said, as he entered and sat behind the desk.

A raised eyebrow was his reply.

"The housekeeper and Linette were there earlier this evening. One or both could still be there."

"So, tell me everything. Start with the bank." Wally hunched over a yellow pad.

Skye related what her cousins had said, then asked, "Didn't Yates report this?"

"Nope, first I'm hearing about it."

"Isn't that odd?"

"Nope, bank would be afraid to say anything that could cause a run on the deposits." Wally looked up and grinned. " 'Course they're pretty silly to think the tellers wouldn't talk — especially your cousins."

Skye shrugged, avoiding that slippery slope. "Do you think the missing money has anything to do with Lorelei's murder?"

"Possibly. Now, tell me about the diary."

Skye confessed everything, and waited for his wrath to descend.

Instead, he said in a mild voice, "You should have come to me last night when you first found the diary."

"And what would you have done?"

"Read it."

"Ah, but would you have let *me* read it?" Skye asked.

"If it contained something I thought you could explain or help with."

Skye was silent.

"On the other hand, I will admit that we would probably never have found it without your snooping around." The chief smiled slightly. "So, what's your take on it?"

She explained her theory.

"That's a lot of speculation and conjecture. Especially your idea that Lorelei didn't know she was pregnant."

"Believe me, a teenage girl would definitely mention something like that in her diary. Maybe in the outside world she'd act like nothing was happening, but she would pour her heart out on those pages."

"Okay, that clears Troy, but Kent still has a motive."

"What?"

"He was dating a student and could have lost his job."

"No, see here's the thing. He couldn't care less about losing his job. His dad is making him work. He'd love to be fired and go home. His family is filthy rich. Which means no motive for him either."

"Let's say you're right. Who does that leave?"

"I think I've eliminated Mrs. VanHorn and Zoë."

He raised his eyebrow again.

Skye tried to remember when she had found that characteristic gesture sexy instead of annoying. She explained her visit to the VanHorns' and the juice bottle.

"Again, who does that leave?"

"You're not going to like this, but remember what Sherlock Holmes said? 'When you have eliminated the impossible, whatever remains, however improbable, must be the truth.' "

"I'm waiting."

"Okay, but listen to all my reasons before jumping down my throat." Skye sat straighter. "I think it's Mrs. Ingels."

The chief was silent for a moment before saying, "Why?"

"The strongest evidence is the juice bottle. It's a very rare brand *and* the label was peeled just like the housekeeper said Lorna Ingels did. Then there's the diary. It clearly shows how controlling Lorna was, and how ticked she was at Lorelei for dropping out of the pageants and cheerleading and all the other stuff that was so important to the woman. That gives her motive and opportunity. She certainly had access to Lorelei's diet pills, so that gives her means." As Skye finished listing her case, it sounded measly even to her.

Wally rocked back in his chair and stared at the ceiling. "There's just not enough evidence. A juice bottle with a peeled label and a mother who doesn't like the fact that her daughter is gaining weight is not enough to arrest her on, let alone get a conviction." He stared a while longer. "Even if her prints were on the bottle we found at the murder scene, and we find a bottle of the pills in her medicine cabinet, there could be a logical explanation."

"So she gets away with it?"

"Unless we find some hard evidence." Wally gave a dry laugh. "Or unless she confesses."

"Maybe I could get her to confess. Unless, of course, she's in Bolivia by now."

"Not a good idea."

"Do you have another plan?"

"No." The chief stood. "But I do need to look into this bank matter, so if you'll excuse me . . ."

Skye followed him down the stairs, waving to her mom on the way out.

Wally walked her to her car. "Go home, get some sleep." He put his hand on her cheek. She felt the calluses in his rough palm. "Please don't put yourself in danger."

She swallowed a lump in her throat. "I won't if you won't."

He leaned closer and pressed a soft kiss to her temple. "Let's both be careful."

Chapter 23

A Thing of Beauty Is
a Toy Forever

At five the next morning, the phone woke
Skye from a light doze. She had spent another restless night before finally falling
asleep around four-thirty.

"Skye, you awake?"

She was too tired to come up with a
smart remark to her mother's dumb question. "Yeah, what's up?"

May was whispering, which meant she
was still at work. "Allen Ingels really has
disappeared. Car's gone, safety-deposit
box cleaned out, and closet empty."

"Wow! What about the rest of the
family?"

"Lorna claims she doesn't know a thing
about it." May's voice got lower and more
serious. "Looks like he took Linette, too."

"Oh, my! Mrs. Ingels must be frantic."
Skye wondered if Allen knew his wife had
killed their older child. Maybe he was
trying to protect his youngest daughter.

"Not really. Wally said she seemed almost like she couldn't care less."

"Mmm. Why don't you meet me for breakfast at the Feedbag? I want to run some ideas by you."

"Okay. I'll keep my eyes open." May sounded energized.

"Great. Say, how about calling Charlie and Vince, and seeing if they can join us?"

"You have a plan?"

"Part of one, but this time Wally's not going to be able to call me the Lone Ranger. If I go in, it'll be with backup."

After the call, Skye took a leisurely shower and examined the possibilities. She coaxed her hair into a chignon and put on her most expensive outfit. She didn't dare wear fake jewelry, so she put on the only real ones she had — the Leofanti emerald ring and a string of pearls her parents had given her for graduation. She wished she had some of the pieces her ex-fiancé had given her, but he had taken them when he moved out on her. Skye thought Lorna would be more willing to talk to someone who seemed her social equal.

After calling the school and telling Opal she would be making home visits that morning, she tucked a small tape recorder into her purse and drove to the restaurant.

411

Her troops were already assembled. Skye pulled out a chair and sat facing the three expectant faces. "Mom has filled you both in?"

The men nodded.

"Great. Here's the plan." Skye outlined what she wanted the others to do while she was attempting to get Lorna to confess. "Any questions?"

Vince was the first to speak. "How can I hear anything if I'm hiding in the bushes? How do you know she'll 'entertain' you in the library and not the living room?"

"By the looks of the living room, no one ever goes in there. And as to you hearing, I'll tell her I'm warm, and ask that she open the window a crack." Skye looked around. "Anything else?"

"Why do I have to stay in my car?" Charlie pounded the table. "Are you thinking I'm too old to really help?"

"No. If I thought that, I wouldn't have had Mom call you." Skye patted her godfather's arm. "You need to be on your CB in case we need Wally fast. You're the only one who's got any pull with him."

Charlie grinned. "Ain't that the truth."

"Mom, you okay with watching the back of the house?" Skye suddenly looked worried, thinking maybe she shouldn't have gotten her mother involved. "I could get Trixie if you want."

May huffed. "The day I can't take a walk in the cemetery is the day you bury me there."

"Great. Vince, you take Mom and pick up your old walkie-talkies, so she can alert you if she sees anything. If either of you thinks there's a problem, Vince tells Charlie, and Charlie calls Wally."

Everyone nodded.

"Vince, remember that if I say, 'Oh my, look at the time,' I'm in trouble. Get help." Skye looked around the table. "Since the cemetery is the only place where we can inconspicuously park cars anywhere near the Ingelses', we'll meet there in fifteen minutes."

Skye went over her plan in her head as she pulled into the Ingelses' driveway. Her mom should be in place with binoculars, Vince would be along the library side of the house in the bushes, and Charlie would pull into position as soon as Lorna shut the door after Skye.

She rang the bell. No answer. She rang again. *Boy, will this be embarrassing if Lorna isn't home.* She looked at her watch. Almost eight. It should be the perfect time. Lorna should be up and dressed, but not have gone anywhere yet. One more ring. This time the door was inched slowly open.

Not a good sign. Skye was already wrong about one thing. The woman wasn't dressed, and she doubted Lorna had been up yet. *Shit!*

"Mrs. Ingels, I don't know if you remember me. I'm Skye Denison, the psychologist from the school."

The woman turned and walked away, leaving the door ajar. Before following, Skye thumbed up the button in the knob, disengaging the lock.

As Skye trailed Lorna across the foyer, she noted that the woman had continued to go downhill since the last time she had seen her. Today her blond hair hung in hanks, with one side flattened. Her skin seemed to have coarsened, showing large pores, discoloration, and wrinkles. She was dressed in a stained floor-length bathrobe, with bare feet peeking from beneath the hem. Skye felt a momentary twinge of sympathy. If Lorna had killed her daughter, clearly she was suffering for it.

Lorna shuffled into the library and curled up in a wingback chair. She finally spoke. "What do you want?"

"Ah, I was wondering if I could do anything to help you."

The woman glared. "Can you bring back my daughter . . . daughters?"

"No, but perhaps I can help you locate Linette. Do you have any idea where her father might have taken her?" Skye reached into her purse and clicked on the tape recorder.

"No." The word was whispered so low Skye wasn't sure she had heard it.

Skye perched on the coffee table, which brought her knee to knee with Lorna. She took the other woman's hand, "Do you know why he would take Linette and leave?"

Lorna jerked her hand away and grabbed a nearby wineglass. "No, why would I?" She gazed into the red liquid as if she would find the answer there.

"Could it have to do with what happened to Lorelei?" Skye persisted gently.

"No." The woman shook her head wildly.

"Maybe Mr. Ingels thinks he's protecting Linette by taking her away."

Lorna's head snapped up, and she narrowed her eyes, her whole body stiffening. "Why would you say that?"

The swift change in Lorna was a bit

frightening. Skye stood to put some distance between them. "Ah, it's really warm in here. All right if I let in a little air?" Without waiting for an answer, Skye moved toward the window and lifted it several inches.

Lorna's mouth tightened. "I didn't say you could do that."

"Sorry, thought I was going to faint for a minute there. Can't stand being hot."

"You'd better leave now." Lorna rose, finger-combed her hair, and straightened her robe, seeming to notice the large red wine stain near the waist for the first time.

Skye forced herself to go on. "I know this is hard for you to hear, hard for you to think about, but I found Lorelei's diary. I know what you did."

"Where? How? You can't!" Lorna flung herself toward Skye. "I don't believe you."

Skye took a hasty step back, but Lorna had grabbed her wrist in a clawlike hold. "The diary was in a gap between the wall and her cheerleader locker. It tells everything," Skye said.

"You had no right to read that." Anger seemed to revitalize Lorna.

"Maybe not, but the police do have a right."

Lorna's flushed cheeks paled. "The police?"

"Yes, they'll probably be here to arrest you at any minute. I just thought maybe you'd feel better if you talked about it. I can't imagine what it would be like to kill my own daughter. It must be tearing you apart inside." Skye felt a little queasy, as if she were pulling off the legs of an insect. But Wally said that they needed a confession, and it wouldn't be fair to Lorelei if her death went unsolved.

"I never meant any of this to happen." Lorna wilted again, releasing Skye's hand. "A month ago I had a successful husband, two beautiful daughters, and a life that everyone in Scumble River envied." She was silent for a moment before continuing, "You know, you can do something in an instant that will give you heartache for a lifetime."

"Sounds like you were living a fairy tale. What made things go wrong?"

"It was all Lorelei's fault." Lorna sank into the love seat, facing away from Skye.

Skye was forced to move away from the door to see her face. "Lorelei's fault?"

"She was a beautiful girl. And so smart and talented. She had everything. Sometimes I even thought she might be psychic."

Skye blinked. *Psychic? Please.* "Sounds

417

like she had it made."

Lorna nodded eagerly. "That's right. And was she happy? No. I made sure she had the most beautiful clothes. And for the pageants, she never had to wear a costume twice. I did everything to ensure she'd win. She could have been Miss America, but she wanted to throw it all away. I couldn't let her do that."

"How could you stop her?"

"I talked her out of quitting cheerleading and the play, and made her promise to do one last pageant." Lorna gazed feverishly at Skye. "I figured if she won Miss Central Illinois, she'd see how important it was to go on, but she made sure she'd never get that crown."

"By gaining weight?"

"Yes, she just kept eating. I knew that if I didn't do something right away, she'd end up as fat as you. She wanted to eat three meals a day, for godsake. And she'd hardly exercise anymore. She was down to only three times a week at the gym. But that wasn't the worst part."

Skye overlooked the personal insult and guessed, "Lorelei stopped taking the diet pills?"

"Yes." Lorna shook her head. "She got so fat. She went from a size two to a size eight in a matter of three or four months. None of her clothes or costumes fit. It was a nightmare. And she still wouldn't take the pills."

"It must have been hard to watch." Skye hoped she wouldn't gag on the words she was forcing out of her mouth. "So, you just had to do something to stop her."

"To help her. I did it to help her." Lorna suddenly lunged forward and grabbed Skye by the shoulders. "You've got to make sure everyone knows I only did it to help her."

"Help her?" Skye tried to back away, but the woman was stronger than she looked, and her nails were digging into Skye's flesh.

"Yes, I started slipping the diet pills into her food, but the dose she had been on before wasn't working." Lorna's hands tightened on Skye's shoulders.

"Lorelei didn't know you were feeding her diet pills?"

"No, of course not, she wouldn't have taken them if she knew."

Skye tried to edge toward the door. "Oh, I see. So what happened?"

"I kept giving her higher and higher dosages. Then that Wednesday I was going to be away all afternoon and evening, and I was afraid she'd really binge if she didn't get her pills."

"How often did you feed her those pills?"

"Three times a day. Anyway, where was I? Oh, yes, so I took a bottle of her favorite juice and added a handful of crushed pills. After I met with the other cheerleaders' mothers that morning, I found Lorelei and gave the drink to her. She loved that juice, and usually I didn't let her have it since it was three hundred calories a bottle, so I knew she'd drink every drop."

"Then you went out of town so you'd have an alibi."

"What did I need an alibi for?" Lorna let go of Skye and looked confused. "I went to get my hair done."

"An alibi for the murder of your daughter."

"I didn't murder Lorelei. Why would I want to kill my own daughter? It was an accident. I just wanted her to stay beautiful."

"But you killed her." The words slipped out before Skye could stop them. And judging from the look on Lorna's face, they were a mistake.

Without warning the woman lunged and wrapped her hands around Skye's throat.

Both women toppled to the floor. Skye tore at the other woman's hands, panicking at the sensation of not being able to breathe. It took her a moment to realize that Lorna was about half her size, and by flipping the smaller woman on her back, Skye easily pinned her to the ground, using her weight as leverage.

Lorna let go of Skye's throat and started pounding on her chest. "You cow, get off me."

Skye wished she had an extra hand to slap the hysterical woman. Instead she shouted, "Oh, my, look at the time."

"What? Are you crazy? How can I look at the time with you on top of me?" The woman struggled. "You're breaking my back. I'm going to sue, you fat cow."

Skye ignored Lorna's curses and threats. She had a bigger problem. What to do? Vince must not have heard her. For now, Lorna was secure, but if Skye got up off her, the woman would either run or attack again. They were at a stalemate.

Before Skye could formulate a plan, the front door slammed open, and Vince ran into the room saying, "Skye, something's wrong with Mom. I heard a scream on the walkie-talkie and now I can't get a response. You run for Charlie. I'm going out back to see what's —" He stopped abruptly, staring.

Lorna grew still, and her demeanor changed instantly. "Vince, darling, your sister has gone crazy. She's hurting me. Please help."

Vince frowned and flicked a look at Skye.

She made a face. "Vince, get something to tie her up with."

He looked around. "What?"

Her mind worked frantically. "The electrical cords on the lamps."

Lorna yelped, "Don't touch those lamps. They're originals by Tiffany."

Vince ignored her, ran to the nearest end table, and yanked the wire from the base, returning with the cord. Even though she fought him, he easily secured Lorna's ankles, and then repeated the procedure for her wrists. As soon as he was finished, Skye jumped up and between them they tied Lorna to the desk chair with the sash from her robe.

Within minutes, Vince and Skye were running toward the cemetery. They arrived at the end of the Ingelses' property at the same time. Vince had longer legs and was in better shape, but Skye was still jazzed with adrenaline from her wrestling match

with Lorna. A few inches in front of them the graveyard began.

Skye paused, listening. Which direction? Sounds of scuffling indicated the way. She slowed down, picking her way carefully among the plaques and grass-covered mounds. Vince followed silently. As they advanced, Skye began to hear voices and she slowed further, going from headstone to headstone, crouching behind the granite markers.

A huge gray marble slab with a teardrop shape cut out of the top allowed her to stand upright and peek through it without being seen.

May was sitting on a flat headstone, and Allen Ingels held a pistol pointed at her head. May was speaking. "You never answered me. What did you do with my money?"

Allen looked a wreck. His hair was in disarray, allowing his bald spot to show through. The knee of his suit had been torn, and the lining of his jacket hung beneath the hem. He wiped a soiled hand across his eyes, leaving dirt on his cheeks. "Shut up. I've got to think. What am I going to do with you?"

"Give me back my money." May cocked her head. "It's not right what you did to this town."

"You're forcing me to shoot you," Allen gritted out from between clenched teeth. "You're just like Lorna and Linette — totally selfish. If that little brat hadn't insisted she had to have her crown, we could be in Mexico by now."

"Why did you take her then?"

He looked puzzled. "I couldn't leave her with Lorna. Not after she told me last night about 'accidentally' killing Lorelei with those damn diet pills of hers. She'd already started Linette on them. What was I supposed to do, wait for another 'accident'?"

May reached out as if to pat his arm, but he stepped back, out of contact. "Save your pity. Linette and I will be just fine as soon as I take care of you."

May clasped her knees. "Why did you do this, Allen? You had money. You didn't need ours."

His laugh was raw. "That's what everyone thinks, but when the bank was sold last year, the new company cut my salary in half right away. We couldn't live on that amount."

"But your family has had money, what about that?"

"With a wife and kids like mine, that money was gone long ago. We live from paycheck to paycheck." Allen's voice was dazed.

"Look, why don't you just turn yourself in? I'm sure Wally will see that things go okay for you, especially if you give back the money."

Allen clutched his head with both hands, momentarily directing the pistol away from May. "Shut up! You're driving me crazy!"

As soon as Allen's aim drifted from May's head, Skye signaled Vince and they darted forward.

But before they could cover the uneven ground, Wally stepped out from behind a small group of trees and leveled his gun at Allen. "Drop it."

Allen stared at the police chief for what seemed an interminable second before he let his weapon fall to the ground.

Officer Quirk and a couple of county deputies emerged from their cover in the foliage. They handcuffed Ingels.

"You might want to pick up Lorna Ingels too, " Skye said. "She's in the house, tied to a desk chair in the library."

Wally shook his head. "What have you done now?"

Skye explained about the confrontation and handed over the tape recorder containing Lorna's confession.

"Okay, men, take Mr. Ingels away, and while you're in the neighborhood, pick up his wife."

Skye heard one of the officers reading Allen Ingels his rights as they walked away.

Vince and Skye had been standing with their arms around May. Now, they all spoke at once.

Vince gave May a hard squeeze. "I was so worried."

Skye patted her mother's back. "How could you say those things to him?"

May looked them both over, and said, "What took you two so long?"

After a few minutes, Vince led May away. Skye turned to Wally, who had been leaning against a tree trunk, silently observing. "How did you end up out here? Were you following Allen?" she asked.

"Nope. I was following you." He straightened. "What did you expect after our last conversation? I knew you'd go after Mrs. Ingels."

"You didn't have to do that. I had my own backup."

"Are you referring to the Three Stooges? A seventy-year-old man sitting in a Cadillac, a defenseless middle-aged woman, and a hairdresser?"

Skye crossed her arms. "Who does that make me? Shemp?" She was none too happy about being called the fourth stooge, even if Shemp was her favorite.

Wally grinned. "If the stooge fits."

Epilogue

It was hard for Skye to drag herself to school on Friday. Her throat hurt from Lorna's attempt to strangle her, and every muscle in her body ached. Worst of all, her four-hundred-dollar suit was ruined. She was seriously depressed.

She vowed that she would go to work, do what had to be done, and sneak home early. The most urgent item on her schedule was to talk to Lorelei's friends . . . and enemies, so they could have closure. There would be an assembly first hour to tell everyone in the school what had happened, but the kids most closely involved deserved to be told in private.

Skye arranged for extra chairs to be set up in the guidance office and asked the various homeroom teachers to send the teens on her list to the guidance office as soon as the bell rang. They filed in silently. Zoë and Frannie immediately claimed the two seats across from Skye's desk. Troy drew up a folding chair just behind Zoë, and Justin did the same on Frannie's side. The rest of the cheerleading squad and

Chase occupied the remaining seats.

Skye leaned forward. "I'm sure many of you have already heard some version of what happened yesterday, but I wanted to tell you the true account. Mrs. Ingels was arrested for the *accidental* death of her daughter. Lorelei had stopped taking a prescription medication that her mother wanted her to take. Without telling her mother, she started to take it again. In the meantime her mom had begun to put it in her food. She ended up with a fatal overdose."

The teens remained silent. Their expressions ranged from boredom to incredulity.

Skye went on. "To add to this family's tragedy, Mr. Ingels embezzled the bank's money, took his youngest daughter, and tried to leave the country. He was caught when he came back to retrieve one of Linette's belongings. Both Mr. and Mrs. Ingels are in jail, and Linette is staying with a relative in Chicago."

Zoë yawned. "And you're telling us all this, why?"

"Well, Zoë, partly so we can all have closure. Lorelei was a big part of everyone's life, whether they liked her or not. But I guess partly because I thought you all might gain some insight from this mess."

Justin gestured with his head. "That's asking a lot from these guys, Ms. Denison. They all have hipatitis."

"Hipatitis?" Skye asked.

"Yeah, terminal coolness."

Zoë narrowed her eyes. "Are you getting smart with me?"

"How would you know?"

"This is exactly what I mean," Skye said. "You all make judgments about each other based solely on appearances instead of getting to know each other as real people. I was hoping you would learn something from Lorelei's tragic experience."

Justin spoke again. "That's like saying that someone like Zoë, who looks perfect, could ignore the fact that I don't look like a Ken doll, and actually date me. It'll never happen."

Zoë shrugged. "Sorry, I don't date out of my species."

This was obviously a waste of time, Skye decided; she wasn't making a bit of difference in these kids' attitudes. Maybe she was being too subtle.

"I guess that's that then," she said. "But think about these three things. First, TV is not real life. In real life, people actually have to leave the coffee shop and go to work. Second, and this one is especially for you, Zoë, be nice to nerds. Chances are you'll end up working for one, or wishing you had married one. And last, if you think your teachers are tough, wait until you get out in the real world. Bosses don't have tenure, so if their team members don't work up to their capabilities, they're fired."

Later that night Skye, Vince, Charlie, Trixie, Loretta, May, and Jed sat around May's kitchen table snacking on salami, cheese, and crackers.

"I still don't understand why you didn't call me to be part of your backup team," Trixie said, pouting like a two-year-old who had been denied a trip to Toys R Us.

"It would have been too hard for you to get off work," Skye answered, before drinking from her glass of pop. "You know how Homer is."

Charlie puffed out his chest. "She didn't need more help. The Three Musketeers did just fine."

Skye hid her grin and did not share with Charlie what the chief had actually called them.

"I can't believe you talked me into handling another case down here in Skillet River," Loretta said. "I thought when they released Kent, I was home free."

Skye slapped her friend on the arm. "It's Scumble River, Ms. Big Shot. Besides, you like it down here. You get to be a giant catfish in our itsy-bitsy pond."

"It is kind of fun riling up that cute police chief of yours. He's single now, you know." As if they both weren't well aware of Wally Boyd's marital status.

Skye's thoughts flashed to Abby. "I think he's dating someone," she said.

"Dating isn't married." Loretta grinned, took a sip of ice tea, then turned serious. "I'm surprised you wanted to help Lorna by getting me to represent her. Isn't she everything you hate?"

Skye squirmed in her chair. It was hard to put what she felt about Lorna into words. "I guess so, but I think she's a product of our society. The media, the magazines, everything tells us if you aren't thin, you can't win. Did someone like Lorna ever really have a chance to think any other way?"

After a pause, Trixie broke the uncomfortable silence. "Speaking of Kent, have you heard from him since he went back to Boston?"

Charlie took a swig of beer and answered, "I met with him after he had been questioned by Wally, and we decided it

432

would be to our mutual advantage if he forgot Scumble River even existed."

"Mutual advantage?" Vince asked.

"Yeah. He'd get to go back where he fits in, and I wouldn't tell his father that he'd been screwing teenagers." May coughed, and Charlie added, "Pardon my French."

Skye turned to Charlie. "Did you know Allen Ingels was embezzling from the bank?"

He shrugged, a smug look on his face. "Maybe, maybe not. Let's just say I knew he was up to no good. Wasn't sure exactly what."

"With both her folks in jail, what's going to happen to Linette?" May asked.

Loretta crossed her legs. "Her grandmother is too frail to take care of her, but her mom has a cousin in Chicago. The little girl's going to go live with her for now, until we see what happens with Lorna."

"What do you think will happen to Lorna?" Skye asked Loretta.

"Hard to say. She could get off with probation, or she could go to prison for a long time."

It was the first Saturday in May, and Skye, her mother, and Vince were attending Scumble River High's production of *Sleeping Beauty*. Jed had declined to join his family for a night of live theater, stating he preferred his La-Z-Boy and TV.

To everyone's surprise, Abby had volunteered to direct the musical after Kent was removed from duty. Zoë would be the star and Frannie Ryan had taken her role — the evil fairy.

Justin greeted Skye and her family at the gym door. He had signed up to usher. "Ms. Denison, I saved some seats up front for you."

Skye smiled at him, blinking away the tears that threatened to leak from behind her eyes. Justin had come so far from that boy who would barely speak. His grades now reflected his IQ rather than his depression, he had joined a couple of clubs, and while still not the most popular kid in his class, he had made a friend or two. It was a moment before she could trust her voice to speak. "How nice of you, Justin. Do you know my mom and brother?"

He ducked his head and said to the floor, "Sure. Mrs. D works at the police station and Vince cuts my hair."

Skye shook her head. She should have known. It was hard to find two Scumble River citizens who hadn't met each other.

Justin showed them to their seats and

said hurriedly without looking at them, "Frannie's in the first act. She's the best one." Before they could respond, he turned and ran back to his post by the door.

They sat without speaking while the gym filled with spectators. Skye finally said, "It's hard to believe that only a month ago I found Lorelei's body on that very stage."

May shook her head. "You need to forget about all that."

"I can't. I thought I knew all about the problems between parents and children, but nothing prepared me for the blind self-ishness that ended up killing Lorelei."

May patted her hand, and Vince put his arm around her shoulders. They sat quietly until the lights dimmed and the music started to swell.

Suddenly, May said, "Well, I feel sorry for Lorna's mother. That woman sacrificed everything so her daughter could get out of the trailers and have a better life." May tsked. "But no matter how you try to protect your children, they still eventually get themselves arrested and end up in the local paper."

Skye and Vince looked at each other in disbelief, then exclaimed in unison, *"Mother!"*

The employees of Thorndike Press hope you have enjoyed this Large Print book. All our Large Print titles are designed for easy reading, and all our books are made to last. Other Thorndike Press Large Print books are available at your library, through selected bookstores, or directly from us.

For information about titles, please call:

(800) 223-1244

To share your comments, please write:

Publisher
Thorndike Press
295 Kennedy Memorial Drive
Waterville, ME 04901